Valley of the Moms

Also by Hannah Selinger

Cellar Rat: My Life in the Restaurant Underbelly

Valley of the Moms

A Novel

Hannah Selinger

LITTLE, BROWN AND COMPANY
New York Boston London

The characters and events in this book are fictitious. Any similarity to real persons, living or dead, is coincidental and not intended by the author.

Little, Brown and Company
Hachette Book Group
1290 Avenue of the Americas, New York, NY 10104
littlebrown.com

First Edition: June 2026

Little, Brown and Company is a division of Hachette Book Group, Inc.
The Little, Brown name and logo are trademarks of Hachette Book Group, Inc.

Book interior design by Marie Mundaca

ISBN 9780316596558
LCCN 2025941242

Printing 1, 2026

LSC-H

Printed in the United States of America

To Dan, Nathaniel, and Miles

Valley of the Moms

Prologue

A BODY. OR what used to be one. This time of year, winter, is unforgiving — a canvas of white too frigid for humanity. If a body might become bloated in Massachusetts' humid summer, the opposite is true in the coldest month of January. Here is a person that looks more like a porcelain doll, with pale, blue-tinged skin, and the dull, cloudy eyes of a fish you wouldn't bring home from the market.

The Ipswich River no doubt holds many secrets, and it has held hers for days, until now, when it has released her from its frozen bottom. The first real hard cold — an eruption — will do that. The river tracks forty-five miles from Burlington through its namesake's Great Marsh, meandering through the small towns of Essex County. It's mostly shallow, a canoeing spot for locals, certainly not as dangerous as the nearby Merrimack, where the Coast Guard is regularly dispatched to rescue boats that have been caught in the dangerous choppy waters where the river meets the Atlantic.

And yet. A danger, clearly, a pernicious river, a body of water that consumes and conceals. This frozen relic, she has arrived at the once-muddy banks, herself a new mystery. In small towns, where the daily drone of life is everyone's business, a woman does not just show up on a riverbank in the middle of the winter, expelled from the ice and snow and mud. In a small town, there are no accidents or coincidences, only things that have not yet come to light.

Walking past the canoe launch on a snowy Saturday afternoon, a couple stops to admire the light. It is yellow, it is orange, it is somehow also almost blue. They take out phones to capture the flakes dancing off the trees, the once-sunken river that is now almost overflowing with recent rains and snow, so different from a drought the year before, and then they see her, a doll, hair beneath a layer of ice, Ophelia in winter, with the vermilion sun setting, and it is beautiful, and it is criminal, all this loss, all this that goes unanswered.

Part I
Winter

Chapter 1

NO SNOW, NOT through the entire wretched month of December, nor into January this year, which has been unseasonably warm. Awake before the alarm, Anna looked out at the trees that faced her bedroom window, tall, grim, gray specters. When she was growing up in Massachusetts, she could depend on one thing in these cold, bare months, and it was the pleasure of waking up to unexpected snowfall. Heart racing, she would turn on the television to watch the scrolling of town names, alphabetical, a crazy-making exercise. Her town began with an *N*, Newburyport. It was always promising to see Essex County rival Amesbury closures up toward the top of the list. That meant mostly good news: a snow day, or at least a delayed start, with parents off to work and the exotic, silent, snowcapped world all to herself for the day. But sometimes the South Shore towns got hit harder, or Newburyport's coastal location created a sort of buffer of insulation. You were sure to end up in school if it was six inches or less. No magic in walking up the streets in boots over flared jeans, that was for sure.

What she would give, she sometimes thought, to relive those mornings. Even a dusting would feel prophetic at this point, a sign of the mere existence of winter and not climate change and rot. Anna's house, which she shared with her son, daughter, husband, and dog, was perched high on a hill and looked down onto Hamilton's busiest road, which was, in the quickening dawn, slicked by rain. A kind of bruising sky, she noted, has started to emerge in the direction of Cutler's Pond, where she once imagined her children would learn to ice skate, but she had put that vision away, along with other feeble notions of parenthood. Sometimes, it was good enough just to survive.

"So early again," she heard her husband, Denny, say, as she skipped the lights in the bedroom and attempted to tiptoe through the dark, making more noise than she meant to. It did seem like each day the clock ticked back earlier and earlier, but what was she to do with all of those extra minutes — those extra hours — anyway? This time, it was not useful. When we want things to slow down, she thought, we cannot, and when we want things to speed up, they only drag on, like heels through wet sand.

Only after she had closed the door to the dark primary bathroom did she turn on a sconce and study her face. Forty-two years old. Fine lines just starting to crawl out from around her mouth, but otherwise — this she would confess — she wasn't bad-looking. She had not fallen even a little gray yet, only dyed her hair to get rid of the ordinary brown color her mother used to refer to as mousy. (The first time: eighth grade, a semi-permanent dye called "Glints" by Clairol that turned her hair a shiny and forgiving auburn and that washed out in under three weeks.) Up it went now, into a loose ponytail, a honey-brown blond that looked like it had spent time in the sun, even in the Massachusetts winter.

Hazel eyes stared back at her from the long, flat mirror in the bathroom, where everything needed to be replaced, if they ever got around to it: the greige bathroom that they inherited from the Greek owners before them, the ones who preferred to keep their furniture large and at odd angles, who liked light fixtures encrusted with fake gems, who decorated in colors named after vegetables. *Aubergine. Bell Pepper.* She and Denny had chipped away at the rooms one at a time, building a Farrow & Ball fantasy: high-gloss, wallpaper, brushed brass, their living, breathing masterpiece, part of the pretension of existing in this wealthy New England town, where you had to dress up to walk the damn dog, for Christ's sake.

Downstairs, Anna enjoyed her favorite five minutes of the day, before Denny, before the dog, Hank, and his clawing at the slider, before the kids and the backpacks and the school lunches, and even before the hum of the very expensive automatic espresso maker that cost over $2,500 but leaked onto the counter every time they refilled the water canister. The kitchen was silent, and a little bit dark, and a little bit cold, and Anna Plummer, a small, average mother, did the thing she did every single morning when she came down here into a room that she liked well enough: sighed deeply, looked around, and felt precisely nothing.

There was nothing wrong, and if she were the kind of person who measured out her life in spoons — good or bad, depending on how you read the metaphor — well, even she would agree that there was enough to be thankful for. A sea of bluestone pavers extended out from beyond the sliding glass doors. Past the pavers was grass that had seen better days, the edge to the cleared property, where oak trees rose up from the soft and fallow ground. The January rains had made everything wet and tender, springy and covered in mud. She had a job. Boring, yes, but it paid okay, and it was predictable. Copywriting, some might say, even used the part of her brain that mothers in wealthy towns felt went dormant after too many years spent rearing children. Driving carpool. That sort of thing.

Anna twisted the oval engagement ring around her finger again and again. Force of habit — she never actually took it off.

She glanced at the clock on the stove. Not quite six. Would Di be awake, she wondered? Should she chance it? It wasn't really like she had anything all that important to say. More like she wanted company in this desolate skeleton hour, and Di, with two kids and a cold and achy house of her own, might be awake, too, watching the steam rise off her coffee, thinking about the time that seemed to go nowhere at this hour of the morning.

Did you watch? she texted, meaning the latest episode of a Real Housewives franchise that they're extremely *into* right now.

No, and no spoilers. I mean it. I know how u are.

Not even a pause between texts. Anna did feel gratitude that she was not the only one up in these dark hours, driving her husband so crazy, even if her best friend of thirty years wouldn't let her gossip about television strangers.

Ok, ok, but what else am I supposed to talk about

Idk. Your annoying husband. Your annoying kids. Whatever ppl talk about when they're not talking about tv

Fine Louisa threatened to cut her hair yesterday and I told her over my dead body and I think she considered it

My turn. Henry is so bad at soccer that the coach suggested he switch to t-ball.

Ok that's genuinely embarrassing Di I'm sorry

Three dots lingered for a minute — Di was writing something or thinking about it and erasing it — but then the text chain went still. Truth was, Anna didn't have much to say, either. She was just killing time, waiting for the dawn, for something wild and interesting to happen, and it felt like it was mostly like that these days, on the precipice of a story that was about to be written, if only someone could figure out how to start writing it.

When she was young, Anna wanted to be an artist. It wasn't that she possessed any more or less talent than the average student. She hadn't mastered perspective particularly early, nor was she adept with a pencil. But there was something romantic about distilling life into an oil painting. And it was oil that drew her — not the cheap paints known as egg tempera. Tempera could be washed out. There was a reason that the classic artists all painted in oil, that the resounding and resilient art that lasted for centuries — that was painted upon frescoes and that was painstakingly studied by art historians — was produced in oil pigment, powders from nature's original colors mixed with, yes, oil.

Anna had experimented with all kinds of art: fan brushes, palette knives, pointillism, collage, even a phase where she just threw paint at the canvas like Jackson Pollock. That phase had been inspired by his 1998 retrospective at MoMA, but if she was being honest, she had never heard of Pollock before, had just read about him in the paper and had followed the trail of hopeful academics, and had been just as enthralled as the glamorous then-couple Uma Thurman and Ethan Hawke as she had been by the art itself.

It was a little different, years later, when the Gerhard Richter exhibit came up. By then, MoMA had been renovated, she was deep into an unofficial minor in art history, and halfway through a class on German Expressionism that threatened to turn her off art altogether, something about Richter's candle painting — the one from Sonic Youth's *Daydream Nation* — arrested her. Some artists see a master in real life and chase the high forever. The actual thing — the painting — reignites their passion. For Anna, it was a recognition that she would never paint like that. She could never make a candle look like it was absolutely glowing on canvas. That kind of talent was like a haunting, supernatural spirit. Eventually, she packed up her oils. Art was just another old and abandoned dream.

There was no reason to consider the abandonment of childhood ambition in this specific moment, although Anna had spied a tangle of art on the kitchen island, her son's. He had a natural fluidity, an ease with a pencil. He could see a thing and translate it without looking down, a trick she remembered hearing that Picasso used to train his own eye: Put the pencil to paper, stare at an object, and don't look down at the paper itself. Make the line do the work and live with the results.

Her problem, when she thought about it, was that she had never quite been satisfied with the results. The perfectionist in her had always overtaken the process, and she had yielded too completely to that inner voice that made her throw away anything that wasn't a Platonic ideal. Back in New York, in their former small town in the Hamptons, it had been easier to discard any true notion of perfectionism. The women there were impossibly rich, for one thing. Unattainably rich. Billionaire rich. You could freely show up in sweatpants in public and know that it didn't matter; one of them might own a major sports team, for all you knew.

But here in Hamilton, the playing field was actually level. These women, much as Anna hated to admit it, were her peers. They looked nothing like her, lived nothing like her, spent their money on things she didn't really relate to. But they were all around the same age, probably from the same wide circle of communities north of Boston, had eaten at the same Dunkin' Donuts growing up. Christ, they probably all knew that chocolate glazed was the best donut in existence, when it came down to it. So, yes, you did have to perform, all in a way she hadn't been expecting when she proposed they move back up north. She had to strive for the fucking Gerhard Richter, and all that striving was exhausting. She had always believed that people should be allowed to be whoever they wanted, even if what they wanted was kind of ordinary, something she wouldn't often admit about herself, except when she was alone.

When she and Denny planned this big escape, she had been thinking about Patagonia fleece vests and L.L.Bean flannel and the kind of down-home life that removed the pretense from wealth, but okay, that was unrealistic, because to live the kind of unflappable

East Coast life that you see in Instagram reels — even the kind that she herself grew up with — you had to be kind of upper-crust. Fighting any of it was just an uphill battle. Now here she was, fighting some other battle to fit in. No one wore flannel shirts, it turned out. You just couldn't get away with being the kind of person that Anna Plummer had aspired to be.

Her son, Ben, who was only five, stood in the entry to the kitchen, a halo of light surrounding him. Everyone talked about freezing time, and during the first years of his life she had only wanted to speed it up, to catapult through the messiness of diapers and strollers and naps that commandeered the day. But now, all these years into parenting, she could see her children needing her less, the softness from them evaporating. And she wished that she could go back to that place that she had been so desperate to escape.

This was the central conflict of motherhood: the inability to enjoy the moment you're in because you're always looking backward, constantly searching for a moment that has already receded into the rearview. Ben, dressed in dinosaur pajamas that said *snore don't roar* — tiny T.rex prints all over top and bottom — clambered toward her, in a nearly kneecapping embrace. Little kids have no boundaries: They run in when you're in the bathroom, knock the door down while you shower, will move mountains just to tell you that they had found a purple Lego and that it was a different shade of purple from the other purple Lego they found last week. All this can be annoying or special, depending on which day of the week they catch you — the way they need to include you in all of it, the way they can't stop talking about the world, the way you're the most important person in their lives.

"I'm hungry," he said, burying his blond head in her legs. She leaned down and tousled his hair.

Aggravation. Obligation. Privilege. Parenting never ceased to be all three. "What moves you today?" she said, knowing the question would mostly elude him.

"What, Mama?"

"What are you hungry for? What do you want for breakfast?"

"Toast," he said. "Cinnamon toast."

She didn't know why she asked when the answer was always the same. He was her less adventurous child, prone always to eating the same few things, to less experimentation. In the '80s, when she was a kid, parents didn't give in to the whims and wants of children, but these days, it was different. If Ben wanted to eat toast and bagels every day of his life, well, it was food, wasn't it? Throw a bunch of grapes in there and you've got half the nutritional bases covered (she pictured the triangle she learned in grade school, but then again, they used to drink cans of juice with dinner, so what did they know about nutrition, anyway).

Louisa, seven and always late, showed up in the kitchen with Barbie dolls in each hand. She had the Malibu Dream House that she would have murdered to own forty years ago, but the whole point in having kids, Anna thought, was to give them a better shot. Malibu Dream Houses for everyone. Cinnamon toast and grapes. Live large, kids. You only get one chance. A sherbet-pink sky outside, even on what had promised to be a gray morning, both her children, noiseless, at the kitchen counter, and maybe January was just a word, maybe January didn't have to be thematic, maybe January was not as restless as it felt when you woke up in the dark.

Chapter 2

AT FIRST HE didn't recognize the lights for what they were—bleeding into the snow, a flash of mostly blue with hints of indigo and scarlet. Denny thought his eyes were playing tricks on him. Fresh snow often gives the illusion of being blue, after all, and he was tired. So tired. The lights were yet another sign that his body was exhausted.

But no. It was a throb of lights. Sirens without the sound. The unmistakable pulse of a noiseless police car, parked outside his home. A tear in the fabric of his life. Something just beginning to unravel.

The second week of school after the holiday break had just started. On Thursday, the first day that Anna was gone, he remembered that his daughter had library and tucked her book for return in her backpack, he made the lunches and threw a load of laundry in before he left the house to drive the kids to school, and he had done it all unprompted not because his memory was getting any better but because she hadn't been there to remind him. Also that day he had left cash out for the cleaning lady, and had texted

Anna again: Where are you. At first, he thought she had just been out late with friends, but then he had gotten increasingly worried. While his mother-in-law watched the kids, he had circled the blocks repeatedly. He had screamed – however unreasonably – into the woods behind the house. There were acres all around them. Could she hear him? Finally, he had driven down to the local police department to file a report, but they seemed unconcerned. Bad things did not happen in small towns, or not towns like this one, where many of the property lines included two rolling acres and glossy SUVs, and the kinds of good graces you read about in a Robert Frost poem.

Good fences make good neighbors.

At the police station a good ol' boy from a few towns over – Rowley, where Anna always loved to go flea-marketing in spring and summer at old Todd Farm – hitched up his pants and said, "Just cooling off, they do that, we see it a lot." Then he picked something he must have found offensive off of the corner of his tongue, grabbed a notebook from the back pocket of a pair of navy department-issued pants that were too tight, and made a show of taking notes that Denny was sure the officer would never again look at.

Anna's temper ran hot, flame-hot, everyone knew that, and maybe it wasn't unlike her to drive to the woods and take a walk to cool off. Maybe it wasn't even unlike her to turn her phone off for a few hours to make the people around her feel a little uneasy. But to disappear? That wasn't like her, no. Her social media bore no trace of her. She hadn't posted any snarky memes or liked anyone's political commentary. She had simply vanished.

Now blue light bloomed on the snow outside, and Denny dreaded whatever came next: a knock, an apology, a conversation with his own small children, who were down in the basement watching TV with his mother-in-law, an extra, worried set of hands to help out during the nightmarish past few days. Denny sat facing the window, wondering how long it would take the officers to summon the courage to face their own demons, to admit that they had been wrong. She hadn't just been *cooling off.* Denny had spent half the week driving the roads of Essex County looking for her, looking for her Volkswagen, but it was as if the world had swallowed her up, and it would take a lot to make a woman like Anna Plummer turn small, turn invisible, turn into nothing at all. It would take an act of God, a catastrophe so consuming it would take the icy fingers of the Hamilton Police Department itself — those dang blue lights — to make someone so large in this life disappear. After all, only a force larger than life could change the color of the snow. Only a force larger than life could make Anna Plummer disappear.

A door on the Crown Victoria opened. Denny watched the perfect snow absorb one man's footsteps, then another. In Christmas carols and movies and poems, snow was always soft, he thought, but this was animal snow, crunchy and savage, the kind that held weight, the kind that held memories. Despite an unusually warm winter, it had snowed the week earlier, and hard, the kind that Anna had always described with a sort of childlike innocence when recalling her youth. The annoying kind of snow, thick pack, stuck in the spokes of tires, the kind that didn't go away, no matter how warm it got. Denny got it now, what New England really was, how haunted by this principle of the weather, how it defined the people here. He finally understood.

There was a knock at the door, and Denny rose to open it. Before the welcome mat at his home — her home, really — were two men he had never seen before. They held winter beanies in their hands, out of respect, he assumed. He almost laughed. Anna had a distaste for authority, and she particularly disliked the police. She would have found this funny, the cops there, at her house, where her BLACK LIVES MATTER sign still lived on the frosty lawn. How many times had she uttered responses under her breath to "thin blue line" flags as they drove through neighborhoods populated by officers? How many times had he convinced her not to share her feelings about the cops at dinner parties or social gatherings? It had been a mistake, he now realized, reining her in all those times, telling her what she should or shouldn't say. There had been no real point, after all. You end up with the cops at your door either way.

Denny looked out at those cops now, studied the men he had never before met, despite his own trips down to the police station in search of his wife, this apparition.

"Mr. Plummer?" the taller of the pair asked. "Are you Mr. Plummer?"

"Denny," he said, shifting his weight.

"Do you mind?" the second officer said. He was short and kind of squat with a mess of graying hair plastered across his forehead. He was gesturing inside. "Can we?"

"Oh, yes, of course," Denny said.

Denny walked the officers inside, past the small foyer, with its convex eagle mirror that Anna bought because it reminded her of the one that she had as a child in her ship captain's home, and past the vintage bread box that she picked up well before she had children and that she had always used to store dog leashes and treats. He brought the officers into their kitchen, where reminders of his wife were also everywhere: Here were the blue velour bar stools that they quarreled over at West Elm (too expensive, too hard to clean); here, in the center of the island, in a blue ceramic bowl, were the potatoes she bought for last Sunday's dinner but never ended up cooking. The officers stood around the kitchen island.

"Can I get you anything?" Denny asked, though it was mostly a formality. They demurred. They seemed equally unaccustomed to accepting things at people's homes.

"Mr. Plummer," the taller officer began.

"Denny," he corrected.

"Right, Denny." The officer cleared his throat. "Sir, we're here about your wife."

But Denny already knew this. He wanted to fast-forward, like in the old days, the VHS days, when you could watch everything move forward quickly, with white lines striped through the video. It was less traumatic that way. He wanted to move through this conversation three times as fast and without sound, get to the part where they hand him the information that matters, dispense with the courtesies. They were just doing their jobs, of course. They couldn't help it.

"We have, ah, located a body," the shorter officer said. "We believe we have located your wife."

Body first, wife second. That order was striking. Death eclipsed life. Denny could feel every muscle in his body vibrating, a will to stay upright. Somewhat resistant to emotion by nature, he was now fighting his own synapses, at war with impulse. *No one tells you how you turn to jelly,* he thought. *No one tells you how you just want to sink into the floor.*

"No," Denny said. "That's not possible." She had just been there. It had only been a few days. The police had told him — they had *told* him — not to worry. *Cooling off.* Their words. Not his.

"Mr. Plummer, we're very sorry."

"But we...we have a family...we have children." As if this somehow precluded tragedy. As if tragedy was somehow reserved for people unlike Anna. Anna Plummer could not be dead. Anna Plummer was not the type of person, Denny reasoned, who could even die.

"Do you need help telling your children, Mr. Plummer?" the first officer asked.

It had not, in this exact moment, occurred to Denny that he would have to tell his children. This seemed like a unique and excruciating torture. Raising his children alone? Impossible. He opened his mouth to say something and found that he let out an involuntary shudder. The grief in him was wide, so wide that it catapulted out. He could hear a cry that sounded like it came from someone else in the room. He looked around, scared by what he had heard, until he, Denny Plummer, realized that the guttural sound had come from his own body, realized, too, that he was lying on the floor. He had, in fact, collapsed. The officers were standing by him now, grabbing him from beneath the arms and assisting him into the living room, where an armchair awaited.

"Where was she?" Denny asked, waving the officers away once he was settled. Even Denny did not know why this was the first question, why he didn't want to know, for example, how she died, or when, or who found her. Where: It felt like the most important of these questions, came tumbling from him with such urgency that he didn't even realize that he had asked it until it had already been loosed from him. Anna had gone out with friends on the night that she disappeared, and that fact had felt ordinary until it hadn't. He now wanted to know this information, where Anna's last moments had been lived, and he hoped, in the seconds before the answer arrived, that it was an answer that would bring him peace. *She was asleep on a bed at the Four Seasons in Boston.* Or, *they found her at the Garrison, in the tea room,* not a stitch more explanation than that, just the understanding that she had been having tea one minute and then, the next minute, she was gone.

But Denny knew better. He understood from the way they were looking at him—not at him, but through him—that there were secrets he didn't need to know.

The first officer dug a toe into the wood plank flooring. "Unfortunately, a few passersby saw her in the Ipswich River. We'll still need to do forensics, of course, but her Volkswagen was parked nearby. Near the canoe haul-out," the officer said. "There is more investigation needed, but we believe she died of exposure."

Exposure. A polite way of saying *frozen to death.*

The haul-out wasn't far from the road, wasn't far, in fact, from civilization. And yet, Denny's wife had, to hear the officer tell it, frozen to death. Where had her phone been? Why hadn't she thought to call anyone?

He had spent too many hours, he thought, staring up at the ceiling in his bedroom, circling the drain, trying to remember about Spanish class on Mondays and library books on Tuesdays. He was caught in an endless loop of responsibilities, mad at himself for not having paid better attention, for all those times that she scolded him, mad now because there would never be another opportunity even to argue about it. He saw, so clearly, the blooming blue light on the snow, and, no, he could not accept that his wife had simply turned ice white from the cold. This felt like an objective impossibility.

"I fucking reported it," he said. "I came to you. *Just cooling off.* That's what the department said. I drove around looking for her. I screamed into the trees."

The officers looked at one another. "We understand that there was a report," the squat officer said. "We did make the search a priority."

"Maybe not enough of one," Denny said. He was pale still, though regaining some color. The shock had started to fade and had been replaced with anger. These officers — they had come in the middle of a nightmare only to replace one terrible outlook with a worse one. "I want to know what happened to my *wife*."

The squat officer softened his stance. He looked more like an ordinary guest in the Plummers' comfortable living room now. He put a hand on his hip. "Well, there's gonna be some more investigating."

Denny nodded. He knew the officers didn't want to tell him whatever the brutal truth was. A body. *Her* body. "Do you have any other... details?" He practically choked on the last words.

"Mr. Plummer, I really am sorry for your loss," the officer said.

"Was she... Was it fast?"

"I'm not sure we have too much information on that yet, Mr. Plummer."

"I just...it's just that I once read that if you . . . I once read that with hypothermia, you go to sleep? That you don't feel it?" He felt like he was bargaining with the police for an outcome. He needed them to tell him that it had been painless, that it had been quick, that she had felt nothing, that sleep had come first, that everything had just slowed down until there had been nothing at all.

"For now, Mr. Plummer, I suggest talking to your children and taking some time as a family. And we will get back to you as soon as we know more," the officer said. He would provide no comfort, Denny could see. No guarantee.

"I appreciate you coming out here to tell me in person," Denny said, even though he knew this is what officers did, what they were trained to do. They were not extending him any specific kindness, nothing they wouldn't do for any other victim on any other street on any other January evening. His anger had receded, somewhat. He was beginning to feel something else, something darker, the knifepoint of pain, the truth of what he had just learned, that Anna was really and irrevocably gone. The house was so large. The house was so large without her.

The squat officer put a hand to his head and rubbed it. He looked uncomfortable, itching to go. Like he wished he could be back in the field, investigating car accidents, clocking high-risk drivers. Anything but this.

"I'm sorry we had to bring you this terrible news," he said.

Denny heard an echo rise from the television in the basement, where his children were temporarily sedated with his mother-in-law as stand-in mama bear, in these last few moments of hope before their world effectively ended. That was their blue light, a happier version. Later, he would have to bring them into this very room, with its deep green walls where the fireplace was, and explain that the absence was more than a break, that it was forever, that this life, it was theirs now — an inheritance, a permanence.

"I guess we'll be going now, Mr. Plummer," the squat officer said. He just could not bring himself to call Denny by his preferred name. "Leave you to it." Whatever *it* is when you've just lost a wife, when you've just lost a life. They both made hat-tipping gestures and turned their backs as they headed toward the door, and Denny was thankful for that, to be left alone, and there he was, staring into the gray, his face as wet and slick as the bleak January snow.

Chapter 3

BACK IN THE dark space before she had children, she would have told you this: *I will never spend an afternoon hitting refresh on my computer to sign up for a fucking school dance.* And yet there she was, refreshing, trying to get past what was some kind of nightmarish virtual line for the Ziti with Your Sweetie Dance for her second grader, a dance that she wished she knew nothing about, except that, unlike Denny, she read the bulletins sent out by the PTO. There had probably been one bulletin, actually, where she gleaned something about early ticket release, but it had slipped through her soft mothering brain, like so many other things did these days. And somehow, her daughter also knew about the dance. The kids: They talked. Why there are not just traditional sign-ups like back in the '80s, well, Anna would never understand. She remembered a time when permission slips used to make it from backpack to kitchen counter and seamlessly to a teacher's desk without question or recrimination, even with a check attached. The Internet changed all that.

Refresh. Refresh. Refresh. Anna had spent over half an hour clicking on the stupidfuckingbuttons before she was allowed into an even more ridiculous waiting room. Queue after queue. That should be a band name, by the way. She went to select four tickets, but, wouldn't you know it, the fucking thing glared an angry red slogan back at her: SOLD OUT. How could a dance for elementary school students, hosted by the PTO, be sold out? On sale at noon, sold out five minutes later, in a town where not one woman she knows appears to have an actual job. Click, click, click. Lost to the stay-at-home moms. Maybe she should have paid more attention to that newsletter, with all of those technicalities about *early ticket releases* or whatever it had said.

She was in her first-floor office, on a cold and rainy day. It was painted Hague Blue, Farrow & Ball, maybe appropriate, she sometimes thought. The Hague. Who would name a color this, anyway? Okay, fine, it's a blue-gray city in the Netherlands, but that's not what anyone thought of when they thought of the *Hague.* They thought of the International Court of Justice, or, more appropriately, they thought of war crimes, of people doing terrible things, of nations holding one another accountable. Still, her office looked like one of those rooms that might appear in an issue of *Architectural Digest:* glossy paint running all the way up to the crown, all the way up to the ceiling. Her desk faced the yard, one-hundred-foot pine trees that grew taller here than they did in New York. One bad storm, Denny always liked to say. Whoosh. They could take down the whole house. Sitting in one place too long could make you start thinking the kind of thoughts that did no service to anyone. On Facebook, Anna looked up the PTO's page. Everyone was complaining about the tickets. They had sold out in minutes. In seconds. In nanoseconds.

"This is why you have to get the premium membership," one woman had written. "The pre-release was yesterday, over email."

Anna could hear Denny in her ear. *Don't respond. Don't get into it. Let these idiots have their premium PTO membership and just LEAVE IT ALONE.*

"Oh, shut up, Denny," Anna said to the empty room. She typed in a comment. Deleted it. Typed it again.

"Do you mean that in a public school u can pay more to get early access 2 events that all kids shld b able 2 attend," she wrote.

Five minutes. No response. Anna stared out the window. Probably not worth the irritation. A cardinal had appeared out of nowhere, had perched itself on a teak chair — Denny had meant to cover it but never mind — outside her office window. The bird was motionless, stark red against a gray January landscape. They were supposed to be mean, she seemed to remember. Or was that the blue jays? Or the robins? All the birds you saw in Disney movies, the ones that flitted about: You'd never want to encounter them in real life.

A red number appeared.

"Uh yeah that's what PREMIUM MEMBERSHIP means."

Wow. Just wow.

"That seems insane 2 me," she wrote back. "Not everyone can afford a PREMIUM MEMBERSHIP."

It was more than that, too, of course. It wasn't just the parents who couldn't afford the premium membership, but the kids who were left out. She thought back on the kids who had been left out of things when she was small herself, the ones she knew were from poorer families, who wore secondhand clothes, who lived in houses down along Washington Street. Their parents rented, didn't own, and you weren't supposed to talk about it, because you weren't supposed to talk about money. But those same kids had grown up with less opportunity, and it was always apparent, from the time they were seven to the time they turned seventeen.

Anna was thinking of those kids now — the ones she knew from childhood who would never be able to recapture the things they had lost, or the ones who would be edged out of the Ziti with Your Sweetie Dance due to some pretentious and unaffordable membership. Now she was off and running. The messages came fast and furious. *Premium Membership Hamilton PTO*, she typed into her browser, and there it was, staring back at her, just a few hundred dollars every year for early access to events, better seats at the graduation, and possibly even a rental house on the Cape for the summer if you won the raffle. It hadn't been an accident, all those people crammed into one virtual queue at the same time for the dance tickets scraps. It had been organized mayhem. Want a better shot? Pay the money. Feed the machine.

It was a horrifying idea, of course, that in order to gain equal footing in second grade, of all places, you would be required to pay the piper. That kids had to suffer as a result. Anna folded her hands in her lap. She felt a familiar rage unspool, a fire flower, like the kind Mario ate in Super Mario Brothers, except this one did not make her shoot hot balls of supersonic flame from her hands; all it did was make her burn hot from the inside. If she could rip everything from the walls of her Hague Blue office, she would (what was stopping her besides pride?). Comment after comment defended the PREMIUM MEMBERSHIP as some genius hack. Why stand in line for hours when you can just toss a little money at the system, her mothers-in-arms reasoned.

She looked at the time at the top of her computer. Two o'clock. She had been at this, she realized, for over two hours, fighting back and forth with other moms — under her real name — about the stupidfuckingschooldance. There had got to be a better way! Finally, she decided to put an end to it.

Google: Who is the president of the Hamilton PTO?

Answer: Mimi Mar, elected January 2016.

Bingo.

Of course, now that she had the answer, what exactly was she going to do with it? She did know Mimi Mar. Everyone knew Mimi Mar. Not two weeks ago, Anna had taken the kids over to the Ackerman Playground at Boy Scout Park, over in Boxford, the *big* playground, the *nice* playground, the playground where all the parents dressed up, like it was some agreed-upon precept. You had to wear your best boots, your fanciest puffer, and put on makeup and two-carat diamond studs before stepping out of the damn house. Yes, she had all of these things. No, she did not dress up to go to the fucking playground in winter, so she sat on the bench in the cold, scarf wrapped around her head, looking like a vagabond compared to extremely well-heeled women with designer fanny packs, and there, of course, was Mimi Mar, blond, fine-boned, in Michael Kors and some kind of very ridiculous Gucci situation, including a very *Gucci* belt that could literally strangle a person, it was so thick and wide and strong. She was petite – the kind of petite that came from regularly holding your hand up at the end of a meal. *No more for me, please.* Salads and Diet Cokes and an hour on the Peloton each day. Housewife thin. Her daughter was in the third grade, not at all Mimi Mar thin. That probably killed her. Well, it *would have* killed her, except that, somehow, Mimi's daughter was still the most popular, *and* captain of the elementary cheer squad (a thing Anna did not know existed until she moved to Hamilton), *and* a blue-ribbon equestrian, *and* the reigning Top Student at Winthrop, an award given out to the elite academic top performer in each grade every year. Harper Mar had snagged it every single year since kindergarten.

Mimi held a coffee – not Dunkin', probably because it was somehow beneath her – and chatted with other women who also wore designer outfits that were meant to be seen at the playground. Anna could hear words here and there. *Playdate. Dance. Soccer. Vacation plans. Skiing.* Small-town repartee. Louisa had found a friend near the swings and they were imagining an entire world for their dolls. A world, Anna guessed, where Barbie goes camping in extremely expensive boots.

Anna could have made small talk. It's not as if Mimi wouldn't have played along. A lot to be said for that, after all, in this kind of town – playing along, inventing some kind of role for oneself.

Maybe Anna was the problem and not Mimi. Ask the other women, who had assumed their roles in the Hamilton rankings with alacrity, and that would have been their take. Anna had befriended one or two. Ellen Wilson, who seemed like she was the most down-to-earth, who pulled her hair back into a ponytail, and wore — God forbid — a pink Red Sox hat to soccer practice, and who didn't even have a gunite pool or a very expensive SUV. She was the mother of one of Louisa's friends, and every once in a while, they texted back and forth.

I just can't get into the whole scene, Anna wrote one time, looking for solidarity.

They're not so bad!!! Ellen wrote back. It was a lot of exclamation points. Ellen was a classroom mom, someone who voluntarily signed up to go into the school and set up parties for the kids, which was a nice gesture, Anna had to admit, and something that she herself didn't have the bandwidth for. Everyone just wants to fit in here I think!!! Is anyone even really from hamilton?

Maybe not. Maybe everyone suffered from the same condition. It was like living through high school all over again, except they were supposed to know better now, since they were older. Tolerance, acceptance, letting people into a widening circle. Those were the values you learned once you went out into the world and came back to settle in a small town that looked and felt a lot like the small town that you yourself had grown up in. But, of course, the guys were all just grown-up jocks who liked to play sports on the weekends and the women were all competing for some kind of award for best-dressed or most-liked.

One thing most of these women also had in common was that they were somehow involved with the PTO. Anna was compulsively adherent to an adage she had learned from old Groucho Marx movies: Never become affiliated with a group that would have you as a member. It went something like that. If you were a child of the '90s who listened to grunge and wore flannel and drove up to Salem, New Hampshire, for underage piercings, chances were you still had a streak of subversiveness running through you. Growing up, you were either Contempo Casual or J. Crew, and it was unlikely that you traveled seamlessly between these two definitions of self. Were preppy people self-actualized? Had grungy people truly found themselves? Who was to say? But there was a certain truth scratched out beneath the grimy CDs they listened to in basements or in attics, achy, melodious, filled with the rawness of being teenaged and a little unloved.

You don't really leave that part of you behind, the part where you're the outcast and dig metal tacks into your shoes, tap dance down the abandoned hallway that no one gives two fucks about because it's just a place where the undesirables go at lunchtime, the dark hallway that only matters during Friday Night Lights — yeah, it's that kind of town. Anna hadn't, anyway.

Now, in her Hague Blue office, midday January light streaming through, Anna considers all of this: the chatty mothers at the playground who had never once asked her to participate; the text messages from Ellen, who had always been straightforward and kind; the blinking messages on Facebook, alerting her, over and over again, to the mounting crescendo of the school dance; the imbalance of all of it, the place they had chosen, the circles on the map they had drawn and the school districts they had researched, and the inevitability of landing somewhere that was both a choice and an accident. Were there any accidents? Nothing is ever an accident, nothing is ever a coincidence: That was something that had been burned into Anna's brain from childhood.

In her email, she fumbled, opened a message, closed it, typed a sentence, deleted it, typed it again. Angry mothers have words with administrators all the time, but was she going to write to Mimi Mar? That was the question. *Opening up some kind of can,* she could picture Denny saying. He liked to take a well-loved expression and turn it on its side. It wasn't even like he was from the south, unless Pittsburgh qualified. Some kind of can. Not *a can of worms*. What kind of can was this, Denny?

But she knew, by instinct, what he would say, that this would be difficult, that she was only going to make living in a small town harder, that she was always getting herself stuck in things for no good reason.

Mimi Mar's precious little third grader was going to be at that Ziti Dance, of course, dressed up like a drag queen under layers of tulle, and there were kids — Anna was sure of it now — who had missed out on the opportunity to do any of it.

Hi Mimi, she wrote, but erased it. She erased everything, typed out a million introductory sentences, started over, wished she still smoked the Parliament Lights that she gave up years back, because they always offered a fresh start, a new perspective, and anyway, weren't writers meant to smoke? Even if she was only a little bit of a writer — the kind who worked as stringer for the local paper, the kind who wrote obituaries of people who had lived somewhat small and ordinary lives, the kind who mostly made a living through soulless copywriting — wasn't she supposed to keep a stash of cigarettes crumpled in a desk drawer somewhere?

When they moved, she threw the last pandemic pack in the trash, and that was really it, for smoking, for the old life, for the dream of being an artist, or any real kind of journalist. Parting with dreams: not so hard. Parting with the notion of everyone getting the same shake: much harder.

We should talk about the PTO, she finally wrote. *It's starting to become a real problem. — Anna Plummer*

Chapter 4

DENNY HAD MET Anna Denton at a Montauk bar when she was thirty-two years old. He was five years older, coming out of a rocky and long relationship with a woman who had been a mediocre and overpaid private chef to multimillionaires in the Hamptons. They had never married — his call. Mostly, he never considered himself the marrying type, and he warned Anna of this right from the beginning. It was a pink, frothy day, start of season, as the East Enders liked to call it. Back then, he and Anna had both lived in the city but had found themselves out on eastern Long Island by chance, dragged out, both of them, by friends, crashing at underwhelming houses for the holiday weekend.

He had once accused her of sorcery. "You're a witch," he said. "There's something about you," and she didn't deny it, but instead tipped her head to the side and looked at him, the light picking up in her eyes, turning them green — they were prone to changing color — and dusting the accusation off.

"Witches aren't real, Denny," she said.

"You're real," he told her. "And you're a witch."

He didn't exactly believe that, though. He didn't believe in any mysticism, or in religion, not since Catholic school had turned him sour. His own parents still attended mass daily, still kept rosary beads roped around every available surface in their Florida Gulf Coast condo, but mostly Denny believed in magnetism and a certain order of the universe. That Anna had convinced him to live this life with her was part of her outstanding magic. He had been a head-down bachelor on the heels of a bad relationship, with a dog and a little bit of credit card debt, and she came along one May afternoon with smooth, tanned legs and something he could not quite put his finger on. Persistence might have been the word for it. She liked to tell people that she was terrible at taking no for an answer, and he had been all no, all resistance, all loner in his little life-for-one until she hammered her way into his heart.

"Don't get involved with me. I'm an accident waiting to happen," he said on the day that they met. Then he raised his margarita, rimmed with salt, even though he pretty much never drank stupid drinks like that, and toasted to her, and to the very pretty background scene unfolding behind her: rosy sky, cerulean water, people dancing like they'd never left the city before.

"It sounds like a warning, but I'll take it as an invitation," she had said. She was always saying things like that, cloaked in mystery, and maybe she didn't even know she was doing it at the time. He could never quite figure out if she knew her language was like that, always luring people in, making promises, sometimes delivering, other times not.

"I didn't say that," he had replied. There was something crackling that day. Electric. Like, you could almost feel the air snapping. Had he felt that before? A rainstorm on the horizon, except it wasn't going to rain, he was sure of that. One of those afternoons slipping into evening that promised a perfect sunset. (It delivered — he remembered that much.) Maybe they had drunk too much, or maybe they just fit the right way on the wooden benches that overlooked the water, and so, at some point, Denny put a hand on her knee and felt skin that was soft and smooth and even he knew that he couldn't fight whatever magnet was pulling him to her.

Later, he drove her home in his 1971 Chevelle, top turned down, Bose speaker on the dash because the radio had stopped working the minute he inherited the car. She hadn't tied her hair back and he tried not to look at her, but she wanted him to – he knew that much. She was staying in some upside-down house near the F streets, where the weather was always good, unlike the cloudy, rain-befallen area near Ditch Plains, and he pushed her hair back behind her ear. He meant to stop there, but she grabbed his hand. She really was a witch. He believed that. And then there was no turning back, not even when the lights of that upside-down house came on and a voice called out, "Anna, that you? I've been calling you! Where have you been?"

All that, of course, had been a very long time ago. In the in-between, they had settled into whatever the medium stage of marriage is. Anna woke up in the gloom before the sun, Denny rolled over and pretended to sleep for the remaining hour before the house shook with life, but actually didn't, tried to avoid his phone, tried to prevent his thoughts from racing, did none of those things, and finally stabbed around in the dark for a sweatshirt and pants, and then padded downstairs for the first in a long line of duties.

He had worked a series of different jobs throughout the course of their marriage, falling, finally, into computers, but the one he had now, as a self-governed carpenter of sorts, was his favorite. The pandemic brought all kinds of new purposes to the surface, and a weird tick in the Instagram lifeline made him an unlikely influencer, even though he barely knew how to make a reel. He began making things: small things at first, like a concrete patio table that consumed his boredom when he couldn't sit still at home. The base arrived from pieces of black pipe, and he mixed concrete and poured it into a wooden frame that he built out of spare pieces of scrap that had been lying around the basement.

Anna had come out every few hours, staring wide-eyed, first at the mess, then at the mess that had evolved into a developing *thing*. She had always been able to craft things from words, a talent he admired, but he could tell, from her face, and from the way she tilted her head a little to the left while looking, that this was beyond her.

"Well?" he asked. He didn't like soliciting praise, but he was proud of this thing that he had done with his hands.

"It is remarkable, Denny," she said. And then, just a dig, because she could. Always because she could. She looked back at him, turning on her heel, just for a minute. "But you knew that, right?"

Maybe that was why he had started making the reels, anyway. To prove something to her, to prove that he could do this thing and that someone would care about it. For the table he took three-second videos of the concrete, poured out like caramel. A nail gun, puncturing the surface of the wood for the frame. He asked Ben to hold the camera for just a second while he hammered. He spliced it all together and added a bunch of random hashtags and put it up on Instagram, and there it was, his beautiful mess, and he thought not much of it, really, until Anna came out to the patio the next morning, sun on her hair, dress sweeping behind her, carrying the catkins from the oak trees that made everyone sneeze.

"You're viral," she said.

"What?" He was shaking the mold, getting rid of the bubbles before the concrete was fully set. It was one of the things you had to do when you're building a table. It wasn't even done yet. There wasn't even a complete photo of it, just a series of process videos.

"See?" she clicked on the image.

He looked. Beneath the reel, there was a number, indicating

how many people had viewed it. Thousands. Actually, hundreds of thousands, a clear departure from any social media post he had ever put out into the world at this point. (Previous post's likes: thirty-two.)

She looked at him and blinked. "I don't know, Denny. People seem to like it. So keep doing it." It was the closest she could come, he figured at the time, to acknowledging that he was good at something. He considered that a win. He finished the table. It had a creamy gray top, speckled with flecks of pink and white in it. Online, someone offered him $6,000 for it, and he said no, but he offered to make another one if they could pick it up in person, and they said yes, and sure enough, a few weeks later, there was a transaction, masks, and a trailer hooked up to the back of a luxury SUV.

That was the beginning of his weird business, before things took off. He had never believed that the Internet had power like that, had never believed Anna, in particular, when she told him that people could become successful overnight in exactly this way. And then he had done it. But then, she was right about a lot of things, he now realized; she had a gut instinct that guided her and let her see the round and sharp edges of the world in ways that he couldn't.

"It can be as big as you want," she said once. "I feel like this could be a really big business."

"I don't know," he said. He was genuinely unsure about its sustainability. Before this, he had worked for other people. His long-term career had been in IT, and he had been good at that work, because he was a natural problem-solver, but he never quite knew how to ask for more, even when he knew he deserved it. The money was good. Every few years, he climbed up, except for the years when the economy was shit. He learned the things that others were too bored or too lazy to learn, he had a team beneath him, he was an executive with perks now, and that spot on the ladder was safe, so why disrupt it?

But Anna always believed in unsafe choices. "You don't get anywhere by standing still," she loved to say. Sharks die from immobility, and she was definitely a shark. She hated the idea of sitting at home during time off. She hated complacency in any and all forms. Hated people who failed to use their power to change the world. She never saw gray or nuance. It was black or white, good or evil, yes or no, and this kind of quality could be extremely endearing and powerful in a person, and also very frustrating. Still, it pushed him, humble Denny who only ever wanted to do the kinds of creative things that he liked – draw excellent pictures or build things with his hands – but who had fallen into computers as a way of making a living because, well, that's what adults did.

"Just throw everything you have at it and make it work," she said. "People are buying it. Let them overpay. You determine what your work is worth anyway. Capitalism 101." After he sold the table, he built a set of cabinets for a local family, a contract project. It was a business, Anna said. He could do furniture. Mirrors, like the one he once made as a pet project: the pages from *Moby-Dick* rolled up and encircling the center piece of glass.

"And what if it fails?" he wanted to know.

"Don't let it."

The advice always sounded so simple when she framed it that way, because, according to her, there were only two options: You succeeded, or you failed, and the only barrier standing between the two was you. He often wondered if seeing the world the way his wife did was refreshing or heavy. Was it easier to exist in this binary framework, where everything could be placed into one category or the other?

But the truth was, in this instance she was right. Her instinct for his work – that he could pursue the passion of his followers and his creativity – was intuitive. He made things. People wanted them. They paid big bucks for them. Enough for him to leave behind his past life in computers. Down the line, he would even consult for other furniture companies, like Thuma, a company based in San Francisco that made minimalist, low-profile beds and dressers, pieces that people coveted, heavy wood pieces, which Denny sketched out on card stock late at night when everyone else in the house had gone to bed. Once Anna had given him the push, there was no looking back, not at the office job he had held before, or whatever boring job he had held before that. It was like flying, this new opportunity, and yes, he had Anna to thank for the self-assurance to set himself free. She was always like this, igniting something in him that he never knew existed, and it was lovely and beautiful, and also a thing that could really make the wrong person extremely irritated, he knew, because not every person appreciated the perspectives so closely held by someone like Anna Plummer.

Chapter 5

Dear Anna,

Thank you so much for reaching out! I'm always happy to connect about issues regarding the PTO! I have to be honest. You are the only parent who has reached out expressing any concerns about the upcoming dance. Yes it's true that some parents were not able to register in time for the dance this year (we are so sorry about that but there just isn't enough space for everyone!!!), but I think most parents understand that there are plenty of other opportunities available for getting our kids together within the community!!! I haven't seen you at any of the PTO meetings, but I'd be really happy to connect with you in person to talk to you about how you can personally better serve our kids here in Hamilton!

We have so many upcoming events that are

```
great for all of our kids, so I hope you
consider becoming a member or attending some of
our meetings. Happy to send along a calendar!!
  Let me know if you'd like to meet up for
coffee sometime!!!
                                        —Mimi
```

Mimi had taken two days to respond to Anna's email, two whole days to compose this strange and oddly conciliatory note — if you could get past the part where she slyly accused Anna of being the only person in the entire town of Hamilton with any objection to what the PTO was up to. In the meantime, Anna had sifted through her emails, in search of... what, exactly? Evidence of some wrongdoing, she supposed. She had come across that newsletter, the one she had only casually read. An advertisement for the Ziti with Your Sweetie Dance, which was how she had found out about it in the first place. *Early-release tickets,* the newsletter had promised, and there had been a certain vagueness about the whole thing. *Sign up now and make sure to get a spot! Make sure you make this year's Event of the Season!!* No mention of a membership, but definitely a veiled threat about available space. That, in and of itself, Anna thought, was interesting. Who plans a dance for little kids without making sure that everyone could go? Whoever had penned this newsletter wanted to make one thing clear: Not everyone was invited to the party. First come, first served.

And then there was, of course, Mimi's email, itself a study in grammar and tone. In college, Anna had taken an introductory writing course called Logic and Rhetoric, whose purpose had been to arm freshman students with basic writing skills, and Anna could only think about how this email was the perfect specimen for any young professor or TA, with its exclamation overkill, with its perfunctory niceties.

But she had to write back. Of course she had to write back. To leave the email hanging in space was to allow Mimi some kind of upper hand. She could hear Denny in her ear now. *Just send a nice note back. Accept the invitation to coffee.* Anna, with every fiber of her being, did not want to be caught dead having coffee with Mimi Mar, but she knew this might be the best opportunity to get the point across: sit across a table from Mimi, mugs in hand, two adults in a public setting. Lay down the law.

"Fine, fine, fine," she breathed aloud, to no one, because it was early morning, just after the kids had left for school, and she was alone in a cold office, with Denny out in his shed, making God knows what for God knows whom.

> Hi Mimi,
>
> Thanks so much for getting back to me. I really appreciate it. Happy to get together to talk some of this through in person. If you're free today, I can meet at Honeycomb for coffee/lunch. Let me know.
>
> A.

The *A.* in the signature, she thought, made it sound more personal, less intimidating. She was sitting there staring, wondering whether or not she had made the wrong choice, when a response came in from Mimi: four words, indisputable.

Perfect. See you there.

It seemed kind enough, Anna thought, but she knew better. They were each preparing for battle, on not quite neutral ground, Honeycomb being firmly in Camp Mimi. By agreeing to meet, Anna had certainly agreed to *something*, though she wasn't sure quite yet what it was.

* * *

Honeycomb was the kind of bakery that was built to look like a farmhouse. A bluestone paver walkway led up to a door that was painted robin's-egg blue. Anna had actually only ever been to the bakery once before. It was always so crowded, the parking lot overflowing with Hamilton moms and UPPAbabies and glossy Mercedes GLS 450s, one of the many luxury SUVs of choice (All-wheel drive! For the snow!). Inside, a line snaked around a weathered wood table, where pricey home goods were for sale: tea towels and whisks with colored handles; slate cheese boards and little name tags for guests when they came over for dinner parties, although Anna never threw dinner parties. A basket on the floor beneath the table boasted batons of fresh bread, and Anna did fall for that. The breads looked perfect, deep brown and crusty, like the ones you found at boulangeries in Paris.

She bought herself an iced coffee — New Englanders never change, this she knew about herself — and one of the stunning, fist-sized *pains au chocolat,* and looked out for Mimi. Anna hadn't been sure about what to wear but had settled on a fluffy blue and white sweater with a cowl neck and a drippy-looking pattern from Lululemon; black leggings and shearling-lined boots; plus a shiny black coat from Amazon, the coat that had become unpredictably trendy even though it cost under two hundred dollars.

Scanning the room, she discovered Mimi in a corner, near a window, the sunlight enhancing a very expensive blond highlight. Mimi was not looking around. She was instead engaged in what looked to be a very serious conversation with a man in a pinstriped suit and a tiny gold button on the lapel; he was bent over her table, intent on hearing everything she said. She wore large Gucci glasses atop her head, and Anna could tell — even from a relative distance — that she was a woman who invested in eyelash extensions. Mimi hadn't bothered to take off her expensive-looking quilted black coat with fur around the collar.

Anna walked over, coffee in one hand, pastry in the other. The man backed away, an instant ghost. Mimi only looked up when Anna's shadow blocked the ray of sun running across her flawless face.

"Oh, Anna, I didn't see you," she said. Big smile. Big teeth. Maybe veneers. She drew a hand out, expressing to Anna to sit, so she did. "That was... well, I'm sure you already know. Thanks for meeting me."

Anna didn't know. She must have worn a face that betrayed her naivete. A question mark.

"Representative Murphy?" Mimi said, her voice clipped.

"Oh, yes, of course," Anna said. The congressional representative for the third district, their district, Essex County, Thomas Murphy. And here, at Honeycomb, in the middle of the day. *How about that,* Anna thought.

"Just catching up," Mimi said.

"I didn't realize you knew each other," Anna said. She opened her bag with the croissant in it and flakes flew everywhere. Was it her imagination, or did Mimi give her a sideways glance? Maybe members of the PTO did not eat. Maybe meetings over coffee were meant to include only coffee and nothing else. "Sorry about that," Anna said, hastily wiping the crumbs from the table.

"Yes. Well, some people say I know *everyone,*" she said. "But that's just a silly rumor." She brushed crumbs from her side of the table. "What's a little croissant among friends?"

Were they friends? Anna wouldn't go that far. "Well, anyway," she said, clearing her throat. "I just wanted to say, I don't want to get into a big argument."

Mimi raised her eyebrows. "Argument? Certainly not!" She laughed. "In any case, I don't really argue."

"You don't?" Anna was taken aback. What kind of person never had an argument.

"Not really!"

"Oh."

“I just say what I need to say and then I move on!”

Her tone, Anna noticed, was chipper, but there was something beneath it. A message that she was meant to receive. Mimi Mar was the boss – not just of the PTO, but of everything in her life. You agreed with her, or you found another place to hold court. It wouldn’t have surprised Anna one bit to know that Mimi had been, for instance, homecoming queen, or class president.

“I just wanted to talk about the whole thing where parents can pay more money? To be premium members of the PTO?” Anna said. She could hear her own voice, always so completely sure of itself, breaking down. It was annoying, this sense of powerlessness.

“It’s called the Incentive Program,” Mimi said. She placed her hands on the table. Her nails were long and rounded and painted a pale pink, and the diamonds on her left hand – a solitaire in what looked like a platinum setting, as well as a diamond band – were very large.

“I’m sorry, the *Incentive Program,*” Anna said, laughing, and then realizing she was in the wrong company. Mimi did not look similarly amused. “I mean, did you ever think that maybe incentivizing parents to pay money was...unfair?”

“Unfair how?” Mimi lifted those perfect hands of hers and folded them and leaned in close on her elbows. She seemed genuinely interested. “This is the fairest way, Anna. We’re giving parents the opportunity to secure a spot. What is more fair?”

“Fair for the parents who can afford it,” Anna said. “What about the ones who can’t.”

Now Mimi leaned back in her chair. She was quiet for a minute. “Anna,” she said, in a voice that was barely above a whisper, like it was commiseration between friends. “This is Hamilton. *Everyone* can afford it.”

She was almost right. Hamilton’s median household income was $138,000 per year, and it was home to rolling acreage, an equestrian sensibility, a thriving public school system. But Hamilton was also home to the Acord Food Pantry, a thirty-year-old space where locals had been quietly dropping off and picking up things that they needed. There was, Anna knew, an Affordable Housing Trust, run by the town, and, three years earlier, the town had even passed a plan to build more affordable housing for its own residents. Meaning: There was a need. Meaning: Not every single person in this largely white, largely wealthy New England town was doing okay, or better than okay. There were, Anna knew, plenty of parents who kept their struggles close to the vest.

"Not everyone, Mimi," Anna said. "There are families even here who have a hard time. I know that's hard to believe."

"The PTO is always happy to support anyone who needs a little extra help," Mimi said. It was flat, the way she said that. She unclasped her hands and smiled that toothy smile again. Anna could tell that the conversation had reached its natural conclusion. Mimi could not be moved. Pay the money, get the key to the city. Otherwise, admit to the PTO that you were a have-not. These, according to Mimi Mar, were your options. She would not hear of any alternative.

"But then parents would have to come to the PTO and let them know that they needed the money," Anna said. "Wouldn't it just make more sense to charge for other things, instead of access to a dance?"

"But we're raising money *for the kids*. We're doing this for our kids! For your kids! There's no harm in that. Anyway, if a family is struggling a little bit, that's hardly anything to be embarrassed about," Mimi said.

So said Mimi Mar, who had clearly never had to ask for money to assist in her own survival. Anna could not imagine an embarrassed version of Mimi, a version of a story where this woman before her — so calm, so well-kempt — had to slither before the Hamilton PTO in search of charity for her children. A ticket for a dance. Assistance in access to the thing that tax dollars are supposed to secure, even in a wealthy town, or especially in a wealthy town.

"Maybe people who have to ask for help see it differently," Anna said.

"Well, I just think that the PTO is always happy to assist in our community, and it's sort of outrageous to say that we wouldn't all be on the same team," Mimi said. "Right, Anna? We're all on the same team here!"

"I'm just saying..." Anna started, but she could already see that a dullness had come over Mimi's eyes. They had reached an impasse. If Anna had hoped to move the needle, that hope had now been abandoned. Mimi Mar was resolute: The PTO was benevolent. The PTO was grand in its ambition. The PTO was Saving the Children, and Anna Plummer could get right out of Hamilton with her accusations.

"You are saying what exactly?" Mimi asked.

"It's classist. That's what I'm saying. Kids who have no money are at a disadvantage. I'm sorry to have to be so blunt, but that's the truth. Hamilton is wealthy, but not every single person lives..." — Anna spread her hands out to indicate the room, the women, the very town of Hamilton — "...like this."

Mimi smiled a frozen smile. "You know, Anna, I don't appreciate the implication. That we're — what was the word you used? — *classist.* Kind of ridiculous, actually. Of course we want everyone to succeed." She paused for a minute, appearing to consider her next words. "You know, I'd really watch what you say to me, Anna. *Classist.* That's almost, like, a threat, right?"

"I'd hardly call it that, Mimi."

"I guess it just depends on how you take it, then."

"I think we can both agree that we just want some people to succeed a little more than others, right?" Anna said, smiling.

"I don't think we can agree on that, actually. But in any case. I have an afternoon meeting," Mimi said. "So, I do have to get going. I hope we've cleared things up here?"

"I'm just wondering," Anna said. "What if we haven't? Cleared things up?"

It was the first time Anna had seen a change in Mimi. That porcelain face — for just a second — twisted into a contortion. Had Anna imagined it? But just like that, it was back to normal, like a doll you see in a horror movie. Blink once, imagine its disfiguration; blink again, it's as if it never happened. Mimi pursed her lips, which made her cheeks tuck in just a little. She had a dimple on one side, Anna now noticed. People probably thought that was cute and endearing.

"It's best if we have. Cleared things up," she said. There was no room for ambiguity. "And I think we have!" At that, it was as if a switch had flipped. She clapped both hands together and stood up with a little hop, allowing the chair to jump back against the wall of the bakery, and Anna could see that Mimi's boots (also Gucci!) had a heel to them — they were designed for neither snow nor rain. "I'm so, so glad we did this!"

"Right," Anna said. "Me, too."

"I have to run, but you know where to reach me," Mimi said, collecting her phone and her purse. "And I hope you'll consider, you know, *the membership.*" At that, she took a step forward and leaned in and did the thing that wealthy white women in New England towns did, grabbing Anna by the shoulders and pulling her into a half-hug and barely brushing her cheek with the kind of kiss that you offer someone that you don't know very well and don't care to know much better. Anna's body was stiff. She didn't yield to the embrace. Mimi squeezed Anna tight. Surprisingly tight. *She's got a bodybuilder's grip,* Anna thought to herself. *She could wrestle a tiger to the ground.* Then stopped herself from laughing at the thought.

"So *good* to see you, though, Anna," Mimi said, and Anna could tell that she almost meant it, that most people would have been fooled. "We'll have to do this again sometime." She pulled the big black Gucci glasses down over those fluttering eyelashes and then she was gone, leaving Anna Plummer with the crumbs of the croissant and a baguette to bring home, one loaf of bread that she would contemplate tearing into in the car.

Chapter 6

HE WOKE UP in the night, sometimes twice, three times, sticky with his own sweat, imagining a depressed side of the mattress, realizing there was nobody there. The air felt chilled, like he was sharing the space with a ghost, but then, Denny remembered, he *was* sharing the space with a ghost, because Anna was everywhere: in the paint colors she selected, and the upholstery that was her idea (the fucking *velvet,* she loved to announce, to anyone who would listen), and the diffusers that lived in unused corners, smelling of Balsam and cranberry, irrespective of the season, since she had a thing for Christmas.

In the first few weeks, he left the house untouched, as if willing her much-anticipated return. Despite her proclivity for tidiness, a pair of her slip-on sneakers — Vans, inexplicably decorated with bagels — sat on the middle landing to the stairs, and he did not bother to bring them up or down. It was as if he expected someone to come for them. Mornings, he found that Ben came and stuck his feet into them, then took them out, dazed. They were all waiting for something to happen that never did: for Anna to walk through the door, her purple perfume of energy behind her, sometimes a pulsing angry purple, sometimes lilac-hued, soft.

Thinking back on it later, Denny would remember almost nothing about the funeral. The service was at Twomey, LeBlanc, on High Street, in Newburyport, at Anna's mother's request. Anna herself would probably have preferred a party over at the Elks, with free Bud Light for everyone (he seemed to remember her once saying she wanted to have a funeral party at a Chinese restaurant, but good luck finding a place big enough in Newburyport, and anyway, Szechuan Taste had closed down).

There were people he knew and people he didn't, thanks to an obituary taken out in the *Daily News*; he had nothing to do with that, either. The white walls of grief had made him a shell of a person in those first days. He was awake in the morning with the express purpose of dressing and feeding his children. In the evenings, he stumbled to bed realizing that he had gone hours without eating, and then walked down into the kitchen in a daze, picking through casseroles that had been left behind by neighbors and friends, a kindness he felt he didn't deserve.

All of that time was compressed, impossible to parse. The only distinguishable moments, Denny realized, were the ones punctuated by visits from the police, which seemed frequent enough. Denny could feel them poking around like dogs sniffing days-old trash. At first, they had come by only in what he thought of as an ever-widening circle. Evidence, site investigation, procedural stuff, they said. But soon, Denny started to get the sense that he might be a suspect in his wife's murder, and he became gripped by a sense of unease.

The stubbier officer, Denny had come to know by now, was named Malkin, a local guy who once played hockey, and well, too. In fact, everyone called him Sticks, though you'd never know from looking at him. Sticks had stopped by exactly three times since The Night. The first time, it was to drop off a ziplock bag filled with a few things that had once belonged to Anna: a wedding band with five diamonds on top, all adding up to one carat total. Where was the engagement ring, Denny wanted to know? *Musta come off in the river.* Denny didn't believe that part for a second, didn't believe most things cops told him, never had. Despite the officer's kindness on that first night, Denny had grown leery of him. Sticks had the kind of smarmy way of talking out of the side of his mouth that made it sound like everything he was saying was a lie. That ring had belonged to Anna's mother, one large oval diamond in the center, surrounded on the side by two baguettes, as they called them, though it made Denny think of bread, each time, without fail. Now it was either beneath a block of ice in the Ipswich River, or, more likely, sitting on the charmed finger of some police officer's wife, who would never dare wear the thing out in public.

A few nights after the wedding band was returned, Sticks showed up a second time, this time with an officer Denny had never seen before. Sticks held his hat in his hand, much like the first time he had come to the house.

"Mr. Plummer," he said when Denny came to the door. Denny, busy feeding his two children, had taken some time. No use correcting the officer who, he could see, would plainly never call him Denny.

"Did you want to come in?" he asked.

"No, no." Sticks cleared his throat. The other officer looked uncomfortable. He was slightly taller, also round, and stared at his shoes. "It's just . . ." Sticks continued: "We're going to ask you if you can come into the station. Sometime? Maybe this week?"

"You came here at dinnertime to ask?"

"People are usually home at dinnertime," the second officer offered.

Sticks looked at him, and this time not with kindness.

"We're sorry to have bothered you," Sticks said. "We just wanted to ask." And that was it. They disappeared into the January night, which had turned a bruising sort of cold, the kind that burns your cheeks the second you step outside.

But on the third time around, they weren't as kind. The knock came a week later. Denny hadn't been avoiding it. He had only forgotten. Anna had signed the kids up for ski lessons on Wednesday nights. There was Spanish on Mondays, and library on Tuesdays and the gym classes to remember and the snow pants to pack with the regular pants. The groceries, of course, and the laundry. So much laundry. Sheets needed to be stripped and washed, baths needed to be drawn. Here was the grief, hanging heavy like a cloud, thick and dark and impossible to navigate. Before he knew it, another week had passed, another week without his wife, another week without a drive to the station.

Sticks's knock, on this third appearance, was pronounced. Denny didn't need to guess who was at the door.

"Officers," he said, giving a nod.

"Mr. Plummer," the officer said. "Maybe you know why we're here?"

"I assume it's to ask me why I haven't been down to the station yet."

"Good guess."

"I do apologize for that," Denny said. "I did lose track of the time a bit." He gestured around the entryway to the house, which was a mess: papers overflowing on a credenza; a glass of water with a ring of condensation large and wide around its base; toys surrounding the foot of the stairs.

"I see," Sticks said. "Sorry about all this. Just see to it you get in soon?"

"I will," Denny said. "I really, really will." He meant it, too.

Denny was dressed in a flannel shirt over a thermal waffle one, threadbare Levi's, boots, and a beige Carhartt coat. The kids would be at school for four more hours, time enough to get down to the station, talk through whatever Sticks needed so desperately to discuss, and get back.

The police station was part of a complex that included the library and town hall — all municipal needs wrapped into one. You could buy your trash stickers and file a noise complaint at the same time. Plainly convenient in a place where nothing ever really happened.

It was ten in the morning, and Denny was on deadline for a table and chairs for a family down the road in Boxford: $20,000 for a custom set, and he had to get it done by next week. It would cover a few months' mortgage and keep them on steady ground, which was all these projects ever did — pave the way for more projects.

The snow from the week before had evaporated, large piles of it shoveled to the sides of the lot, now turned gray with car exhaust and dirt. Denny parked his Jeep — Anna's Volkswagen had been taken into police custody, though he didn't see it here in the lot — and made his way to the door, when he saw Sticks right before him, heading in, wearing a blue bomber jacket and holding a cup of coffee.

Denny wasn't sure if Sticks had seen him, but the officer didn't miss a beat.

"Ah, there he is," Sticks said, turning and smiling out of the side of his mouth, with what almost looked like a snarl. "The man of the hour."

"A pleasure, as always," Denny said, extending a hand, but Sticks didn't take it, holding up his coffee as excuse.

"Shall we?" the officer said, motioning to the door of the station with his elbow.

Denny nodded.

Inside, the station was painted greige, the same color, Denny noted, as his unpleasant and still-unrenovated bathroom, a project that would now remain unfinished.

"Deb, you can hold my calls for the meantime," Sticks said to a woman behind a thick double-paned sheet of plastic or glass who stood guard at the front desk. She wore her hair in an unflattering '80s style: bangs in two layers, top section a roll formed with what must have been a curling iron, likely held fast with Aqua Net. Her eye shadow was bright blue, but she couldn't have been more than thirty-five. A relic, Denny thought. A whiff of the past right here in the present. She reminded him, in an oddly pleasant way, of his grandmother, a woman with a fashion sense that never accurately represented the time, but who tried, at least, who went to the hairdresser every week, and who wore makeup every day until her last, blue eyeshadow and all.

Denny followed Sticks through a door that led into the back of the station. It was a maze: A long hallway led to a series of smaller rooms that looked like the nondescript, blocky spaces that had so fascinated his wife on the *Dateline* episodes she so religiously watched.

"Right in here," Sticks said, stepping back and allowing Denny to take the lead. The room was small, with no windows, two chairs, and a metal desk between them.

Denny sat down in the nearest chair. The room was cold. The chairs were cold. The room was very bright. He looked up in the corner: camera, green dot. Anna would be proud. *Dateline* had paid off.

"Water?" Sticks asked.

"I'm good," Denny said.

Sticks sat in the opposite chair, taking a second to position himself. "Thanks for, uh, finally coming in," he said, drawing out the word *finally*. He smiled that sort of shit-eating smile again. Denny had come to the conclusion that he did not like the officer, though maybe this wasn't the best moment to have an epiphany of this nature.

"Sorry about the wait," Denny said.

"The reason we wanted to have you in here was that what we originally thought about Mrs. Plummer, well, turns out there are some additional facts," Sticks said.

"Facts?"

"We have a bit of a situation," the officer said. He placed a beefy hand on the metal desk. He still had his coffee, cardboard cup, large, Dunkin' Donuts, smelling like artificial vanilla, gripped in the other. Hard to take a man like that seriously, Denny, who drank only espresso — black, naturally — thought. Anna had sworn by Dunkin' Donuts, as many New Englanders did, but he had never himself caved.

Denny chewed the inside of his lip, a habit he took up while nervous. "A situation?"

"The exposure," Sticks said. "It's a little more complicated than we originally thought."

"Wait a second," Denny said. Plausible, this idea that they were both on the same team, even though, sitting here, they both knew that they were combatants, not friends. "What are you saying here?"

Sticks looked at Denny, tapped an index finger on the table. "I'll get to the point. This wasn't an accident."

"I'm sorry, Officer, I think I'm going to be sick." Denny heaved for a moment, and the officer slid a black plastic trash can toward him, but there was nothing in his stomach to release, hadn't been for days. His sweat ran cold. Suddenly, it dawned on him: He was here for a murder investigation. What had happened?

What was it that Anna was always saying, on Friday nights, on that stupid velvet couch? The husband was always the first suspect. Denny Plummer, called into the police station in Hamilton — now it was clear as day — not to discuss an engagement ring gone missing, or some detail lost in the ephemera of his wife's cut-short life. He was, he now realized, a rat trapped in a maze. He was a suspect. Something had happened that had been unintentional.

His wife had not simply vanished. She had *been* vanished. There had been causality. Intent. He was, he now realized, angry. Not at his wife, but at the so-called situation. The sick feeling that had emerged the last time he saw Sticks had come back. He could feel that same shaky feeling, the feeling of being on the verge of fainting. He could go for that water now, but no one was offering.

"What happened?" he said. He had the sense that his own voice was betraying him. Anna, had she been here, surely would have coached him on how to tamp down his anger and his depthless sadness, on how to appear normal and functional in the face of such an unimaginable accusation. True, the officer had not yet said the words, but Denny could feel them lurking, just another series of ghosts.

"Why don't we start with me asking the questions," Sticks said, interrupting Denny's thoughts. "Like, where were you that Wednesday, when your wife went missing?"

Denny raced through the schedule in his mind. His life now existed on two planes: Before and After. Before, he had a complete life, a life with a wife, a life with a family. After, he had a life that was just skeletal remains. A half-life. Barely a life. What was he doing in those Before Times? Who could remember that far back? Now he had to try. Monday: Spanish. Tuesday: Library. Denny could see the schedule in his wife's messy handwriting. On Wednesday evenings, the kids had ski lessons at Bradford for two hours, from four to six.

"The school bus brought the kids home a little after three," he said. "I remember, Anna told me she was going out with friends and that she wouldn't be home until late and that I shouldn't wait up." He paused. Thought back. It had gotten late. That had been normal. Then, it had gotten *very* late, and it had stopped seeming so normal. He had called her phone, twice, he thought. Sent her a few texts. "We went to Bradford. Ski lessons. I made dinner for the kids. After I put the kids to bed and I got into bed myself and texted her and when she didn't write back, I thought something might be wrong. That's when I texted Di."

"Who is Di now?" Sticks asked.

"Anna's best friend since childhood. They had gone out together. Or I thought they had." *Out with friends.* That was what Anna had said. But which friends? Denny had thought instantly of Di, but Di hadn't seen her that night, she said.

"And Di — is this Diane Maguire?"

"The same."

"She hadn't seen her?"

"No."

"And you don't know who was out with her?"

"I... No, I don't."

"You don't know who your wife's other friends are, Mr. Plummer?" Sticks looked at him with concern.

"She's usually with Di. Di was also worried, and she was trying to help me find out who else had seen her."

Sticks stopped, shook his head, and took a few notes.

"Those skiing lessons are, what, two hours?" he asked, redirecting.

"Yes, plus it takes about a half hour to get there and back," Denny said.

A half hour. What could he have done in that time? How much time had he wasted, not knowing, not acting, not thinking? Sticks, with his questions, barking up the wrong tree, but Denny could not stop his own thoughts from their downward trajectory: *What if it was his fault? What if he had driven around the haul-out? What if he had found her? What if he could have stopped it?*

"Know how long it takes to get to the canoe haul-out from Bradford?"

But how could he have known where to look for her? How could anyone have known?

"I honestly don't," Denny said.

Who had hurt his wife? Didn't he have the right to know?

Sticks leaned back and seemed to consider this. The coffee had created an unfortunate-looking ring on the metal table, sticky. "It takes, oh, I'd say, twenty minutes. Faster than that if you can drive pretty good."

"Before we go any further," Denny said, "do I need to get a lawyer?"

That gave Sticks pause. "I find," he said, "that the only people who ask for lawyers are the ones who are guilty of something."

Denny felt that wave of nausea again. He also knew that wasn't true. People got lawyers to protect themselves. But here he was, stuck between a rock and a hard place. He wanted to be indispensable to the police, mostly because he wanted to know more about what had happened to his wife. He also wanted to loosen whatever tension had suddenly emerged in this bright, windowless room, where he was being treated not as a grieving husband but instead as a homicide suspect.

That tone, anyway. It sent Denny into a tailspin. Few things could make him react — it was a common grievance of Anna's that Denny was too slow to anger, even when he should feel *something* — but the implication that he was somehow responsible brought the blood to the tips of his fingers, up to his throat. He could feel it rising like bile. Maybe that was the intention, he thought, to rile him up, to get him to scream. Well, Sticks was going to get exactly what he wanted, then.

"I'll tell you what you need to know, but I also need to know what happened *to my wife*!" Denny said, slamming a hand down on the table. Sticks looked momentarily startled before twisting his mouth into a grin, and Denny realized that this had been the point, to provoke a reaction, to prove that he was capable of violence.

"Can we go back to where we were, then, Mr. Plummer?"

"Yes, sure, ask me what you'd like to ask, but I'd also like to ask some questions myself," he said.

"We'll see where we get," Sticks said, making no promises.

"You've lived here how long? I mean, probably long enough to know how long it takes to get to the haul-out, wouldn't you say, Mr. Plummer?"

"I know how to get to the haul-out. I don't know it well," Denny said.

There was, Denny knew, a practical problem with Sticks's theory. Even on a good night in January, slick roads eased with salt, Denny would have had to be a mastermind to have figured out a way to drop off two kids at Bradford, get to the canoe haul-out and, what — kill his wife in under an hour, all to make it back in time for pickup?

"You know how to get there, though."

"I know I didn't kill my wife. I know you still haven't told me what happened to her."

"Your wife. She was... well... we thought it was the elements." Sticks was more serious now. Maybe even a little kind. He looked Denny straight in the eye. He was searching — for humanity, or for clues, or maybe just for whatever it is that two people search for when the only thing they have in common is a dead person. "We're trying to establish where you were. We're trying to establish who might want to *do something* to a person like your wife. Following up on leads. Tying up loose ends."

Sticks, for his part, needed an answer, and the easier answer was the better answer. Less work. A more logical conclusion. It was unlikely that he was going to go too far in search of a thing that didn't make sense when the thing that did make sense was right here, a guy in Carhartt, maybe not brutish, but certainly brutish enough. A guy who worked with his hands. Callused. Strong enough to commit a crime, and maybe, like any guy, fiery enough to burst through at times.

This line of questioning, though, infuriated Denny, made him see why Anna had always seen the worst in cops. He would have done anything for Anna, and he had spent the last years of their marriage trying to prove to her that he was worthy. People always said these things when people died, that they would trade places, that they would do anything to have the time back, and he had never really seen it, not until now. But he was useless. He thought of what Anna used to say, a line from a poem, and it hung there, the *foul rag and bone shop of the heart.* It occurred to Denny that he didn't know what that meant, and maybe good poetry wasn't supposed to mean anything, it was only supposed to feel, and that was exactly the point: He was rag, he was bone, he was the foulest without her.

"Did anyone see you? At Bradford? Maybe you have a few eyewitnesses that you can recall that you can get over my way? That would be extremely helpful, you know."

"My kids," Denny said. *They were so small, his kids. Like birds.* "I dropped them off. The ski instructors."

"Right, right," Sticks said. "But what about anyone else. Where were you during the lesson? Did you stand out in the cold that whole time? What I'm saying is: That's a long time to stand waiting on a January night. I wouldn't do it myself, and I played hockey." Sticks laughed, a short honk of a laugh, meaning, well, it wasn't really funny.

"No. Maybe for a minute, I guess. I usually just sit in the lodge."

"Usually? Or that night? Because I'm particularly interested in what you were doing on the night that your wife disappeared."

"Usually. That night. I was trying to get in touch with Anna. I had a project I was working on. I was sending some emails."

"Mmm." Sticks didn't seem happy with this answer. "So your wife, she doesn't come home. Which is unusual for her, would you say?"

"Yes, it's unusual, but since she went out, I wasn't sure when she would be home. At first, it didn't seem so unusual." And really, it *hadn't* been so unusual. She had gone out. She had been out for a little while. It had been late. He had texted her. He had been busy with the kids. Then, suddenly, it had been too late. He had texted Di. Di had offered her help. Morning had come. All of this happened in such a short period of time. A person is there and then she is not. No time to calculate when she has slipped out of the web of the universe. No time to calculate when you could have gone back and done something to prevent the biggest loss.

"And so you spend a few hours on email, or just, what, you can't really recall?"

"I guess I can't recall."

"You know, we've been sitting around here for fifteen, twenty minutes now, and it occurs to me." Sticks picked up the coffee, took a long draw. *Must be cold by now,* Denny thought to himself. "You still haven't asked exactly how it is your wife... expired." Expired. Another strange choice of words. Not unlike exposure. Denny thought of milk, left out too long. It is irreconcilable, his wife, the milk, the greige chamber in which he is now trapped, the metal chair and the smell of fake vanilla, all of it.

But he *had* asked, and Sticks had ignored him. Denny knew it was a setup — another ploy to get him to react — but he fell right into it again, pictured Anna's moon face and her shiny legs and the way she sort of sang the end of a syllable sometimes when she was happy, or the way the light seemed to come up from behind her in summer, how it trailed her, how it almost flowed from her, and from this pool of memories a flash of fire ignited.

"I did!" he raged, and was immediately sorry he had yelled. "I asked from the start! I asked for all of this information from the start! I came in here voluntarily, trying to help you, and now I'm being treated like a goddamned suspect."

"Strangulation," Sticks said, calmly and without being asked a second time. A way with words, this man. "Ligature marks around the neck, but we didn't see those at first, what with the cold and everything. So, as you can see, we have ourselves this ..."

"Situation," Denny interrupted angrily. "You already said that."

Another officer shuffled past the door, which Sticks hadn't bothered to close. This was informal, after all. The officer stopped, did a double take. Sticks nodded. *Sure, man, come in, join the party.* "Mr. Plummer, this is ..."

Denny closed his eyes and massaged the bridge of his nose. *This probably isn't helping,* he thought to himself. It was infuriating, the fact that he was here, answering questions from some bumbling idiot, when he had been stuck at Bradford with the kids when his wife disappeared. Even if you ignored the sheer impossibility of it – driving from Bradford to Ipswich to strangle Anna and back in time to pick the kids up from their ski lessons – there was no earthly reason for any of it. Denny's marriage had not been in trouble. He and Anna had been co-conspirators. She had been a part of him. He might as well have lost a piece of his own body. That was how well he knew how to function in this world without her. And now, in this stained, cold, and ugly station, he was being accused of the worst kind of crime, the crime of degenerates and sociopaths who are willing to give up every single good thing they have in one moment of passion. Denny Plummer wasn't that man. Denny Plummer hated men like that, and he hated the men who thought he might resemble men like that.

"I do have one more question, actually," Denny said, forcing himself to be more calm, before the other officer could begin another line of questioning.

"Sure, what's that?" Sticks said. "We're happy to answer any questions you may have, of course, Mr. Plummer. We understand that you may have some...concerns here."

"Am I being arrested?" Point of fact. He needed to get out of the station. He needed to get back to the house, where his things were. Where his wife had once been.

Sticks smiled. "Now why would we be arresting you, Mr. Plummer? Do you have something to confess?"

Denny stood up, planting both hands on the table. "I just got the feeling that this was going somewhere a little ugly, that's all," he said. "But if there's nothing else, I think I'll go now."

"You're free to do whatever you like, actually," Sticks said. "You, sir, are free as a bird. I just wouldn't go too far."

"I can't go wherever I want, then?"

"Are you planning on taking a trip, Mr. Plummer? That's the kind of thing the Hamilton Police Department might be interested in knowing." Sticks stopped and looked down at the table, picked at something that wasn't there.

"I have no plans to do anything. I'm just trying to establish my rights. I'm not under arrest. You can't tell me if I'm a suspect. And, near as I can tell, I'm a free man. So, I can do the things I normally do. Correct?"

"You summed it up, Mr. Plummer. You can live your life the way that you normally would, and we absolutely cannot stop you," Sticks said. Denny could detect a subtext. Yes, he could go wherever he wanted, but the officer wasn't necessarily recommending it. They'd probably be watching him, though he didn't necessarily care.

"With that in mind," Denny said, standing up, and tipping an invisible hat, "I think I'll be heading out. Appreciate the information here."

He had come in as a volunteer, but they couldn't hold him, he knew that much.

"I do have to get back. The kids. If you find any leads on my wife's murder, you know where to find me." He let the word hang, turned on his heel and made his way out of that maze, door after door, until he reached that thick January sunlight, ice-cold, a drink of which he had never wanted so badly in his entire life.

Chapter 7

IT WAS THE night of the dreaded dance, which Anna had mostly forgotten about. Mostly. Louisa had been keeping tabs, because seven-year-olds forget nothing, locking away every imperceptible slight and wrongdoing in some lockbox of the brain for later use. Honestly, Anna couldn't fault her daughter. She had been exactly the same, had built the same arsenal up against her own mother, using decades-old pain whenever she needed something to be angry about. Today Louisa was sulking around the house in an old pair of torn jeans and a tie-dyed T-shirt from summer camp that said *Camp Chris* across the front, swearing she would never again find happiness.

"Everyone," she said to Anna. "Everyone at school. Everyone! Everyone is going to the dance!"

"Kiddo, I wish I had better news to report, but there just were not enough tickets to go around this year," Anna said. She had watched her bird-boned daughter arc through all of the human emotions of defeat: anger, resistance, denial, an attempt at manipulation. Perhaps they could just show up anyway, she had suggested. No, no, Anna said. That certainly was not a good idea.

"But *why aren't there enough for all the kids?*" Louisa sobbed. "It isn't fair!" Stomp, stomp, stomp. She had made a bit of a game out of this, up the stairs, down, a circle around the kitchen island, the same refrain about the *unfairness* of it (Anna didn't disagree, but she had to lie about it in order to dodge a larger argument). More stomping. A few tears. A little bit of flailing on the floor of the kitchen, which, Anna noticed, was dirtier than she had thought, as evidenced by her daughter's now gray-looking T-shirt. It was a bitterly cold February night. Anna could think of nothing cozier, anyway, than staying in by the fire, like when her children were tiny and only wanted to be close to her, but they seemed to reject her at every turn now, and this was just another rejection.

"There will be other dances," Anna said, a consolation prize at best. "I'll tell you what. You go get changed and we can all figure out something to do tonight that will be even better than having mediocre spaghetti with a bunch of kids from your school."

Louisa's eyes turned big and wet at the mention of the word *spaghetti*.

"But, Mom!" she wailed. "This isn't just pasta! It's a whole... thing!"

Anna knew she had misstepped, and it made her feel terrible to see Louisa like this, broken. Her daughter was dramatic, that was true, but it felt devastating to a seven-year-old to be the odd one out, the excluded party. Louisa had crumpled onto the floor again, a little pile of person, shattered by this stupid, silly little dance, and although Anna had always repeated the same refrain to her kids about life not being fair — about fairness being no measure of anything — she had to concede the point, just this once. It really did suck, all of this, pitting kids against each other for no reason at all. And there would be other excluded kids in other houses, too, ones with less privilege than her little Louisa, and Anna could feel the real injustice of that, a quiet ember burning inside of her, a hot fire, inextinguishable.

Earlier in the day, Anna had picked the kids up from school and she had run into Mimi. It should have been ordinary: two mothers collecting their children after a day of school. But the air between them was frigid. Anna watched the girls exit the doors of the school in unison, Harper her usual, bouncy self and Louisa slightly dejected, and she thought she saw — now, maybe she was imagining it — something coursing between them. Harper's face held, Anna was sure, a slight sneer, and when Anna looked over to Mimi to see if it had registered, she caught a smile on the mother's face. Sanctioned. Approved. A rumble of war had ignited, Anna was certain about that.

Later, at Riverview, in Ipswich, they ordered the kind of bar pizzas that come one pie to a person and leaned back in the red vinyl booths and tried to make small talk to pretend that the night hadn't been a bust. Ben with his pepperoni, and Denny, always with his sausage and black olive and a glass of Miller Light, and Louisa, so particular, cheese pizza, extra-crispy, and Anna, always changing her mind about what kind of pie she wanted, but this night, only mushroom, please.

It took her a minute to notice that her phone was doing something unusual. Buzzing, sure, but then buzzing a lot. An orb of light illuminating the whole table, like a weird oracle. "You wanna get that?" Denny asked, and so she looked down and realized that in the time it had taken to order a few pies and a round of drinks she had gotten, what, sixty-seven notifications? That didn't seem right. She checked again.

The phone was still going, though. Sixty-seven. They weren't all from one place, either. Email inbox: forty-two. Facebook Messenger: seventeen, none of them familiar. Instagram notifications: eight. She took a quick glance. Strangers, all of them. Scanned the titles. Swear words. Slurs. Her first name in subject lines. Her last name. Words she shouldn't be seeing. *Cocksucker. Slut. Dumb cunt. Anna Plummer.* A dizzying compilation of words that all came together at the same time from different places.

"Sorry, I'm not sure why I'm getting so many emails. It must be something work-related," she said, but her face must have given her away. She could feel a creep of red-hot fire fall across her cheeks.

"It's still vibrating," Denny said. "Anna. Your phone?" For a second — and only a second — he looked concerned, but he abandoned it and went back to looking into the distance, thinking about something else, someone else. Anna never knew where he lived when he wasn't living here with them.

Anna's phone was shaking the whole table, actually.

"I think I'm being pranked," she said, feebly.

"What?" Denny said.

"It's just... I'm getting some weird Facebook comments and things."

Denny opened his phone and scrolled to her page. Not all of the messages were visible, but he was able to see some of the comments posted to her page. "What on earth?" he said.

"I don't know. Maybe I got hacked?" she said.

"Looks like local kids," he said. "They're Internet-savvy. They do all kinds of insane things these days."

"I, um, I think I'm just going to shut it off." Her right hand was shaking, and she took a deep breath and went to steady it. She stopped and looked directly in front of her, at the red vinyl of their booth, at the faces of her two children, who were paying attention to their drinks, to the little squares of wax paper that Riverview had given them in lieu of plates, to the loud noises in the restaurant, but not, certainly, to their mother's phone, or to her shaky hand. Denny had stopped paying attention, too, and Anna was relieved by that. She pressed the button on the side and the phone went dark and she sank into a Diet Coke and smiled and looked around the restaurant, scanning it for people she knew.

At the bar, behind their booth, she spotted Rachel Kincaid, who was not necessarily a friend, but not an enemy, either. They had gone to high school together, and Rachel lived in Hamilton now, too, her kids older, out of elementary; they rarely saw one another these days. She was waiting by the takeout window, wearing a crossbody Tory Burch bag and holding a glass of white wine, talking to someone in a cheap leather jacket. Anna waved hello, and Rachel waved back: two girls from the same town, just getting pizza. Maybe she was having an affair. Maybe she was just killing time until her dinner was ready. Anyone, Anna realized, could be a different person here, in Riverview Pizza in Ipswich. Who knew which version of the story ended up becoming the final draft?

Back home, once the kids were cleaned up and in bed and once Denny had settled onto the couch with a martini, Anna begged off on her own. "I'm going to take a bath," she said, kissing her husband lightly on the lips. He didn't look up from the show he was watching about whether or not the Loch Ness Monster was real (spoiler: in fifty-five minutes they gave no answers at all).

"Did all that stuff stop?" he asked.

"To be honest, I haven't really looked," she lied. For whatever reason, he believed her. Denny rarely checked his social media on weekends, and by the time he looked again, her accounts would be gone. *Hackers,* she'd say. Case closed. Honestly, he was probably right. It was probably just a bunch of kids messing around. But better to run it by Di first anyway.

Upstairs, Anna went into her ugly bathroom, with its tiny and dark bathtub, and drew a bath for herself, the water so hot she could barely stick a toe into it. Sitting stark naked on the edge of the porcelain, she paused and then pressed the button on her phone. The Apple icon appeared. Boot up. Then the phone sprang to life, the green icon denoting texts, and suddenly a windfall of new messages. Two. Six. Sixteen. Fifty. Over a hundred and thirty-five. They spiraled in. Emails. Facebook messages. Instagram notifications. Her phone was suffering a full-scale assault.

The texts came from unknown numbers, every one of them similar in language and in detail, as if a script had been copied from a master. You fucking bitch, who the fuck do you think you are. Anna Plummer, watch your back. But they weren't identical. A few contained details about her kids. One offered up her address, another the address of the house where she had lived before, on Long Island. Still another: I hope Denny has a good life insurance policy on you, little sister. She googled a few of them, but they were cell phones and led to dead ends, and she gave up after a few tries. It all felt futile, because the messages kept coming, furiously, stacks of them. She was overwhelmed by the onslaught. So she stopped. Fuck it. She wasn't going to get to the bottom of these mysteries, not one by one, anyway. Looking up phone numbers wasn't going to stop them from barreling forth.

She slid into the hot water, moving the phone to the corner of the tub, where she had room for it. Clearing the phone took time, but she scrolled through the offenses, taking screenshots of the worst of it. She sent a series to Di. No heads-up. Not a simple text with a "whaddya think" preceding it. It was too exhausting. Let her friend see what it meant, all of these messages, tumbling over one another, tripping into the next.

What the fucking fuck is this, Di wrote back.

About a fraction of what has been spamming my phone since 6pm

I mean I think we both know what this is

But Anna didn't know anything. Outside, she could hear a high-pitched whistle, probably a fisher cat; they were deep chocolate brown and larger than a fox, a variety of weasel, she found out when she moved. They could take down a full-size dog. She had learned to identify the noise, but when they had first come here, to these woods, she had thought that sound was something else, someone calling for a dog, maybe even a far-off train whistling in the distance.

I have no idea what this is Di

You do know what this is, Anna, a noise inside her said. Somewhere, little kids were rolling in from their dance, taking off shoes that pinched, wiping their faces clean from spaghetti and ice cream.

To send a person this kind of shit — that was a campaign. You had to organize it. You had to have power behind you. You had to be some kind of, well, organization. Say you were, oh, the *president* of the *PTO* and in anticipation of a hotly contested *dance* you had organized your minions to harass a member. This — this was the kind of thing that might result from such an event. Yes, it was a theory. A wild theory. But Anna knew it could be exactly what had happened. She could picture Mimi getting people on board, telling friends and conspirators what time, what number, what email to use.

Of course, this was all very far-fetched. More likely was Denny's initial suggestion that the messages were from neighborhood kids fucking around. She could picture her husband now. *Stop twisting yourself into a pretzel, Anna. This is all in your head. No, the PTO isn't coming after you. You sound like an insane person.*

There had, though, been just that one flash: Mimi's face, for just one second, an inkling of what was possible. Was it ridiculous? Maybe. Mimi, for all of her peccadilloes and annoying Hamilton mommy traits, was just another mom. She picked her kid up just like everyone else, made sandwiches with the crusts cut off and wiped tears away and brushed hair and stacked pajamas into little squares so that they fit into cabinets and made lunches before anyone else in the house was awake and lived by the same mom promise that they all did: that they would serve their kids first, even when it hurt, even when it broke them, even when it meant that they would have to live a life that was a little less meaningful, or a little forgotten. Mimi wasn't on the other side of some looking glass; she was right there, a slightly altered version of Anna.

Well, that was what she *had* thought, but now, as messages continued to pour in, another and another and another, Anna had a less generous reading. She pictured a snake, she pictured something insidious, she pictured the spread of a virus that could not be stopped. She could not stop the febrile rush, spiders of fire crawling beneath her skin and outward as she contemplated the possible, if improbable truth of it.

The water in the bath looked like a tidal wave, the vibration from her phone was unforgiving, the sound outside — the fisher cat — did not stop, and Anna Plummer closed her eyes and pulled beneath the surface, with her hair loose around her in waves, and the phone pinging incessantly until her submersion finally silenced it, and the drowned-out sound of a wild animal, muted and still in the thick, black night.

Chapter 8

DENNY HAD LEARNED all kinds of new terms since his wife's death, terms that filled up his brain when he should have been doing things like going through her personal effects or thinking about flowers or greeting the people who showed up at the house to pay their respects. He learned about *responding officers* and the *right to know,* about *evidence technicians* and *public information officers,* about the *safeguarding of evidence, trace evidence, evidence control, fibers, notification of next of kin.*

Back in the old version of his life — the *Anna* version of his life, as he now came to see it — he had spent Friday nights watching *Dateline* with his wife. Keith Morrison's voice, smooth as Scotch, oozed over murder. *But was he a suspect?* Morrison loved to ask. If Denny had been in an episode of *Dateline,* a narrator might have asked the same question. Was the Hamilton Police Department focused on him? He couldn't quite tell. In the first frenetic days and weeks after Anna's death, Denny had been preoccupied with the physical details — how to operate his home, his life, the lives of his children. That the police kept showing up every once in a while felt both important and unimportant. Denny desperately wanted to know what they knew, but he also felt unmoored from the burden of his new responsibility.

Back from the interrogation, he felt breathless but also determined. As Denny was walking out of the station, Sticks had softened, if only slightly. Maybe the whole "bad cop" routine was just an act. Maybe he hadn't really been a suspect at all. Sticks promised to keep Denny updated with anything related to the case, though it had been Denny who had checked in with the station every couple of days, asking about potential leads. Had anyone come forward as a witness? (Not a single one.) Had the couple who found Anna seen anything else at the haul-out that day? (No.) Had any fibers or other evidence been retrieved from her body, like material under her fingernails or hairs or DNA on her body? (Negative biological evidence.) Had there been blood or fingerprints detected in her car? (The vehicle was swabbed and found clean.)

In return for his many inquiries, Denny faced a series of his own. Had he found anyone to corroborate his Ski Bradford timeline? (One instructor remembered seeing him picking up the kids.) Would he be willing to submit DNA for a sample for the police? (Gladly.) Did he recall what he had been wearing the night of the murder, and would he be willing to deliver his clothing to the police department for analysis? (He did not honestly recall what he had been wearing that night, no.) Sticks had gotten into the habit of texting Denny with follow-up questions, which Denny didn't mind. It gave him the opportunity to ask questions of his own. He asked about leads on suspects, but Sticks said the police couldn't tell him anything about the current status of the case. It was natural, Denny supposed, to feel singled out in a murder investigation, and maybe also natural to feel like the police department wasn't taking seriously his own sense of urgency. He had read, of course, that most progress in homicide cases happens within the first few weeks, and he was beginning to feel that Anna's case was losing steam.

Maybe that wasn't fair. Or maybe Sticks and the team at the Hamilton Police Department were taking every piece of information he passed their way with a grain of salt because they believed him to be involved. Twice now, Denny had noticed cars passing him on the road near his house — slowly, in the kind of way that a car passes when they've been driving with no particular place to go. They weren't cruisers but large domestic cars, the kind that Denny had always associated with municipalities. Almost certainly unmarked vehicles, he had thought to himself, which gave him even more reason to believe that the police were watching him to see if he was up to anything suspicious. He did have a gnawing feeling, too — something he shoved aside, because to think it was to sink into the despairing realization that he couldn't trust anyone, not even the police — that maybe the surveillance was less about him and more about his being a nuisance, a simple attempt to get him to stop doing what he had been doing, which was sending nonstop inquiries to the police department. In any case, it hadn't worked. It wasn't working.

You said ligature marks, he texted Sticks the first week of February. Can you tell what it was from?

Three dots. Pensive. Then a reply. Sticks did this a lot, like he was considering the nature of his response.

Belt of some sort, the reply said, when it came.

Is there a way to find out what kind of belt? Maybe something about the belt marks? I'm no expert but don't different belts leave different marks?

You're no expert, Sticks responded. So leave the work to the experts.

Denny wanted to help, and he wanted answers. He had left the station bruised, of course, and had even made a call to his mother-in-law, herself a law school graduate who had never practiced (and who sometimes proffered free advice based purely on academics). She was a decent woman who trusted Denny, and she told him to tread lightly with the police but to try to get information from them when he could.

"Stay in their orbit," she said. "You have a right to know what's going on with the investigation, too." There was, she let him know, something called the Victim Bill of Rights in Massachusetts, meaning that he was entitled to know how any criminal case was progressing through the system, if it made it that far. He also had the right to know any details about a case *involving* him, including significant developments. Just knowing this made Denny feel better, even though it infuriated him that Sticks blew off any of Denny's attempts at crime-solving but felt no remorse about tearing up his life piece by piece. Neighbors had left him messages, expressing discomfort over what they called the new "surveillance state" in the neighborhood.

Things around town didn't help, either. The whisperings were like a river.

Denny had grown up in the Rust Belt, where people preferred Springsteen to pretty much any other songwriter. He was the raconteur of the blue-collar worker, penning ballads for those who could never seem to get out of their own way. Trenton, Pittsburgh, Scranton, little cities and towns that ran down through the Tri-State Area and west through Pennsylvania and into Ohio—these were a dime a dozen to the people up in New England. Ask Anna and she couldn't even tell you where New Jersey ended and Delaware started, but every kid who grew up trying to figure out how to turn a quarter into a dollar down through the forgotten states that fell somewhere between the Northeast and the Midwest could sum it all up in a Springsteen song.

"The River" was one of those songs, and even though it came out when Denny was just a toddler, he sometimes felt like it was a song that was meant to express his entire small-town life growing up: people who got stuck in a place for too long, who made one stupid choice and never really recovered. Now Anna was dead, found in a river, and the gossip flowed from that river, tributaries of sound all around him. Every time he stopped to get gas at the Citgo station and every time he went in for a cup of coffee at Honeycomb and every time he bought groceries at Market Basket over in Rowley.

He brought the kids to Market Basket, in fact, on a Saturday afternoon in February. There was snow coming, the forecast said; otherwise, Denny would have waited to shop during the week, like always. Less potential for running into people he knew that way. The parking lot was mostly full when they got there. He had already resolved to let the kids get whatever they wanted. Doritos. High-octane Coke. Ice cream. All of the off-limits junk that Anna had objected to. What were they waiting for, anyway? It was, he now realized, the first real storm since she had disappeared, the first time that they would all be stuck in the house as a family of three. They would learn to survive without her.

Actually, that wasn't quite right. They would never really *learn* to survive without Anna. They would accept it. Denny himself had been accepting her absence in the same way that a patient, newly emerged from surgery, accepts the information about the loss of an important body part. His phantom limb haunted him, day and night. It pained him. It was visceral. Sometimes he found himself doubled over in the kitchen, heaving with it. He worried he might vomit in front of the children, and he steadied himself from memories that came on so urgently and thick that he wasn't sure where they had been hiding. A pulse of lilac – but from where, in the middle of winter? – triggered a memory of walking with Anna in late spring to watch the sunset at the Montauket, with too much time on their hands, nowhere to go, no one to care about but themselves. One night, the smell of mushrooms on pizza catapulted his grief back toward a tavern in New Haven where they had stopped on the way home from a long drive, where coal-fired pies had greased their fingertips and burned the roofs of their mouths.

The reality of living without her had started to settle on him. Not just the everyday living so much as the darkness that seeped into every single corner of his life. What was it like when someone shut off the lights, when your favorite person wasn't there anymore? So many times, he came home thinking of the things he needed to tell her, and she wasn't there, she would never again be there, and he had to remind himself, in the throes of his burgeoning grief, that it would always be like this, that he was training his brain, once again, to live the way that he had lived in the days before he had ever known Anna Denton. It was a process.

Denny hadn't seen Sticks since his visit to the station, but he knew the officer wasn't exactly done. It wasn't just his imagination that people from town had cooled to him. In the first days after Anna's disappearance, there had been a warmth from the community. An empathy. That feeling had faded. Now, everywhere he went, he was Denny Plummer, Prime Suspect, and he knew this, just as surely as he knew that he had done nothing to his wife.

"Grab a cart," he told Louisa as they got to the door of the grocery store. He could already see two people he knew, Matt Lennox, a local dad from the softball league that Anna had convinced him to join in their first year, and Karen Pistoulia, a PTO member he had never really talked to before. Matt wore a backward baseball cap — Red Sox, typical, Denny thought — and a ski jacket over a pair of jeans. It was a very specific look, a very specific nod to how wealthy he was and how subtly he wanted people to see it. Those jackets: five hundred bucks apiece, Denny knew.

Karen Pistoulia, who stood near the seasonal items, to the left, was a completely different story. Floor-length puffer coat, Moncler, at least two thousand dollars, and she wanted everyone to know it. She was talking to someone he vaguely recognized – *Please,* Denny thought, *let this conversation last long enough for me to get past unnoticed* – but the man, who was bulky and looked to be in his mid-fifties, ducked out of the way as they approached. Denny tried to keep his eyes trained to the ground. Just then, Ben jumped onto the back of the cart as they made their way through the store and the cart, unevenly balanced, took a nosedive forward, and the noise of the commotion drew everyone's attention. And there was Karen, looking straight at Denny, with her honey-brown hair, almost the same color as Anna's, swept up into a messy ponytail.

There was no avoiding her. Denny had to push the cart aside to avoid a collision.

"Karen," he said, nodding. He had intended to keep going, but she put a hand on his shoulder.

"Denny," she said. She had a weird half-smile on her face, like she knew something he didn't. She brushed a strand of hair away from her eyes. "How are you? How are the kids?" She looked down at Ben and Louisa and made a motion as if she was going to hug them, but then held back.

The attorney general. That had been the familiar-looking face, Denny now remembered. Denny had voted for him, maybe, or seen him on TV. "We're okay. We're all okay," he said, trying to make quick work of the conversation. "Hanging in there."

"I hear the cops have . . ." She hesitated, letting the word *cops* twist for a minute. "Well, anyway. If you need anything, I hope you know that the community is here. The PTO is here!" She smiled. Her teeth were very white. Anna was always saying that, that the women of Hamilton had extremely white teeth, like they all used the same toothpaste. It had made her uncomfortable.

The cops, it was true, were still sniffing around. But they had stopped short of calling him a suspect. Don't go running off, Sticks had told him yet again over text, but Denny was officially free to do as he pleased. He hadn't been arrested, and even though he knew the police were watching him, he lived his life as if they were not.

"Can you bring her back?" He sort of half smiled as he said it. It was funny — before, every once in a while Anna would catch him doing something like this. She loved it about him, that her normally demure husband would just *once in a while* go off-course. Karen Pistoulia never would have expected quiet, grieving Denny Plummer to ask a Hamilton Mommy to conjure his dead wife from thin air, but here he was, doing just that, in the Market Basket, of all places.

"I'm... I'm so *sorry,* Denny!" she stuttered, the words hissing out of her. She was cornered now, stuck in the store's goddamned Valentine's shit.

"Oh, I'm sure you are," Denny replied. "Everyone is *so sorry.* Hey, don't forget the conversation hearts!"

She backed away, and Denny started to laugh. It was a little funny, this outburst, and he felt a tiny bit bad about it, but he could imagine no circumstance in which he would go to Karen Pistoulia for any kind of comfort. Her husband, Greg, was a burly Greek guy, and every summer they went off to Santorini for two weeks with their three kids, posting photos of creamsicle sunsets and round blue rooftops and octopus drying in the sun. Anna hadn't trusted Mimi Mar, but Karen Pistoulia — well, Karen she straight up disliked. Denny had never seen it, exactly. He had believed that his wife's proclivities for drama outpaced her capacity for reason. But now it was as if he could hear Anna in his head, merged with him somehow. There was something he hadn't seen before — something in the performativeness of that coat at a grocery store before a major storm, picking up cans of, Denny saw, tomato soup. He didn't like her. She wasn't just some Stepford wife. She was looking at him with judgment, making her own private case for his condemnation.

What was it about her, he thought, that had triggered him so completely? He had only ever seen her a handful of times before, at school events mostly, and they had been cordial. But today he felt revulsion toward this woman, like he had somehow swallowed the feelings his wife had felt for her all this time. All those comments Anna had whispered under her breath about *inequality* and *cliques* and *keeping up with the Joneses* seemed to sink in right this minute, right now, at Market Basket, over the NECCO conversation hearts and stuffed teddy bears holding pink messages of endearment. *Forget me not. I love you. Be mine.*

Karen Pistoulia's cart hadn't been full of valentines, and neither had Denny's, and it was a sad state of affairs, being stuck together in that tiny section of the grocery store, commiserating over all of the junk that people would buy and eventually forget. Last year, and the year before, and the year before that, he had been the one buying it, too. Karen's house was probably the kind, Denny thought, where long-stemmed roses arrived in a skinny white box at the doorstep, but Anna always preferred Russell Stover chocolates, which reminded her of the times when she worked at a Hallmark store in high school, listening to rom-com movie soundtracks and eating expired candies.

Anna had wanted the world, but really, in the end, she had been easy to please. A box of cheap chocolate, that had done the trick. She was no Karen Pistoulia, and standing there, surrounded by the Pepto-Bismol pinks, he became aware of a deep ache that he had not addressed, the realization that he would see Anna's ghost in every Hamilton mom, that every moment going forward in this life without Anna Plummer was a moment of persuading himself that he was thriving when he was merely surviving, living a life that used to be light and joy and pleasure and was now just air and food and water. And maybe his eyes said all of this to Karen Pistoulia or maybe they said none of it, for he felt, in that moment, like a shark who had died, who had simply stopped moving in the water, dead shark eyes, black and hollow, dead.

Karen was still looking at him, in the way that people looked at him ever since Anna died. With pity. With derision. With blame. As if his face contained a question mark. Fuck all of it, he thought. Fuck every last bit of it.

Chapter 9

IN HER MARRIAGE, there were things she told Denny Plummer and things she kept to herself. It wasn't that Anna didn't trust her husband so much as the fact that she considered herself the self-reliant type. She had sworn, in the years leading up to her engagement and marriage, that she would never become the type of woman who fell too hard for a man, that she would never become the type of woman who lost her grip. Finances: She shared these with her husband. Travel plans: Of course she shared. What she intended to make for dinner: Everyone was in on this, to avoid any possible fuss. But if there was something that bothered Anna Plummer – truly bothered her, down to the core of her being – she might sock it away, bury it the way her old pet Russian tortoise had buried himself beneath layers of substrate to keep warm.

She had debated telling Denny about the rest of the messages. There had been so many of them, after all, it had been hard to keep track. But the more she thought about it, the more she was sure that he would only weigh in on the matter in a way that would not be helpful. *You should never have opened this box*, he would have told her, or *I did tell you to just let this one go.* She could picture him sitting on the couch, looking straight ahead, not bothering to see the injustice she felt, scolding her, as if this had somehow been her fault. As if she deserved it.

It was easier, then, to disable the social media accounts, and to change the settings in her MacBook, one by one, blocking every single unknown address from contacting her. It took the better part of the next day, a Saturday, but she had sent Denny and the kids up to Salisbury Beach to the arcades to get energy out. She had to work, she told them, a deadline for a copywriting client.

After they left, she made herself a coffee and stared at the computer. Where to begin? Facebook account: delete. Instagram: comments deleted, settings privatized. One by one, she ticked away at them until there were just a few manageable emails left to go. Things had slowed down from the night before, and she felt less like a stranger in her own skin. She had blocked over forty-seven accounts, though she wasn't really sure what to do now. Her phone was dead, her only text capacity on her computer. She'd have to go to the Verizon store tomorrow with Denny to handle that piece of the puzzle. An accident, she'd say, and he'd be pissed, but he'd get over it.

Di texted to ask what her situation was. How many more???

Oh hundreds but I just finished blocking most of them

Not enough!!!

Leave it to Di to be the better angel. Anna was content to leave the conversation at that, but her friend wasn't done.

I'm on my way, the kids are at that methuen trampoline park lol bday party

How many times had Anna thanked her own lucky stars that she hadn't become a baseball mom like her best friend, since the sport was interminable, and yet on this cold Saturday morning, Di had somehow been strategically relieved of her sports momming duties, just ten minutes down the road and on her way, somehow intuitively aware that Anna was here, alone, staring at the

MacBook and not quite sure how to purge the menace from all of her electronics, Gen X Luddite that she was.

One thing Anna was good at: making notes. She opened a Word document on her computer and wrote a stupid little note to herself:

> Note to self, February 12, 2022, tons and tons of emails, messages, facebook scam replies, totally and completely unhinged messages on Instagram, and text messages from unknown numbers. Have blocked all of them, disabled FB, changed privacy settings on Instagram, etc., last nite threw phone in bathtub (lol oops it's me I'm the problem it's me) but just making a note *in case of emergency!!!*

She saved the note into a folder on her desktop that was marked MISC., where other notes she had written to herself lived, notes about passwords and about what she wanted to do if she ever won the lottery and about her hopes and dreams for her children and about where she had buried the time capsule in the backyard, because she was certain that she would forget (and it was true; she had forgotten).

Di let herself in without knocking. She was tall and ruthlessly thin, about six inches taller than Anna if she stood without hunching, which she rarely did. Ever since they were younger, she possessed the kind of unaware beauty that made people stop and look at her. She could command attention in a pair of Adidas track pants and an old ratty sweatshirt, which was equal parts infuriating and admirable. Today she wore loose jeans and a hooded sweatshirt from American Eagle that she must have brought along with her from the Dark Ages, from before they had kids, from college, even. She looked like a teenager despite two unmistakable diamond earrings peeking out from beyond a blond bob.

"Well, I know what we do first," she said, marching into Anna's office.

"You could bring coffee, you know," Anna said.

"How do you know that wasn't the 'do first' part?"

"If it was, it had better include a donut, because I'm starving."

"Fine, but don't tell my kids."

It was more like Don't Tell the Hamilton Mommies, because they would be horrified to know that anyone would go to get a chocolate glazed donut at Dunkin' rather than a *pain au chocolat* at Honeycomb, but girls from the North Shore, they knew better. Di got her coffee iced and light, no matter the season ("regular," actually, in Massachusetts-speak, which meant cream and enough sugar to kill an adult from diabetes if they drank it every day, and Di swore she didn't, but she ran pretty regularly, so who knew if it was exercise or just genetics that kept her looking like she wasn't drinking bad coffee and sugar in her free time).

"So what's next?" Anna wanted to know. She had a feeling she was not going to like the answer, just like she hadn't liked the answer when they were teenagers, borrowing her mother's Mercury Villager minivan for what was just supposed to be an hour and ending up across the border in New Hampshire with a carton of P-Funks for under twenty dollars, smoking butts in the back of the car, legs up on the sea wall at Hampton, home late, her mother smelling the smoke, getting caught even though she had set the clocks back a little, always getting caught because her mother knew to watch the 11 p.m. news.

"The truth is, we gotta report it," Di said. "Simple as that."

"Report what to who?" Anna said. Big ideas, always, Di with her big ideas.

"The calls. The messages. All of this shit. You have *got* to file a police report. If you're not going to talk to Denny about it, well that's one thing. I can't talk you out of that, I guess. Your marriage, your mess. But you can't just put your head in the sand here. These people are doxing you. How do you know someone isn't going to take things to another, crazier level? It's just stupid to let this go." At Dunks, they had parked in a space designated for takeout orders, but the lot was mostly empty. Anna's Volkswagen ticked. She had gotten in an accident, side-swiped by a pickup truck on 113 in Newburyport in the fall, and ever since, the car made all kinds of bad noises. Unholy noises. Rattles. It shook on the highway. She sometimes wondered if a tire would just shimmy loose from the friction. Right now, the ticking felt like some kind of warning.

"It's ridiculous, all of it," she said. "You don't really think these adult women are responsible for this, do you? And, let's be honest. It's not scary as much as it is immature. My address ..." Anna paused and laughed, because, truly, it was actually almost funny. "I mean, all of this stuff is public information! If these people are people who know me, they already know where I live. Plus, this shit is all on the Internet anyway. What is the fucking point?"

"I think the point is to scare you."

"It's not scaring me. It's *annoying* me. I'm annoyed. Mission accomplished."

"I still think it's worth going to the police," Di said.

"Is that really necessary?"

"What is it that people always say?" Di said. "When people show you who they are?"

Anna knew the expression. Believe them. When people show you who they are, believe them. Mimi's face, twisted up, like the knot from a balloon. Believe them. Believe that they are who you think they are, she said to herself, but believing something like that meant stepping into a place where terrible things were possible, things that Anna didn't want to accept.

"I know what you're saying," Anna said. "It's not like I'm trying to be generous. I'm just trying to be realistic. I don't think these are serious threats. The only thing I have to fear is fear itself."

"And maybe the Hamilton PTO," quipped Di.

"It seems unlikely that the PTO is going to plot my untimely demise, Di. We're talking about women who don't even do their own nails."

"So, realistically," Di asked, "do you think that timing is an accident?"

Accidents. Were there any accidents? Anna thought it was possible — possibly possible — that the attack, if it was, in fact, an attack, had been planned to coincide with the dance. But what if it wasn't that? She could hear Denny in her head still. What was more likely was that this *was* just a kid. That this *was* just a prank. That this *was* just some stupid overreaction.

"And realistically," Di continued, "do you think there are that many people out there who have your phone number and a big Rolodex of people who they can give it to?"

It was that last part that stuck with Anna. The access. The assault. The PTO, they had strength in numbers. But then, the kids in Hamilton, they had Internet-savvy, too. They could just as easily rile up a crowd. She wasn't sold. "I'm not convinced that Mimi Mar is smart enough to be able to execute this kind of thing," Anna said.

"Maybe you're underestimating her," Di said. "I don't really know. I don't know her that well. But she's on, what? Her third term as president of the PTO? Six years? She's been in the PTO for practically her entire time as a mom. That sounds pretty powerful to me."

"I'm not sure how much power I want to give to a parent-teacher organization, to be honest," Anna said. "It gives me the creeps."

"Fair enough," Di said. "All I'm saying: Maybe give the blonde the benefit of the doubt." She shook her own shorn blond hair like a little wet dog. Anna giggled. Di was anything but a prototypical blonde.

Maybe warnings were everywhere. A scrim of ice, creeping across the windshield, formed a bony finger. "Would you look at that," Anna said.

"It's pointing right at us," Di said, and it was true; it really was.

* * *

Di had always been a gifted partner in crime. She was born to do it, as the youngest child. Diane Foley, before she was Diane Maguire, forgotten child, tomboy in childhood who had somehow outgrown ugly duckling status far earlier than the rest of their motley crew. She had been the first to be noticed by boys, but she never let it stop her, never let the attention divert her from hijinks and adventures. Maybe it even made her a bigger prankster than the other two: Anna and Kaitlin Connors, who had died of a heroin overdose back in the early 2000s, when the stuff was consuming all of the northern New England towns, back in a bleak winter that was not unlike this one. Stuff like that, stories like that, were what bonded Anna and Di together after all these years, Anna sometimes thought. It was why they were here, at the Hamilton Police Department, on a Saturday morning — okay, fine, call it early afternoon by now — rubbing hands together in the cold, looking at each other for confirmation. *Are we going to do this? Okay, fine. Let's do it.*

Inside, they asked to speak with an officer and were directed to have a seat: two filthy and nubby orange chairs that looked like they had never been reupholstered, like they had been there at least since the 1970s. In time, a short, meaty officer with a crooked name tag that read *Malkin* came out and shoved a paw at them.

"Ladies," he said. "Right this way."

Perhaps predicting what she was thinking, Di jabbed an elbow into Anna's rib cage, like they were thirteen all over again. A mistrust for authority, that's what she had always been accused of possessing, right or wrong. There was the old *Wayne's World* joke: smells like bacon. Cops. Pigs. Anna thought of it now. Wrong time to piss an officer off, of course. She knew that, though she couldn't help but think of the cops as the enemy.

"Thanks for taking the time," Di said, putting on her best Hamilton Mom performance.

"Ever been in the station before?" Malkin asked, making a joke about upper-middle-class mothers from Hamilton and the station, and this time Di elbowed Anna hard. Hampton Beach, 1998. Weed wasn't legal yet. A joint. Officers' flashlights right in their fucking *eyes.* Locked up and cuffed to a metal bench for two hours until they paid bail. Plus, the assholes grabbed their fake IDs and threatened them with possession of false identity, a felony.

"Now what would two fine upstanding women like us be doing in a police station, officer?" Di smiled her best mom smile, flashed her perfect white teeth, which she now got bleached regularly by a very expensive North Shore dentist. Her husband was a corporate lawyer, and she could afford to do that, even if she didn't wear Moncler every single day. She was no Mimi Mar, but she could perform with the best of them.

"You'd be surprised," Malkin said. "You sure would be surprised." He laughed a tinny little laugh, ineffectual for a man of his heft. It made Anna want to laugh, too, but she didn't. She stared straight ahead at the narrow little hallways with their yellow-white light. Malkin took the lead and opened a conference room for them. "Right in here," he motioned.

Inside, at a table meant to look like wood that was actually plastic, Anna filled out five pages, signed her scrawled cursive signature. *Anna Plummer, February 12, 2022,* beside a long and detailed accounting of every message and threat sent to her.

"We'll handle it from here," Malkin said. "I'm sure you'll have no more trouble, Mrs. Plummer."

"You can call me Anna," she said.

Chapter 10

OUTSIDE, THE FIRST flurries from the storm scurried like they were fake, like they were part of some movie set. No sign of the police today, trailing him home or parked anywhere near the house. Sticks had sent an obligatory text earlier in the day to report only that Denny's DNA swab had come back negative. No surprise there, Denny thought. He himself trusted his own innocence, even if the cops and the town did not.

Denny had received a text about an Amazon delivery at the front door. Louisa and Ben were reading *Dog Man: Fetch-22* in the playroom, offering up a rare moment of silence. All of the things that Anna had once spent hours shopping for, Denny now bought last-minute: toothpaste, detergent, dog food, socks. Prime next-day delivery had been saving his life, another marker of his wife's absence, of the hollowed-out space where she had been. He could only show up. He could not be her. Ordering things online was no true replacement for a parent, and he mourned what his kids were losing in the kind of mom who went out to actual stores and hand-picked the things she knew they loved. But he felt like a hard-tapped spring maple, too tired to produce even one more ounce of usable sap. Of what use was he now? He could make his tables and chairs, feed his kids, and hold their hands at the bus stop, but he could not be Anna Plummer. He could not be that.

And so, Denny ordered the toothpaste, detergent, and dog food, and they arrived in large cardboard boxes. His wife would have been horrified. Retrieving the boxes, Denny noticed that the door looked different. Scratched across the hunter green paint, as if marked in blood — but no, it was just paint, Denny thought, holding his breath for a minute — was a scrawled word. *KILLER*, it read, right there, across the door to his house. The indecency of it. The gall. That someone would come right up to the front steps, as he stood not feet away, talking on the phone, in his house, where he made breakfast every morning for his kids — Ben's *frupples,* the word he still used instead of *waffles*, even though the kid had long ago learned to pronounce it correctly — it was a desecration, an invasion.

The Amazon delivery person had just been there. Could it have been? But no. Denny checked his phone. He had received a notification for the boxes, and, what's more, an email with a picture: boxes propped against the front door. That was a coincidence, yes, but the door in the grainy photograph was the same door that he had left behind, and anyway, what delivery person would jeopardize a job that could so easily get them fired?

No, there was obviously another explanation, a more insidious one. Whoever had done this thing had been there just seconds before, had missed Denny by a hair, which made the skin on his arms grow prickly. How had Denny missed the culprit? How had this person had time to violate his home and slip so quickly and so quietly into oblivion? The house was set on a hill. Any car would have had to have been parked on the busy road below. In the settling dusk, Denny saw scuffed boot marks, large, leading down the steps toward the driveway, where they evaporated into thin air, as if they came from a ghost. He could not understand it. The timing, the footprints, the cat scratch on the door: It made no sense, but it had clearly been done to provoke in him a sense of fear, in this snow-lit witching hour, his wife's spirit haunting the walk, surely telling him something that he could not quite understand. Men's boots, they had to be, he thought, but no man could simply cease to exist, no man could be there at the door one minute and then gone the next. An impossible feat. A violation of time and space and physics.

Something deeper had started to sink into Denny's consciousness, a vague feeling that maybe — and perhaps it was paranoia, he couldn't be sure — he was being set up. To stage such an act of vandalism took real skill. Professional skill, Denny thought. A cop might be good at replicating a phantom. A cop might be able to get up to a home without anyone noticing. A cop might be the perfect person to wipe evidence clean and make sure none was ever found after the fact. That his wife's murder investigation was unsolved had opened in him not only a chasm of grief but also a deep mistrust for everyone. He couldn't be sure that Sticks was doing his job, that he could trust anyone in this small town, that scraping away the patina of Hamilton left behind anything but rotten framing. And that was what scared Denny Plummer the most: that somewhere, buried in the architecture of power, lay things he did not want to know, did not need to know, and was in danger of finding out about. Of course, thinking this — any of this — was ridiculous, and Denny knew it.

He stood looking at the door and the boot marks and the snow, which had started to fall a little faster now, catching the day-end light. Under different circumstances, it would look pretty, he thought, the kind of magical snow that always arrived at this time of February, when everyone was just about fed up with winter. Six more weeks of it? You could barely stand it, could barely hang on in the cold, and then there you were, struck speechless by the diamond glisten of that stupid snowfall. It was coming down now, harder than ever. For once, the weathermen hadn't been exaggerating. The promised snowstorm had finally arrived.

The children were asleep. Sticks had come by to take an official report about the door but had seemed untroubled. The officer was worried about the things that seemed to matter least and was unconcerned about the ones that seemed to matter most. Someone had been here, on this property, while Denny was in the other room with his own kids, but Sticks had shaken it off as if it had been just a childhood prank. Not *Killer* with a capital *K,* no, just *killer,* like the adjective, because words, he assumed, could have so many different meanings. It was a punch in the fucking gut, was what it was. He could see, from the officer's eyes, that he was not being taken seriously. That he was a *suspect,* not a *victim,* and it made him *angry,* even though he struggled labeling his own emotions (he was getting better at it, he had to admit, since Anna was no longer around to pull it out of him, almost as if he had absorbed this part of his wife in her absence, this ability to see his own deficiencies and proactively work on them).

Since his wife's death, Denny had avoided her glossy blue office, and he had made it a point to walk through different parts of the house. That space, where she so often stared out from her desk at a square of lawn and the staggeringly tall pine trees, had been a place for her own contemplations. It was where she went, he guessed, to think about the work she could have done if she had been a little braver. Next to her desk was a collapsed portable easel that she had given up on years before. He couldn't remember the last time she had rescued her paints from the abyss.

Tonight, he turned on the overhead light in her office. Denny had forgotten about his wife's backup computer, the one he had urged her to buy just in case the first one crashed. She was, after all, a copywriter. She needed a backup plan. And there it was, right where she had left it, top left drawer, a gold MacBook, lifeless in its case. He propped it up on the ergonomically correct stand that he had gotten her two years earlier. The stand was on top of her mid-century desk, along with the other ephemera of her life. A faded photograph of her parents on their wedding day, cutting a very tall cake. A black porcelain Crate & Barrel crock overstuffed with pens and pencils, many of them broken. A letter organizer with all manner of papers inside: self-adhesive postage stamps, tax information, unread magazines, pieces of artwork created by their children that had no other real home.

He turned the laptop on and entered his wife's password. *Glazed.* So stupid, this inside joke, that she would even dedicate the password to a donut. But look at him now, in this moment of silence, thinking of her and her donuts. Glazed. She had had the last word, all right.

The desktop was meticulous. She had been an organizer, even on the digital side. A single folder marked "documents" stared back at him on the home screen, and he clicked on it. He had no idea what he was looking for. Should he be in here, looking through her personal effects like this? What if he found something he didn't want to see? And also, would there be anything here? Sticks had her computer, didn't he? Wasn't this just a backup?

Email, he remembered. Her email would be saved on both computers. If she was smart — and he knew she was — she would have mirror images of most documents and programs on both, for safekeeping. That was exactly the kind of thing that Anna would have done.

Just then, Denny stopped. Her email, he realized, was where he wanted to look first, but he had been hesitating, because email was the window into everything, where everyone kept their secrets. He and Anna had never hidden their passwords from one another, and so he knew exactly how to get into hers, but he had never been tempted, had never had any concerns, not until now, without her here to stop him. Bottom of the page. Google Chrome. Browser open. Gmail. It would take just one minute to open her entire private life, to sift through anything that she had kept from him in their years of marriage, and now he would have to ask himself the truth about all of this, which was this: Did he really want to know it?

The only thing worse than the worst-case scenario, of course, was not knowing at all. Denny plugged his wife's information into Gmail. Password *Dunkindonutsfann.* Another stupid joke staring back at him from beyond the grave. He had warned her, too, that her password was hackable because it included not a single symbol or number, a password left over from the good old days. But she had refused to budge. *But it's true, it's me, I like it, I can remember it!* On she went: There was no stopping her, no changing her mind.

In the inbox he found nothing unusual at first. A million unopened emails. Pleas to donate from the Democratic Party. Can't you just spare five dollars today? He could not. She could not. They could not. Emails from websites she had once ordered holiday gifts from. A completely impersonal list of impersonal correspondence to someone who would never again see this de facto proof of her own nonexistence. Spam, it turns out, doesn't just end when you die.

For a moment, he didn't see the folder she had created — this Luddite wife of his — where all the other emails lived. But then, one click and he was in there, in the nightmare that she must have lived in, emails reciting back the private details of her life, emails wishing her dead, emails about her children, emails stripping away her decency, so many emails, 187 of them, the folder said, all catalogued in her mysterious and meticulous way, perhaps without emotion, because she was good at that, at removing the feeling when she needed to.

They all came from the same two-day span, in February of 2022, just one year ago. He couldn't place it. What had they been doing that day? Why then? And why had she done this, put these emails in a folder and not said a thing to him, her husband, about the torture and the harassment, and the words coming from these strangers on the Internet?

I hope you die
You deserve what you get
Dumb bitch
You moved to the wrong town
You'll see
You'll see
You'll see

Anna had been the type of person who wasn't particularly spooked by threats or accusations. Self-sufficient, she always liked to say, and so maybe her secrecy had been just that: a form of taking care of herself without bothering anyone. Except that this was definitely cause for alarm, all these emails, all this hatred flowing inside her personal email, bile she could not expel. Except, except, except. She could have told him, and she hadn't, and he was sand turning to glass, pressed down, molten, one element changing into another. *You aren't supposed to be angry with the dead.* He knew this, of course, but it was impossible not to feel a white flame, a lick of anger, like all the trust they had between them was only an illusion. What else had she been hiding? What other secrets lay in wait?

He went into the outbox and scrolled back to February of 2022. He found work emails, messages to copywriting clients. Nothing interesting there. And then, a series of emails caught his attention. She had emailed Mimi Mar. A meeting at Honeycomb right before the harassment started. She never told him about that. And before that was another email, this time to complain about the school dance.

That one, actually, he remembered.

He had come in from the shed late and found her red-faced and furious about tickets to a pasta dance.

"They're charging parents a premium to be members of the PTO so that they get early access to the dances," she practically spat. "This fucking town!"

He didn't really know what she was talking about. He had just finished — now he had to think about it — a set of Windsor chair reproductions for a friend of Diane's that were meant to look like antiques, with a black stain that he sanded off in spots. They were beautiful, period correct, and he had been so proud that he wanted to call Anna out to the back to see them, but she was so mad.

"Who? Who is charging parents?" He could see she wasn't planning to see the chairs, which was a shame. She had started dinner, pounded chicken filets fried with sage and deglazed with gin and chicken stock, and one of the filets had started to burn. Also a shame. She was an excellent cook, when she was paying attention, but in the heat of her anger, she was only thinking about one thing, and that was the dance.

"The PTO! I said that!"

"You didn't. You just said the dance. Something about a pasta dance." He realized, as soon as he said it, that it was a mistake, that what he had tried to say was not what she needed to hear, and that all of it was going haywire, the way conversations do when one person is more angry than the other one, so he turned his back to his wife and the billowing smoke coming off the range — as usual, she forgot to turn on the hood vent that had cost a fortune to install — and started to wash the stain from his hands, which was less of an actual attempt to remove the color than it was an attempt to avoid eye contact or any brewing explosion.

"Maybe you should try listening, Denny," she said. "Maybe just actually listen to what I am telling you for once!" More smoke. More hissing from the pan. The chicken, he imagined, was done for at this point, and they would eat it anyway. It was what they did, a concession, their family's love story, what they did for her in their own bout of self-sufficiency, how they took care of her when she didn't realize they were doing it. That was love. That was marriage. That was his way, even if she didn't see it.

"Okay," he said. "You're right. I'm sorry." And he was, but not in the way that she thought he meant.

This memory, which had been unimportant, came back in a flash: hot steam on the window, acrid smell of burnt chicken and gin, a bitter dinner, Louisa's pout over a dance. Denny had been there, but also not, still preoccupied with the Windsor chairs, thinking about the stain and if the color was right, and the wear patterns created by the hand sanding and his labor and what project would come next, and so he had not been listening — she was right about that part. He had been guilty of that plenty in their marriage, of paying attention to the wrong details, of no details at all. Now, in the blue light of her computer screen, he felt as if he were completing an autopsy. It was all here, all the cancerous cells that had been growing inside Anna this whole time, the lecherous threats perpetrated by foreign entities, and whatever else Anna had kept to herself: personal grievances, aches and pains, things she pinned to the inside because she believed that it was stronger and smarter not to reveal them to the person who was supposed to understand her the most.

He should have been listening all this time, and he hadn't been listening, not about the PTO or the dance or any of the other things she had been talking about. Not that night, not so many other nights. Why did it sound so much clearer now on replay? Why could he smell the chicken? Why could he see the outline of his wife's body as she stood on the blue rolling library stool that she kept in the kitchen, fanning the kitchen hood to prevent the smoke detector from going off? This memory was the kind of disposable moment that you don't even think about — that is only the daily fabric of a day, of a marriage — but it lingered, every mortal moment of it, and Denny Plummer felt the heaviness of the memory. Opening the email was like unlocking a box. He felt feverish, anxious to head back in, a compulsive desire to sift through everything that had once belonged to his wife. He wanted to know all the parts of her that had been concealed from him, wanted to read the emails, and the notes in her drawers, to have access to the pieces of the puzzle.

Denny closed the laptop for now, but he knew he would be back; he had started something, and now he would test the limits of his own obsession. The blue light of the computer faded from the room. Hague Blue looked black in the dark, and now, yes, it was dark inside, dark outside; the snow might as well have been mud outside the window — he couldn't tell either way. All these days that Anna spent at this very desk, writing ideas for other people, pushing her own creative impulses down while he was out in the shop inventing, doing, making. She had stared at the snow, or the muddy soil getting ready to spring green, or the oak trees flush with new growth.

Whatever she had been thinking, he now knew, was a relative mystery. He had known her, but also, he had not — she had kept her own secrets and now they were buried down in that cold, hard space. Eternity. Forever.

Part II
Summer

Chapter 11

LATE MAY'S HOT sun and cold ocean made a formidable combination. The pool they had started last fall was almost done, but not quite, thanks to a battle with a local contractor, so Anna had joined a gym in Peabody with the hopes of becoming a more fit version of herself. Truth was, at Life Time, the ten-thousand-square-foot complex with its smoothie bar and saunas and cold-plunge pools and spa, everyone joined to use the sprawling outdoor pool and waterslides. In summer, the pool was the central gathering space of half of Hamilton, Boxford, Topsfield, and Middleton.

"For just five hundred dollars a month, you, too, can parade around in a bikini among Hamilton's finest dad bods," Di said to her to try to get her to join.

"Is this supposed to be a selling point?" Anna asked.

"It's not *not* a selling point."

Earlier that day, Di had sent her a screenshot from PTO darling Karen Pistoulia's Instagram account. Ever since Anna had deleted her social media, Di had been doing this—sending along good material, the kind that she knew would make Anna laugh. The image in question was a selfie, which magnified Karen's moon face. Next to her was a skeletal Tom Brady, New England's most famous sports personality. The caption just read: *GOAT.*

See what you're missing, not being on the Internet, Di had written, as if not seeing the Hamilton Mommies flaunt their celebutante connections was going to leave some wide and gaping void in Anna's life. Di hadn't approved of Anna's decision to abandon Instagram and Facebook, and her screenshots were gentle reminders that there was a whole world out there.

I'll survive, Anna wrote back. Anyway, her promise to Di had been to meet somewhere in the middle. No social media to track the inane social climbing of her "friends" and neighbors, so Life Time would have to do. Why not meet the hornets in their nest?

Di didn't have a pool of her own, and she rarely drove up to Newburyport or out to Ipswich or Gloucester for the beach anymore. "Too much work, too much sand," she said. She had become persnickety in her old age — old age being her forties. Instead, Di, along with all of the other wealthy moms from the middle North Shore, preferred to pull up a lounge chair at Life Time, where, for a hefty fee, you could order a cocktail, a plate of chips and guac, and Pirate's Booty for the kiddos, all charged to your account, *thankyouverymuch*. Country club life without the astronomical $10,000 club fees of the Ipswich club, which, sure, some people did join, but that was a different stratum altogether.

Anyway, she had ended up joining, mostly because she did love the water, and she wanted the kids to have a summer, and because the beach...well, it was beautiful, but cold, New England being what it was. Getting used to being a member of Life Time was like getting used to being a different person. Every day, Anna looked through her clothes and asked herself: *Is this okay?* Was the cover-up from Target enough? Did she need something more...Tory Burch? More...Prada? To live up to the expectations of the women she saw parading around the gym — and it really was a gym — could set her bank account on fire. And yet she still felt compelled, in some magnetic way that made no sense, to normalize herself, to fit in.

Ever since the emails and the police report, Anna had done her best to become invisible. Despite Di's bid to convince her, no, she didn't think the PTO was behind it. But maybe it was better to take a break for now, to fade into the tapestry of summer. There had been that look in Harper Mar's face, that sneer, that permission granted by Mimi, and it had all burrowed quite deeply into Anna, even before all the calls, even before the dance. All of it felt deeply connected, even though she hadn't talked it through with anyone, not even Di. Anna wanted things to be easy, at least for now. She wanted things to be seamless. She wanted to soften the edges of Hamilton. To disappear at drop-off and pickup. To send Denny to birthday parties. To beg off commitments. She was busy! So busy! If Di had noticed, she said nothing. And she was pretty sure Denny hadn't noticed, which was useful in keeping up her charade. She had been the perfect exterior parent, planning everything, executing plans and attending almost none of them, a background actor, an extra, tiptoeing around the perimeters of her own life.

But now it was the Friday of Memorial Day weekend, and her kids had the day off, for some obnoxious reason, and there was a heat wave, and she'd have to be seen in public eventually anyway. She had made a good effort not to run into any of the PTO moms, but she couldn't avoid it forever, and every time she stepped into Life Time, she knew she was stepping into the hornet's nest.

Di had already gotten seats when Anna arrived late in the morning. Life Time was mostly full, swarming with moms and kids. Some days were like this, though Anna didn't mind it. The chaos almost made it easier not to see anyone she knew.

"What a day to be alive," Di said. She was wearing a long-torso single-shoulder swimsuit in black, with rouching and white piping along the seam, along with a wide-brimmed seagrass hat that made her look straight out of a 1960s movie. Every once in a while, Anna wondered if her friend was real. How could someone look so effortless all the time? How could she go from an old sweatshirt with holes in it to this look — whatever this was — without missing a beat? From a canvas bag monogrammed with her initials, DEM, she produced a full bottle of rosé, a wine opener, and two insulated pink travel cups.

"A little early, isn't it, Di?"

"No way. It's rosé." Di winked. One of her boys, Brian, was in the pool with another local Hamilton kid, Anna could see, searching for batons with a pair of goggles, his navy blue and white swim shorts emblazoned with the high school's logo: the Hamilton-Wenham Generals.

"Where's Henry?" Di's youngest, Henry, was a few months older than Ben, five.

"Upstairs. He didn't feel like swimming today." Upstairs meant daycare, and a hands-off morning for Di. *Rosé indeed*, Anna thought, though she wasn't interested in a midday buzz herself. Leave that to the moms of Hamilton, to escape the pretty prison that they had all created for themselves, even Di, even her perfect and wonderful friend Di.

"Is he okay?" Anna asked. "He hasn't been over much lately. It's almost like he has a whole new group of friends." She had noticed that Henry had been around Ben less and less this summer, and that his interest in sports had suddenly exploded. Henry was young, true, but he had always presented as bookish, which had concerned Anna's naturally athletic friend, who had hoped that both of her boys would naturally gravitate toward fields and teams.

"Actually, he's reignited a passion for soccer," Di said.

"I thought the coach had suggested T-ball as an alternative," Anna said with a quick snort.

Di gave her a look. The look said: *You must have been mistaken.* "The coach says he's unbelievably gifted. They're looking to bump him up to first-grade level. They think he could play a goalie position. Go for captain, too."

I guess things can change, Anna thought. For all she knew, Henry had latent skills buried deep inside that had never been extracted. And now, what more could her friend have asked for, after all, than two sons with advanced athletic skills, besides a pile of money, a day in the sun, a large and fancy pool, and all the chips and guac she could reasonably charge to her account? And they had that, too. Not a bad day after all, if you could stand it.

"Hurry up, come get sunscreen on," Anna called to Ben and Louisa, then pushed them toward the shallow section of the pool where the guards were. For her own part, she had selected a conservative one-piece, not at all *Hamilton Mom* of her, no one-shoulder business, more like Marshalls chic if anything.

"I see you haven't updated your bathing suits this year," Di said.

"Very funny."

"Don't look now, but the enemy's here."

Anna did look now, actually, and when she snapped her head up — purely by instinct — there were three women walking her way, a trio, like Mean Girls, but in real life, and not in pink. This year, everyone only ever wore black, just in case she hadn't gotten the memo. Mimi Mar, hair pulled up into a petite banana clip, was in front. Two-piece, of course, so that no one missed out on the hard work that went into the body. A slip of a cover-up, just enough to go below the waist. To her left: Karen Pistoulia. A little pink-looking, Karen, with a hint of sunburn and a scoop-neck suit and a long, flowing sleeved cover-up that trailed behind her like some kind of weird veil. And Ellen Wilson. Did Anna even know they were friends? Poor Ellen looked a little like an ugly duckling, scurrying behind these two, a little overweight, stuffed into a suit that was probably the wrong size, black with a ruffle around the collar, pretty if outdated. They were looking right at Anna, three sets of bug-eyed black sunglasses, or they were looking right through her. Hard to tell.

"If it isn't Anna Plummer!" Mimi said, as if they were old friends. "I did *not* know that you were a member here!" She stood over Anna's chair, shading her eyes with her right hand. The effect of three women standing over her was like having the sun hide behind a storm cloud; for a moment, she felt dark and cold.

"New Life Timers!" Anna said, with faked enthusiasm. "We did it for the water bottles." All members were issued free insulated bottles, white and red, a sign of brand allegiance. Around town, you could spot a Life Time member from a mile away by those water bottles. *A club that would have me as a member* was what Anna was thinking. Who even wanted to be in with this crowd in the first place?

"Well, the smoothies are just to die for," Mimi said.

"That's not a lie," Karen said. "There's this peanut butter one, and sometimes I drive all the way over here in the mornings just for the smoothie."

Anna nodded. She believed this, actually, although, it did seem pretty unbelievable to drive twenty minutes for a smoothie.

"We haven't seen you at any of the PTO events," Mimi continued. "Right, ladies?"

Karen and Ellen nodded.

"I've just been so busy," Anna said.

"I hope we've... resolved all of our differences from earlier this year." Mimi put her hand down. Now Anna could see nothing but the brutal ball of sunlight behind the three women. They looked like photographic negatives, silhouettes in the sun, unclear and unfocused figures before her. "I think it would be better for us all to go back into the school year with a fresh new start."

"Of course," Anna said.

"Anyway, good to see you, as always, Anna." Mimi reached down and put a hand on Anna's foot. The gesture took her by surprise. The intimacy of it, the quickness. Mimi was nimble, did things you wouldn't expect. Quick as lightning, she had turned on her heel and hopped off in the other direction, minions at her back, none of them — not even Ellen — bothering to say goodbye.

That could have been the end of it, and really, it would have been just another strange late-May day, a posse of uncomfortable Hamilton women at Life Time, if the next series of events had not unfolded, quick as a summertime thunderstorm. Every hour on the hour, the guards blew the whistle and called all the kids out of the pool for ten minutes so that the adults could enjoy the luxury of the pool to themselves. So at two o'clock the guards blew, and all the kids came swarming back to their parents, like ants on sugar. Ben and Louisa and Di's son Brian shook off in the sun and sent water spinning across the chaises while their parents went to swim by themselves. Anna was on her back, staring up at the sky, two cumulus clouds that looked a lot like the kind of fake clouds you saw in video games. That was how perfectly formed they were, with just a shade of gray on the lining. A designer could not have invented a better set of clouds.

The guards blew the whistle again, and before Anna had a chance to flip from recumbent to standing, her own kids were running toward the pool, and that's when she saw it, out of the corner of her eye, just a flicker, just a small thing. Or did she? It looked, from her vantage point, like Mimi Mar had hip-checked Louisa, sending the bony girl tumbling forward to the edge of the pool. All the kids had been rushing, and Mimi had appeared from nowhere, a specter in black, and there was Anna's daughter, stumbling forward until her heel caught the concrete edge and over she fell into the clear blue water.

Anna quickly swam to where Louisa had fallen in, but by the time she reached the edge of the pool Mimi was gone and Louisa was up at the surface catching her breath.

"Are you okay?" she asked, breathless, grabbing Louisa by the wrist.

"Yeah, Mom, I just tripped," she said. "So embarrassing!" She covered her eyes with both hands.

"You just...tripped?" Anna asked. She had seen it, though, clear as day, the image of the woman, black on black, grazing her daughter. It was a taunt, a warning. And then she was gone. But that couldn't be real. It would be a deranged thing to do, after all, to hip-check a little girl into a pool, and Anna was starting to wonder if she had seen it or if she had imagined it. There was the heat, the flurry of people, the chaos. She couldn't be sure. And yet, there was that moment, too, lingering in Anna's memory — the smile at school pickup. That was equally unhinged, if she thought about it.

"I caught my foot." Louisa held it up as proof; a nick on her heel was bleeding.

"We should get you out."

Di was oblivious, afloat on a haze of rosé. She hadn't seen a thing, or, if she had, she wouldn't remember it in the morning anyway.

Louisa was prattling on, concerned about whether other second graders had seen the mishap. Humiliation loomed large in her elementary school life. For a minute, Anna believed her daughter's account. It had been an accident, a stupid accident, and the vision — well, that was just her imagination, running wild as usual.

But then, just as Anna was climbing the ladder to leave the pool, with Louisa ahead of her, Anna saw, at the far end of the pool, two open doors. Mimi Mar waved and held a hand to her mouth, and then Anna was sure.

"It was good to see you, Anna Plummer," Mimi called. "Don't be a stranger now."

Deranged. That was the word that flashed through her mind again. The woman was deranged.

Chapter 12

IN THE AFTERNOONS, before he picked the kids up from camp, Denny drove the back roads of the North Shore: Ipswich Road through Georgetown and Boxford, or sometimes, if he was feeling particularly prone to wandering, the rolling passage through Newburyport and into West Newbury that snaked around the Artichoke Reservoir. This was always Anna's favorite place, particularly in summer, when a plumage of purple flowers erupted in the old farming fields. Sometimes she would have him deposit her here in the afternoons on the way home from a beach adventure so that she could run a quick four-mile loop. He'd take the kids for ice cream at Hodgie's, over in Amesbury, and be back to pick her up just in time to watch the sherbet sun sink into the water, his sweaty wife bent double as if she had just conquered the world.

The Artichoke hadn't changed in the months since Anna's death. Same rolling hills that traced the water. Same group of kids with their legs kicked out over the bridge, fishing, catch-and-release only, every summer, just like always. Same purple flowers, tall and spindly, growing mysteriously from those fields. It had been six months and Denny still had no real answers about his wife's death, though Sticks had mostly stopped coming around. Last winter Denny had turned over one of Anna's computers to the police, believing that giving Sticks this information would help solve the case of Anna's murder. Instead, it seemed to stall it. He hadn't been cleared as a suspect, but the long bouts of silence he received from the police department led him to believe that no one was really looking very hard into Anna's death these days. She was just another woman who had gone quietly into that good night.

The case's stalling had inspired in Denny complete and total wrath. In the days and nights since he discovered the hateful messages on Anna's computer, he had, he supposed, gone a little rogue. He stayed up late, scouring the Internet. Was he becoming a vigilante? Maybe. It felt counter to his nature, but there he was, as obsessed with his wife's murder as his wife herself had been with Friday-night *Dateline*. She always seemed to know the outcome of a case only a quarter of the way through, and Denny hoped that he, too, could reach the conclusion in time to achieve some kind of justice. Besides his desire for justice was a kind of anger that was unfamiliar to him. Denny Plummer was *mad*. He was *livid*. He felt robbed of time, and he was determined to figure out what had happened. The perversion of justice — the murder of his wife — caused him acute pain, but if he could only put things back in order, maybe he could reverse the order of time. This was a way to bring Anna back, as ridiculous as that sounded.

Of course, Denny knew a few things of his own. Every day, on his drives, he thought of more things that might be useful. He kept a notebook in the Jeep and pulled over, jotting down notes when the thoughts occurred to him. By now, the notebook was nearly full of handwritten notes to himself, half-thought-through ideas that led to no significant conclusion.

Handed computer over February 2023
Anna, coffee, Mimi Mar, February 2022
What do I know about Mimi Mar

That last one stuck in his mind like an upturned tack. Mimi Mar, Mimi Mar, Mimi Mar. She had become his foil, his heartburn, his agita. Mimi Mar stuck in his craw. He couldn't shake the feeling that something about Mimi was just not right. Mimi wasn't a local, Denny knew that. She had moved to Massachusetts for college and had met her husband, Franklin Mar, in 2003 at a bar in Boston. By 2007, the two were married and living in a condo in Charlestown. By 2009, Mimi had quit her job in public relations, and by 2012 they were living in Nancy's Corner in Hamilton in a three-million-dollar house. Two years later, she was pregnant, and her trajectory was complete. College grad to the PTO in just a few easy steps.

What Denny didn't know about Mimi Mar was what concerned him, and although he knew that maybe there wasn't much rational about his dislike or distrust for her — except what he had inherited from his wife — he felt a compulsion to keep digging. He needed to find out more about her — where she had lived before Massachusetts, and what her parents did — but she was practically invisible. Search anyone on the Internet and you're bound to find a trail, but Mimi wasn't like that. Her life began and ended in Massachusetts. It was as if her past had been engineered to fit this adult version of her, as if she had scrubbed whatever came before, projected a new and improved part of herself onto the world. And Denny wanted to know more about what came first.

He had heard rumblings that she was from Baltimore. But the trail then went cold. What he needed, he realized, was someone as inquisitive and bold as he wished he could be. He needed Anna, of course, but, in a pinch, he could use Di, the enigmatic best friend, who was fearless and bold, and never afraid to find trouble, even if trouble was happy to find her first.

"The first thing I would do, personally, is a good old-fashioned Facebook stalk," Di said. She arrived at the house with corn from Meadowbrook Farm, first of the season, along with blueberries and biscuits, Richardson's vanilla ice cream, steaks, handfuls of fresh basil, a bag of tomatoes, her two boys, and her husband all in tow. "Take this," she said, foisting the groceries upon Denny and moving right into the house as if she owned the place, ever her signature move. Outside, it was balmy still. The cicadas were singing. The construction around the pool was finally complete, and the backyard had been transformed into a serene oasis, bluestone pavers leading to a cerulean pool that sparkled in the late afternoon sun. Squinting, Denny could almost see a completely different reality, all of them sitting down for a July dinner, his wife emerging from the pool, the steaks hissing on the grill.

"Meaning what, exactly?" he asked.

"Meaning, who she is friends with can tell you plenty about who she really is. Maybe you can't find anything about *her* online, but you can probably find out about *them*." Di had already made herself plenty at home, rooting around in the fridge for a bottle of rosé — old, unopened, Anna's — and a portable insulated cup that was half of a set the two had shared.

The kids ran around outside, jumping in the pool and savoring the delights of late July. July was Denny's favorite month, and he usually hated to see it go, but this year time seemed to mean nothing at all. Coming home, there was no joy in that. You could not look forward to the next steps, it turned out, when you hadn't resolved the last ones. They were loud and preoccupied with the pool, setting up camp at a far table.

"We'll eat out here," Louisa called, and Denny knew the adults would have plenty of time — and space — to themselves.

When he finished grilling, Denny came back to Di's proposal.

He hadn't thought much about how hard Mimi had tried to erase herself.

"Di, do you think she did it on purpose?"

"Anna never trusted her," Di said. "Especially ..."

"Especially what?"

Di's husband offered a look. He reached a hand out, as if to say, *No, don't,* but it was too late, the conversation was too far gone.

"There was just an incident. At Life Time." Di and her husband, Mark, exchanged looks. He had been a friend of Anna's, too, all of them childhood friends, and sometimes Denny felt as if he had been on the outside looking in on some multisided relationship that he could never quite crack.

"When?" Denny asked. "Why am I just fucking hearing about this now? Sometimes I feel like it was a vault between you two, a vault I can't pry open, even after Anna's death ..."

"I think," Di said, "because we weren't exactly convinced, at the time, that it was real."

Mark — prototypical New England type, preppy, swoop of brown hair, loafers, an accent that could never disappear despite accumulated wealth, swaddling a beer — tapped the ring of condensation his drink had left on the teak. He didn't make eye contact. He had known about this, Denny surmised. Whatever this was.

"I still don't really understand what we're talking about here," Denny said.

"There was this day at Life Time, right before Memorial Day last year," Di said. "Anna and I were in the pool. Louisa tripped running to get back in after the guards blew the whistle."

"I remember that," Denny said. "She came home bandaged up."

"That part she told you," Di said, looking at Mark again.

"I assume there's a part she didn't?" Denny said.

"At the time, I didn't really believe her. She swore she saw Mimi hip-check Louisa," Di said.

"*Into* the pool?" That was a wild revelation. Denny could feel his heart beating twice as fast as normal. His daughter pushed into a pool by none other than Mimi Mar. That instinct, the one that kept him up at night, hadn't been wrong, but now it pulsed into overdrive, firing on all cylinders. If his friends hadn't been at the house, he would have raced upstairs and set about investigating this new information, crawling into a whole new wormhole. He could picture his wife's backup laptop, asleep in her lacquered office. What secrets could he uncover with this new information?

But Denny felt something else, too, beyond his anger at his wife's murder. There it was again, that familiar sadness. Here was something else that Anna had withheld from him, something else she hadn't trusted him with. Maybe she thought he would think she was losing her mind. Maybe she just thought it wasn't important after all. Whatever it was, she hadn't told him about it, this *incident,* this *thing* that haunted her, the pool, the moment that happened — or maybe didn't. He ached for Anna, and for his daughter, for the things he had missed when his family was whole.

"It seemed pretty hard to believe, to be honest," Di said. "Even for Mimi."

But now, in the pink light of evening, nothing seemed hard to believe, certainly not a grown woman sending a seven-year-old spinning into a pool with the nudge of a hip. In fact, it seemed to Denny very easy to believe. What if it had been a warning? What if Anna had misjudged the potency of the message? What if to misunderstand the enemy was to do so at your own peril?

"Explain this. Explain why she didn't tell me these things," Denny said.

"You know what she loved about you?" Di asked.

"Honestly?" Denny said. "Sometimes I really do not."

"She loved that she didn't have to tell you all of these things. She loved that there was a whole network of complication and that you were not part of it."

"Di, that doesn't make me feel any *fucking better.*" He stood up and drained a glass of rosé. He wasn't even sure it was his. He often felt that Anna had misjudged him, that she had fallen in love with him because she liked that he was some of the things that she was not: even-tempered where she was outraged, cool where she was hot. But she misinterpreted his quiet for a lack of depth. She misinterpreted his evenness for an incapacity to experience rage. But he had that capacity, and she had seen it a few times, when he would turn funny or weird or sarcastic or angry. He just did a better job of concealing it than she did.

"Maybe she just didn't think you'd react the way she'd want you to react. I don't know," Di said.

"Maybe you have to give someone the chance in order for them to be proven right or wrong," Denny said, walking into the house. "Maybe it's easier to say all these things because she isn't here. Maybe, maybe, maybe."

Once Di and Mark and the kids were gone and his own kids were in bed, Denny took the opportunity to look into Mimi Mar again. He was back on his own computer now, and in his own office, no more than a corner of his bedroom that he had converted into a workroom of sorts. He could no longer face the Hague Blue walls or the abandoned books or the artwork that had once been hers. Anna's office was a place where no one went.

On the nights when he could not sleep — and there were plenty of those now — he had built himself a slip of a desk, which looked out onto the sloping lawn below, and onto the deep blue pool, backlit by the installed lighting that the pool company had talked Anna into. In the end, despite his protestations about the cost, she had been right; it looked like moonlight dappling a lake, just spectacular from this angle, and maybe she, too, would have spent thick summer nights looking down at the project that she had most wanted to see complete, perfectly executed, fully formed, beautiful. And yet, the pool, which was her dream, had become his inheritance.

From his office now he could watch all the plans she had made finally come to fruition, despite the fact that she hadn't lived long enough to see any of it herself. When he was feeling ungenerous, these small and aching twists of fate made him the angriest, not only that her dreams had outlived her, but also that he had been stuck with them, this constant, persistent reminder of her that he could never escape.

Denny logged into Facebook and looked up Mimi Mar again, a search so familiar that computer completed it for him, filled in the blanks before he even had the chance. Following Di's instructions, he went to her long and curated lists of friends, plenty of Hamilton faces he knew, people from school events and softball games, sharp-featured parents who were always well dressed and who drove expensive SUVs.

Mimi Mar was friends with everyone who was anyone in Hamilton, Massachusetts.

Chapter 13

DI SAID SHE was spiraling. Losing her cool. But despite Louisa's recounting, Anna was convinced that it was Mimi who had sent her daughter flying into the pool on that May afternoon. They were lucky that it hadn't been worse. Afterward, Anna had scooped Louisa up and inspected her foot — it was a deep cut, but nothing too serious, even she could admit that — and had gone into the women's locker room while Di watched Ben. She bandaged it with the help of one of the health club attendants and then called it a day, a day ruined by Louisa's "accident."

"It was just an accident," Di said. "Kids trip."

"You don't understand," Anna said. "First, she comes up to me with that weird speech. Then I see her, and then ..." She trailed off. Mimi had been sending a warning, waving at the door. She *wanted* Anna to know that it was her. But why? What was the point of all this? It had been half a year since the drama surrounding the dance. Anna had kept her head low, avoiding practically all of Hamilton. The police report was old news at this point. What could possibly be accomplished by any of this?

"I think that the best thing to do in all of this is to just let it go," Di offered. They had met at Stiles Pond, in Boxford, where a mutual friend was a member. No more Life Time for Anna, she decided. No more risk-taking this summer. She would find somewhere else to swim, and Di was up for practically anything. Hadn't they always been experts at seeking out the best swimming spots as kids, anyway, even when they didn't have pools of their own? Anna would return to her roots, then, rely on her wits to get her through the hot summer, avoid Hamilton and its *ladies* like the plague.

Except. Except, except, except. Mimi Mar waving at her from the doors. Anna couldn't let that image go. A woman unafraid to send a child into a pool like that was probably unafraid of pretty much anything. And Anna, too, had always considered herself the kind of person who was unafraid of bullies. Mimi Mar was a bully, and Anna had never had much use for those types.

Coursing through Anna's mind were all the possible and probable remedies. Complain to the school. (Useless.) Post to her (since deleted) social media. (Social suicide.) Reach out to the state or local government. (Possibly helpful.) File another police report. (Unclear about its efficacy.) Demand that the superintendent remove Mimi Mar due to dereliction of duty. (Maybe the smartest option.) Once again, she considered Denny's reaction to all of this: *no, no, no, no, just do not do any of this*. But he was non-confrontational, and where did that ever get you at the end of the day? Problem-solving with a person like Mimi had to be aggressive, it had to be finite, and it had to involve a third party.

Denny had his own expression for Anna when she was agitated like this. *Poking the bear,* he liked to say. He had grown up in the kind of house where everyone had been better served to keep a head down and mind his own business. It hadn't been the same, in Anna's freewheeling childhood, where her hippie parents had encouraged all manner of free expression. Her mother had wanted her daughter to become the kind of fully realized creative person that she herself had never gotten to be.

Gerhard Richter she was not, of course, and her dried-up paints—well, they could attest to that. But Anna Plummer had certainly lived up to the part of the expectation set by her parents about speaking her mind. She was, in this way, a ruthless interrogator, unwilling to give up if she felt some wrong had been done. And here was her bruised Louisa, the girl not even aware of the crime perpetrated against her. Anna couldn't let it go. The more she wrestled with the idea of doing nothing—of letting it go—the more stuck in her conviction she became. To walk away was to give Mimi exactly what she wanted: a crack at power, the knowledge that she had intimidated them in precisely the way that she had desired. And Anna simply couldn't live with that.

Kick a hornet's nest and you must expect hornets. It's simple physics, though Anna did not know, exactly, how fierce or angry these hornets would be. She wrote a letter—quickly, without thinking much—to Superintendent Morris about Mimi and what she had seen. She wrote about the incident at Life Time. About Harper and that look and the smile—proof of nothing, Anna realized, but still, it had felt like something, and wasn't something... *something*? She wrote about that newsletter, offering access to some, though not all. About the police report. She attached some of the screenshots. The accusations. Anna even mentioned the meeting she had with Mimi at Honeycomb, how Mimi had denied that Hamilton had any problems at all. How could the president of the PTO claim perfection and still claim to be fit? She wasn't fit, Anna knew; she should be removed. Of course, Anna already knew that she now seemed like the deranged one. The one trying to prove the unprovable. Still, she included a formal request that Mimi be removed as the president of the PTO.

She was sure there would be consequences. To sit by idly, though, allowing Mimi to parade around with her posse of women, dictating the rules of Hamilton – who could stay and who could go – *that* Anna couldn't stand for. She thought about how many other girls had been tossed aside, how many mothers had come before, brushed up against the wrath, had cowered in deflection, had been scared silent. Surely there had been people before her, women who had seen the flash of anger and who had walked away instead of confronting it. It was never true, Anna knew, that a person was really alone in a battle, only that she was the first in pushing through the door.

Hitting Send on the email felt like a relief. Whatever came next, that was the decision of the school, administrators, policymakers, the people who held other people accountable. She had done the right thing, she was convinced, had told the truth when it was hard to come to the surface against people who were cruel for no reason. She was always telling her kids to do things that were brave and uncomfortable, even when Denny was saying the opposite: that to ride the wave to completion was better than getting caught in the tumbler of it, better than getting caught in the bone-crusher, laid to waste over the rocks.

Later, Anna dropped the kids off at Di's house for a playdate and drove out to Newburyport for a run. It was a long, out-of-the-way place to go if you were just looking to knock off four or five miles, but Di got it; she understood this need to be alone, to get away when you were mobbed by feelings and family. On the exit ramp, Anna's was the first car at the light. A bearded man stood at the corner, where a guardrail separated the highway. He held a sign.

> **I'm just trying to get through the day. Need some money to eat and survive.**

Anna reached for her wallet, and then she stopped. She pushed the button that locked the doors instead. What was this impulse inside her, the one that made her see the worst in people? This man, standing out in the June sun: Would he do it if he wasn't earnestly in need? And even if he was lying, so what? Why not give people a chance, like Di and Denny were always telling her to do? The man with the beard locked eyes with her, but she looked away. The truth was, she felt bad — about herself, about the fact that she would no doubt go on her run and stop for a donut afterward, about how just one split-second decision could have changed the trajectory of both their days. But then the light changed and she applied just enough pressure on the gas to disappear into the wavy, soft-tar heat of the day, and she never thought of the man or the money or the things she had done or the things she hadn't again.

But then, in the settling, late-day heat, Anna felt the rhythm of the road. Clap, clap, clap, sneakers on pavement, which was a little soft and a little sticky. She looped around the water, stared at the kids smoking cigarettes where the reservoir road dipped down low onto a bridge — Parliaments, of course — and picked up her pace where the maples and oaks created a nest of shade into the backwoods of West Newbury. A calm had settled through her, here on the road. She could hear her own breathing, her own heartbeat, and it was a miraculous thing to know that you had done something brave and smart and protective, that you had made a choice that might rise back up like sewage but that, for right now, rested in the hands of other people. Turning at a fork in the road, she crossed over toward farmland, where a handful of colonial homes sprouted from the ground like the tall grasses that surrounded them, like they had always been there, like they, too, had been planted and nurtured with time.

She could, of course, run closer to her house, in the spiderweb of trails in Hamilton, but there was a certain peace in familiarity, in taking to the road where you had always taken to the road. That's when she saw a familiar face, Rachel Kincaid, formerly of Newburyport, now of Hamilton, wearing a singlet and running toward her. Her mother, Anna now remembered, still had a house over on Carter Street, small and tidy, a Colonial with clapboard siding.

"Rachel!" Anna shouted, with a wave. It felt good to see someone familiar. Running was solitary, but she always liked to share the commiserative pain with someone who understood the sport.

But it was as if Anna's voice had been swallowed up in the dust of July. Rachel kept her eyes to the ground and ran right past her without even looking up. That night at Riverview, back when she was picking up a pizza, it had all been different, but now, the water was tainted. Even her old friends were enemies. Anna kept right on running.

Past the purpling flowers, the small and squat houses, she dipped back into the woods, just in time for daylight to take one final bow, and she tried to convince herself that this would be fine, that she would find resolution, that Mimi would be punished for what she had done to Louisa — and, of course, to anyone else she had harmed in Hamilton — that the world would be slipped back on its axis, that she, Anna Plummer, would come to run this road again refreshed, a new woman, armed with the kind of confidence one assumes when they have done the thing they know was totally and completely and unimpeachably right.

Chapter 14

THE HOUSE WAS cool and dark. Outside, the sky was fading rosy-pink, the same color as on the first night he sat with Anna out on the Montauk docks, looking to the future with that mystery girl, her witchcraft and her charms. Tonight, the light felt decidedly less optimistic. The house seemed closed off, like a fortress, impermeable, cruel, and unkind.

Di had taken the kids for the afternoon, which was both a sadness and a relief. It should have been him, he knew, planning excursions with the kids. They were already one parent down. But he had started to feel like a stranger in his own body, curling back at the edges, a plant that had spent too much time in the sun. Denny looked at a mussed-up bedspread that Anna never would have stood for, Anna and her perfectionism, ever a bone of contention in their marriage and now something he missed constantly. Their messy house — his house, now — was an ever-present reminder of Anna's absence.

While his wife was alive, Denny had been mostly unaware of his own good fortune, but his general lack of perception weighed heavily on him now. Had he been an unfit husband, depending too fully on his wife to propel their lives forward? They had lived well; they weren't wealthy but they were a notch above middle class in this soft and comfortable place. They loved each other. They loved their kids. They had vacationed and eaten lobster dinners near the beach and taken glasses of wine outside in warm weather and done all of the pleasant things that couples in their forties do, and yet: He had missed the signs of her struggle, the throttle of perfectionism, the town closing in on them. He had been too busy enjoying the seamlessness of upper-middle-class life in Hamilton to recognize even the slightest tinge of darkness.

Soon, Denny heard a chorus of voices coming from the kitchen. He met his kids halfway down the stairs and they folded into him, soft bodies that seemed at once bigger and smaller than when he had last left them. Kids were always doing that, surprising you with their overnight changes, breaking your heart with the reminders of how young and tender they still were.

"Daddy, we missed you," Louisa said, clawing at the back pockets of his jeans like she had when she was a baby. She was always trying to find out what he stored in his pockets, the junk that Anna complained about constantly: business cards and tissues, spare screws and quarters, the stuff of life that ended up at the bottoms of drawers or in the clattering trays of washing machines, causing them to clank and stop working for a day or two. Somehow, though, he suspected that even his wife would find pleasure in this corporeal need of their daughter's, a grasping for her dad's body, to hold on to something real, to know that there was a part of them — of their unit of four — that still stood firmly before them.

Denny scooped up both kids, one in each arm, wondering how much longer he'd be able to do it, and kissed each on the top of the head.

"You smell like the sea," he said. Like sunscreen. Like salt. Ben had sand in his hair. "Did Di take you to the beach?"

"Sandy Point!" Ben said. "Then all the way to Salisbury to Beach Pizza."

"I couldn't have designed a better summer day myself," Denny said.

"I took them for a trip down memory lane," Di said. He hadn't seen her come into the foyer, but there, suddenly, was Di, wearing a bathing suit beneath a nearly sheer cotton jumper, along with pink flip-flops. She wore a sporty, expensive-looking visor on her head, which didn't quite mask her sun-licked skin. "All Anna's and my favorite spots from when we were kids ourselves." She looked at Denny for just a second too long, touched a knuckle to her eye in what was an uncommon gesture of emotion — for Di, at least — and then looked away. "Anyway, I have to get going. Dinner."

Denny nodded. Best not to belabor the point. "Thanks. For doing this."

"I hope the break was helpful?"

"More than you know."

"Don't be a stranger," she said. She waited a moment, as if she expected him to deliver a sermon right there. But then, thinking better, she smiled. "Well, anyway. Give a ring." With a salute, she was out the front door, a whisper in the wind.

A few weeks had passed since he had learned about the so-called Life Time incident, and Denny had been turning it around and around in his head. He knew he needed to talk to Sticks about all of this. The next morning, while the kids ate waffles and fought over who had made the better sandcastle at Sandy Point, he texted the officer.

I have some stuff I wanna discuss with you, he wrote. Sticks was inconsistent over text, at best. Sometimes the officer would write back instantly, in a flurry of interconnected blocks — never one-line texts that went on for pages, the way Anna used to write.

Other times, it took hours, or, worse, Sticks would start something, ominous dots of an iPhone messenger portending a response in the queue, and then the dots would disappear and nothing would arrive for days. Denny could never tell if the officer was distracted or plotting, or if he was a little too cautious in what he was committing to the page. Denny had absorbed, he knew, a heavy helping of distrust of the police from his wife, but something about Sticks didn't sit right with him. Still, he was the lead on the case, and Denny was careful not to destroy his only chance of resolving the mystery of his wife's disappearance and — a word he didn't even like to associate with her loss — murder.

Pretty soon, a message did pop up on Denny's phone. He was surprised to see that Sticks was communicative today.

Can meet later today, Agawam in Rowley. 4 or so.

Denny would have to find someone to watch the kids, maybe his mother-in-law, who lived in Newburyport — not so far from Rowley — and the kids hadn't gotten a full day with Gram in a while. After Anna's death, she had finally retired, though she was withdrawn now, suddenly a woman very much settled into her seventies. Anna's Hippie Dippie Mom, as his wife had always referred to her, now always seemed a little unmoored, as if the wind that carried her through life had been subdued. She still dug her hands into the soft garden beds every April through October, but she didn't seem to derive the same pleasure now. She hadn't called to ask if they needed any extra tomatoes, hadn't asked about Ben and whether he was still craving Sungolds or warm green beans straight from the vine this year. If Denny's own small family had been shattered by the loss of their ebullient Anna, Corina Denton had been simply squashed flat.

Denny couldn't make that part right, but he could deliver to his mother-in-law the shiny, bright faces of Anna's children, tanned limbs that made him think of what Anna herself must have been like as a child, leaping into the ocean or diving down to find rings at the bottom of a pool, always in motion, always searching for something, asking questions, seeking the sun like their dog in the slice of winter light in the dining room.

Fine, good, see you there, Denny wrote back to Sticks, wondering how Sticks would consider this wild ride of an idea, that Queen Bee Mimi Mar had some vendetta against his wife, that she had — in front of other people, even — hip-checked his daughter into a pool as some kind of warning.

It was a little unbelievable, Denny had to admit.

And even he struggled to make sense of what Mimi was fighting so hard to preserve.

But Denny believed that Mimi Mar had done something terrible, something she could not come back from. And he intended to prove it.

Corina said to come over with the kids. When they got there, she was wearing a gardening apron made from some kind of thick rubber material. Her gray hair was pulled back in a nub of a ponytail and her hands were covered in gloves.

"My munchkins!" she shouted, holding her arms open as Louisa and Ben leapt from the car, and she wrapped them up in her dirt-flecked embrace, careful not to stab them with her hoe (left hand) or trowel (right). "It has been *too long*! Shame on you, Denny, these kids are practically adults now." She let go and the kids took a step back and she inspected them. "Adults!"

Corina wasn't wrong. Denny hadn't stopped by the house in over a month, not because he was avoiding her exactly, but because he was avoiding talking about Anna, and that was a lot of what they did when they were together. He didn't want to relitigate the past, to slip into memories of his wife when all he saw — in his house, in his car, in his shed — were reminders of his old life. Here, in Anna's childhood home, were just more reminders of a place that no longer existed, a world where Anna Plummer was alive.

"I know, Corina. I'm sorry," he said. "It's just . . ."

She put a hand up. "Don't," she said. "We all have our things."

"I'll probably be gone two hours at the most," he said. "We can have dinner when I'm back. All of us. If you want?"

"That would be nice." She was staring at the kids again, at Louisa in particular, running a thumb along the side of her face, maybe trying to memorize what she looked like now or maybe remembering what another little girl had looked like at this exact same age, so many years ago, in another time, in another universe, when things had been different, when life had been different, when no one had been dead or in pain or left frozen in a river, a mystery for everyone's taking.

Sticks was already at the Agawam when Denny arrived. The old diner, open since 1954, was one of those silver relics with red vinyl seats, the kind that served five different kinds of pie, all homemade, and that only accepted cash and that had rules about what came on a hamburger versus a hamburger plate versus a hamburger club (Denny could never remember the difference). Sticks was staring down at a white, thick-walled cup of coffee, very light and creamy, from what Denny could see, running a thumb around the rim.

"Hello, stranger," Denny said as he slid into the booth across from the officer. Their relationship had mellowed considerably since their interrogation at the police station. Denny would hardly call Sticks a friend, but they had some kind of townie rapport, at least. He was hopeful that the officer would hear him out.

"Well, I'd hardly call us strangers at this point," Sticks said. He extended a hand. "Mr. Plummer. Good to see you, as always."

"Sticks," Denny said. He shook firmly.

"I swear, someday I'll grow out of that nickname," Sticks said.

"Probably not. Or probably not here," Denny said.

"Definitely not here," Sticks agreed. Not in Rowley, his

hometown, where his small-league career on the ice had both started and ended. Sticks for life it was.

"I stumbled on some information recently," he said. "I thought it was only right I pass it on. As a citizen."

"Oh yeah? What's that?" Sticks seemed genuinely interested. He leaned back in the booth, a little relaxed, affect temporarily dropped.

"You ever been to Life Time? The health club at the Northshore Mall?" Denny looked at him. Was it his imagination, or had the officer blinked?

"Can't say that I have. That's a little spendy for my purposes. When I get hot, I jump in the ocean. When I want to work out, I head over to Hard Nock's." He meant, of course, the notorious gym in Amesbury, a haven for townies and muscleheads.

"A one-trick pony, you are," Denny said.

"Let's just say that I like what I like, and there's no reason to change things at my age. I've been coming to this diner, for instance, three times a week since I graduated from high school, and why change now? But anyway. Back to Life Time." Sticks took a sip of coffee.

"My wife was a member," Denny said. "Well, I guess we had a family membership. Have a family membership. I never went there or anything, though."

Sticks nodded. He didn't seem to have any feelings one way or the other about that.

"So. What's the story with it, then?" he asked, tapping his index finger on the table.

"The story isn't so much with it as with a person who's a member over there. I found out about a situation that happened with my wife. It sounds like she was threatened. It sounds like my daughter was threatened," Denny said.

"How do you say?" Sticks said, squinting a bit, and then picked up his coffee and looked squarely at Denny. "You're killing me with the suspense here, Plummer."

"I'll get to the point," Denny said. "The summer before my wife ended up in the Ipswich River, she was threatened in public, at Life Time, by someone who is prominent in our community. And my daughter, Louisa, was, from the sounds of it, checked right into the pool."

"Who's the mysterious offender?" Sticks said. "Or are you just going to keep me guessing?"

"That'd be Mimi Mar."

"That be the same Mimi Mar who lives over on Nancy's Corner?" Sticks asked. "I believe I know her, but she has never had any connection with the Hamilton PD, if that's what you're getting at."

It felt like a strange thing to say—an admission without a crime. Denny stopped for a second. He hadn't asked about the police department, of course. The officer was protesting a little too much. *Tread carefully,* he told himself. *Friends and enemies wear the same clothing.* "The very same Mimi Mar from Nancy's Corner, yes," Denny said.

"Mimi Mar, president of the PTO, Mimi Mar?"

"Yes, sir."

"So you're saying...what, exactly? That she got into some little altercation with your wife at a health club and I'm supposed to look into whether or not she had something to do with your wife's murder?"

Denny went to say something else, but he felt like a wall had come up between them. The mood in the diner had shifted. Denny, the officer was plainly telling him, had crossed a line, but he couldn't stop himself.

"There's more, though. I talked to Diane Maguire," he said. "If you just..."

"If I just what? Start an investigation of a woman who has dedicated her *life* to public service? With no proof except some accusations from the man who we still have been unable to clear?" He sat back with a sneer and a little laugh, folded his arms over his stomach. "You're a smart one, I'll give you that, Mr. Plummer. Probably watch a lot of *Dateline.* Fault of this whole era, thinking they can run one over on the police."

Denny only wanted what any husband would want, what he thought Sticks wanted, though now he wasn't so sure: to find resolution, to finish what had been started, to solve the crime. Anna had always played this stupid song that he hated, over and over again when she had been sad or when she had been stuck on a copywriting assignment that she couldn't get through. He had never understood why listening to the same thing over and over again had helped her over a hump, but now he kind of got it, that she had found new meaning every different time.

Standing at opposite sides / Equal partners in a mystery

But where was his partner in this mystery? Gone, surely gone. If she were here, what would she say, anyway? This was part of the problem. He hadn't really been listening when she was around, and now she wasn't here to share in the thrill of the chase.

"That wasn't my point in any of this," Denny said. "I just think you go as far as you can with every possibility. I think you take every lead to its natural conclusion, and this is a real lead. I looked at Anna's computer, I brought it all to you, and you have done nothing, said nothing."

"We didn't feel that anything on there was sufficient to pursue," the officer said.

"'Sufficient to pursue'! 'Sufficient to pursue'! You said that to me before," Denny said, slamming a palm on the Formica table. "You practically stalked me until I came down to the station, made me feel like I was a suspect...then I guess that didn't work out for you, right? Then I gave you all these emails, all these threats, and then there was proof that she met with—guess who!—Mimi Mar, that she had an issue with one person in all of godforsaken Hamilton, that she reached out to people about it, that people knew, and you are telling me, well, no, no one's gonna do one goddamned thing about it. You might as well just tell me that you have no plans to find out who did this to my wife, because finding out who did this might open a can of worms that you don't want to open."

Denny had a moment of temporary recognition. He thought of the surveillance cars that had stalked his house in the weeks following his wife's death, about the feeling he had back then, that the cops were trying to convince him to stop meddling, about how he had disregarded it. But what if he had been right? What if the police were trying to make him go away? What if the cops were still trying to make him go away? And if they were, why?

"I'd be careful with what you say, Mr. Plummer. I don't appreciate your tone," Sticks said. He was standing now, loosening a tightly impacted wallet from his back pocket. He extracted a wad of dollar bills and tossed them on the table. "I think we're done for today. I suggest cooling off a little. Go for a swim in that pool of yours. Take your kids over to Hodgie's. Whatever you gotta do to get this out of your system." Grabbing his police-issued cap from the hook that hung above the booth, he tipped his head, turned on his heel, and walked out, leaving Denny alone in the Agawam, Anna's intemperate rage coursing through his veins.

Chapter 15

FOR A WHILE, things returned to their natural order. Anna took the kids to play mini golf up at Captain's Corner, in Salisbury, where Ben showed off his natural athletic ability. Afterward, they went across the road to Hodgie's Too and ordered lime and watermelon sherbet freezes, ice-cold drinks fizzy with seltzer. They sat in the sun and watched people eating tall and drippy cones while they got swarmed by yellow jackets.

At dinner, when Denny was done with work, the four of them drove out along 133 to Essex to eat at Woodman's, a yearly tradition. They sat in the restaurant's ancient wooden booths and ordered whole steamed lobsters with drawn butter and, of course, fried clams with extra tartar sauce, and even Louisa, the pickiest eater of all, who always ordered a hot dog at seafood restaurants, tasted the plate of steamer clams that came piping hot and served with a cup of "broth," which was really just hot seawater, as Anna saw it.

Another day, they drove out to Crane's, Anna digging into her purse and forking over the painful forty-dollar entrance fee for the beach, hauling out a rolling Yeti cooler filled with drinks and sandwiches — tomato for her, peanut butter and jelly for the kids — until they were bored with her and with the too-cold water and the too-hot sand, and so she had to do the entire thing in reverse, backtracking through the sand, through the parking lot, her whole life a tape played back in the opposite direction. Then it was a stop at Russell Orchards, this time for tender apricots and green compostable quarts of blueberries, which she allowed the kids to eat in the car, even though she knew she would find shriveled berries under the seats for the next six months.

A typical New England summer, which was all she ever really wanted anyway. It had been the reason she came home, the reason she had pleaded with Denny to move back, all of these sweet things, these memories she would share with her kids and hold on to forever. The beach and the fruit and even the Yeti back and forth on the sand. And she loved every minute of it.

Anna had just about forgotten about Mimi Mar and the pool at Life Time and the letter she had sent to the superintendent. A month had passed. It was mid-July, past the official start to summer. The weather had been cooperative and hot since well before Memorial Day, though she had stopped visiting the health club, had stopped putting herself in the path of any of the usual Hamilton suspects, especially since when she *did* run into any of them, they gave her the cold shoulder. Even sweet Ellen Wilson had been cold as ice the last time she saw her, at the Citgo over on Bay Road.

She drove over to Di's house right after that happened and sat in the driveway until her friend came out.

"What's up?" Di asked, walking out to the car. "You just planning on sitting here forever?"

Anna had the radio on and the sunroof open. "I'm just sitting here feeling sorry for myself," she said. The only thing that would make it better, she thought, was a pack of Parliament Lights, and, just like magic, Di opened her hand, *et voilà:* two cigarettes that might as well have come straight from 1998.

"I come bearing gifts, of course," Di said. "But you have to tell me why you're sitting in my driveway listening to Garbage with the sunroof open."

"I ran into Ellen Wilson at Citgo."

"Big fucking deal. Hamilton's the size of my ass. Which, as you know, is not that big." She put both cigarettes in her mouth and lit them both, before passing one to Anna.

Anna accepted it, looking at the burning ember in wonder. It had been a very long time.

"She wouldn't even make eye contact with me," Anna said.

"I didn't realize you were actually close," Di said. She turned her mouth into a wide O and blew smoke rings, an old and faded party trick that never really lost its shimmer.

"It's not that we were close, but she was always nice to me."

"I'll tell you a thing about Ellen Wilson. I've never met a person so afraid of fucking up in my whole life," Di said.

"What is that supposed to mean?"

"It means that Ellen's entire life revolves around what the members of the PTO think about her, and if you take that away, I swear to God she would die a slow and painful death right in front of you. She's cold to you because her Hamilton life depends on it. She practically doesn't exist without Mimi and Karen."

"That's the most pathetic thing I have ever heard," Anna said, because it was.

"I don't make the rules, I just loosely obey them," Di said.

Anna nodded. The problem wasn't only Ellen, of course. What was irritating her was that it felt like there was a conspiracy of people set up in Hamilton. Everywhere she turned, people were icing her out. Or maybe she had just been having a bad couple of days. "Actually, it wasn't just Ellen," she confided in Di. "Rachel Kincaid, too. When I was out running the Artichoke the other day."

"You didn't tell me that part."

"It was when you were watching the kids for me. I saw her while I was running. I said hi and she just…kept running," Anna said.

"Maybe she didn't hear you," Di said, optimistically.

"She ran right past me, eyes to the ground."

"Okay, well I'll admit, that's kind of bad," Di said.

"It's just that I'm finally starting to realize that I am completely out," Anna said. She could see Henry in the corner of the driveway, dribbling a soccer ball toward the house. She had to give it to Di. The woman certainly had invested in the kid. His form didn't look great, but he did seem passionately invested in the sport. Maybe he had graduated from T-ball, after all. "I'm alone. I'm a ghost in this town. Even with the people who were just a tiny bit nice to me. Even with the people I grew up with."

"You're not a ghost to me, kiddo."

"Careful what you wish for," Anna said. She inhaled once more, and deeply, then tossed the butt out the window. "Stomp that one for me." Winking at her friend, she put the car in gear and headed back out on the road.

Later, Anna took the kids all the way out to Sandy Point, six miles out from the entrance to the Plum Island Reservation, the most beautiful slice of beach on the eastern seaboard, if you asked Anna. Ben came back with a large, gray bone, a vertebra from a whale, and Louisa claimed as her own one of the triangular structures that the locals always made: lean-tos, really, swept away by the wind and sea late in the season, rebuilt by beach masters when the weather perked up.

"It's my Dream House," she shouted with glee, bringing a towel and sand toys inside.

Anna packed up the kids, spent and sand-covered, and drove them down the long road all the way back, through Newburyport and Newbury, through Rowley and alongside the Great Marsh, where the marsh grasses were just beginning to show signs of autumn: golden and red grasses were always the first tells. They drove past the canoe landing, in Ipswich — locals called it the haul-out — where day-paddlers were pulling red and green boats out after a day on the Ipswich River. She remembered a day from long ago, at summer camp, when she had spent a day on that very river, paddling with an inexperienced boater and swimmer. The canoe had capsized, leaving them waist-deep in warm, murky water, an experience that had baked into her bones. She had avoided the river ever since.

They pulled into the driveway at dusk. The Jeep was parked there. Anna could see a plume of smoke coming from the yard: dinner, the grill, more summer memories, and a relief, too, that she wouldn't have to think about it. She stopped at the mailbox on the way up, grabbed the mail, and shoved it in her beach bag without thinking. Inside, the house was cool and dark. It felt like summer.

Much later, when she was cleaning out the beach bags before bed, Anna remembered about the mail. Mostly bills, as usual. Gas. Electric. A few pieces of junk mail. She left the things for Denny on the counter. She was about to toss the rest in the trash when she noticed a piece of mail that was completely separate from the rest. It was handwritten, addressed to her, written in loopy script. *Mrs. Anna Plummer.* The stamp was perfectly affixed. So straight. Unnervingly straight.

She opened it. Inside was a typed note.

Dear Anna Plummer,

We have tried to express to you that you are getting in over your head.

```
  Please try to understand.
  Our generosity only extends so far.
  Consider this the final extension of our
kindness.
                                      —A friend.
```

This is unhinged, Anna thought to herself. *I have to be imagining this. There is no way that the PTO is actually coming over to my house and putting threatening notes in my mailbox.* Even repeating the story in her own head, she wasn't sure if she believed it. Was the note real? Was she holding the paper in her hand? More likely: Some kid had overheard a parent complaining about her and had decided to get in on the fun. It was impossible to take seriously any kind of childish prank that involved a "threat" in a mailbox. In 2022.

"What in the actual fuck am I supposed to do now, anyway?" Anna said to the empty kitchen. Denny had gone upstairs to watch a show about aliens or Nazis. Or maybe both. She knew that she couldn't just let it go. It was not in her nature, it was not acceptable to walk away from this. Plus, that was just giving the bully what she wanted, even if the bully *was* just a neighborhood kid who had overheard a parent talking shit about her around the dinner table.

I'm going about this all wrong, Anna thought. I need to beat the PTO at their own game.

I got another ridiculous message, she texted Di.

What is it this time

A weird note but I think it's just from a kid. But it gave me an idea. I think I should run for president of the PTO. She thought about writing more to her friend. What if the note really was from someone else? What if it was serious? But Anna held back. The less energy she devoted externally to these things, she felt, the less she allowed them into the fabric of her life. It was almost as if she was preventing them from being real by limiting how she spoke about them within her tight circle of friends and confidantes.

Di didn't fall for the bait. What exactly did the note say, she wrote back.

Stupid threat that sounded like it could have come from the PTO or also a teenager hard 2 say

Maybe you should just back off

I'm telling u I don't think it's them

Whatever u say

Let's talk about the PTO and me being president

You literally hate everything that the PTO stands for and also Mimi has been president for six years

THAT IS EXACTLY WHY I WANT TO DO IT! Change comes from the inside. No one owns president. She can't be president forever!

I thought you had to be a member of Chi Omega to be president, Di wrote.

Is that true I don't even know what Chi Omega is or what the difference between any sorority is that's definitely your expertise and not mine you're the one who was in a sorority hahahaha

Idk, pretty sure everyone who has ever been president has been a sorority sister from Chi Omega

There's no way that's a real rule that's just some dumb thing that someone made up

Three dots. Anna hated it when her friend did this. A rumination. Di needed to make sure Anna got the point, whatever the point was. Look if u really want to do it I will help but u know it's the fuckin hornets nest, she finally wrote back.

Now that is exactly the kind of support I needed to hear today, she wrote back. And it was true. Also true: She was scared, not only by the idea of the large-scale project she had undertaken, but also by its inherent challenges. She had to win over strangers, make them love her, overcome a fan favorite, prove her case to a crowd. If she was honest with herself, her chances of dodging defeat were not particularly great. She didn't know that many people in Hamilton to begin with, and the ones she *did* know appeared to hate her. So why was she doing this? Could the force of conviction be enough to move things? Could she be a vehicle for change? She wasn't quite sure, but she was willing to find out.

Anna Plummer needed a plan. She had never run for anything. Not class president. Not homecoming queen. And definitely not president of the fucking PTO. And no, she had never been a member of a sorority, least of all Chi Omega, the largest sorority in the National Panhellenic Conference (she had looked it up). Before Mimi – she had looked this up, too – Laura Cox had been president for a record-holding sixteen years. Cox's predecessor, according to the PTO's website, was Pamela Jansen, 1992–2000. That was as far back as the site provided. Anna googled them both, and, yes, Di was right: Both had been Chi Omega sorority members, just like Mimi Mar.

But obviously this was a coincidence, and not, as Di had implied, a requirement. Anna had known a few sorority girls herself in college – maybe even Chi Omega girls, though, to be honest, she hadn't kept track. The PTO attracted a certain set: women who cared about how they presented in society was how Anna might have defined it. Those same women were more likely than not to have pledged, if she was honest. She didn't need to ask what else Laura Cox and Pamela Jansen and Mimi Mar had in common, because she already knew, and it was a *totally unique* tribal tattoo on the small of their backs, the kind you got on spring break to define yourself as *the kind of girl who got a totally unique tribal tattoo* that would later be referred to as a tramp stamp.

And anyway, like any other position, it appeared to be a popularity contest, and Anna was not convinced of her own popularity. But she was convinced that she was smart and determined enough to be able to convince people to come along with her. She just needed a good campaign. She needed good ideas. She needed a compelling message. She needed people to know that she was running and that her vision for the PTO was a smart, viable, and inclusive vision. And then, she reasoned, people would be on board. Why wouldn't they?

Of course, she envisioned, too, a Tracy Flick–like competition, election in its most divisive and terrible form, Mimi Mar coming at her with all the serpentine desire of a woman who never intended to give up the gig. If Anna brought cookies for a crowd, she could bet that Mimi would follow that move with hand-decorated cupcakes draped with fondant and bespoke lettering. If Anna made posters, Mimi would surely be at the printer with an order for custom booklets about what she had accomplished during her past *term* as president.

Still, she shouldn't let that discourage her, and she knew that Mimi was a force — Anna wouldn't deny it — but it was time that someone stood up to the woman in her own home court. Also, Anna felt sure that there were allies out there, even if she didn't yet know about them: other Hamilton moms who had been berated or terrified or bullied by Mimi, and who were scared to come out and say what she was saying right now by offering to throw a hat in the ring, which was really just that she refused to lie down when someone punched hard to the jugular. And, also, that she believed in more for the community, more for Hamilton, more for her kids. (Even in her own head, she could hear the slogans beginning, which was good, she felt.)

PTO elections ran in January. Anna would have to run a stealth campaign throughout the remaining month of summer in order to convince sitting members to vote for her, and that would take time and dedication. She would have to do outreach, make friends, make alliances, prove her dedication to the cause.

She would start at Honeycomb, which she had been avoiding ever since the disastrous coffee date with Mimi all those months ago. Make it her new satellite workstation. Park there in the mornings once the kids started school. Introduce herself properly to all the Hamilton women. Ask about their sons and daughters. Get to know their peccadilloes. Their lives. What made them tick? What aggravated them about this small New England town? What would they like to see improved? She would take notes, would sit in a corner and watch the season change the way Richard Russo always said he did when he was writing down bits of dialogue and studying language and cadence, preparing for books like *Nobody's Fool* and *Empire Falls* in rusty old Maine diners. She could count on one hand, after all, how many times she had actually sat around and listened to the people in Hamilton — listened to what they wanted without judgment, actually sunk in and stopped and waited to hear the answer without springing to life with an accusation or a thought about how she wished she were somewhere else. It was time, she realized, to give them a chance.

When Anna Denton had moved to Newburyport, Massachusetts, in 1988, she was just about to turn eight. Her parents, desperately trying to save a tumultuous marriage, had sold off a brownstone on Tenth Street in Park Slope, Brooklyn, a house that would become a specter in their family. "If we had stayed in the Slope, the house would be worth over a million now," her father would say in the heat of an argument. By the time Anna was in her thirties, that value had risen to over three million, and her parents' arguments had charted the upward rise of its value in tiny increments.

They stayed together all those years, moving into a heaving, yellow Colonial that had been on the path of the Underground Railroad, half a block from the Merrimack River. At night, when the house was settling, Anna could hear scratching in the walls. "Maybe mice, but nothing to worry about," her mother said, but Anna did worry, not just about mice, but also about ghosts, the hauntings of enslaved people who had never made it to freedom, and the hauntings of whoever else had lived in this place, built so long ago that it had to have seen death in many forms. She wasn't sure that her family, unhappy as they were, was bringing many good *vibrations* – a word her mother loved to use – to the house, and so she worried that she, too, was contributing to another layer of misfortune. A house can only hold so much before it throws its disagreeableness back onto the owners. Well, that's what Anna Denton believed, anyway.

Newburyport, in the late 1980s, was not much like Hamilton. Anna lived in one of the bigger homes. Her parents made more money than most of the parents of kids she knew, drove nicer cars, took nicer vacations. When she said that she liked the New York Yankees, she was ostracized. When she flattened her vowels, the kids picked on her; they dropped their *R*s and spoke sharply, the way their parents always had. All kids played sports: soccer and football in autumn, basketball and hockey in winter, softball in spring and summer. The kids who abstained had no true shot at popularity, and when Anna decided to go out for track and field, she knew she was committing social suicide. A solitary sport? Not a sport, as far as the New England kids were concerned. But she liked the feel of the rubber track beneath her feet, the way it bounced back in return, energy in for energy out, not like the house near the Merrimack, which seemed to suck from her everything she had.

After a year in town, she had made no friends. After school, she came home to that house and sat in a room that her mother had wallpapered in a pattern with tiny pink flowers and played with Barbie dolls and stared out at the street and thought about what the other kids were doing.

"Do you want to do after-school programs?" her mother asked.

"I hate it here. I hate the people and I hate the town," Anna said.

"Maybe you just haven't given it a chance."

But Anna felt the opposite, that she had given it a chance and that there was nothing else to do but wait it out. At night, she could hear her parents' arguments, rising in crescendo each time, each argument louder and angrier, each argument more pointed. They argued about their unhappiness, about the house in Brooklyn, about Anna, about whether every decision they had made together had been a mistake. She was wrapped up in their bad choices without any way out, mired in the middle of someone else's stupid battle. Changing her parents was impossible. Changing the intractable people at school, with their narrow view of the world and their narrow view of her was equally impossible. All she had, then, was the large, gloomy old house, where from the roof she had a perfect view of the rushing blue river, though her parents did not know that she could climb up through the attic window.

For a while, it felt hopeless. Then, a few months later, when summer was once again ceding to fall, she met Diane at a cookout with her parents. Diane, who never seemed bothered by anything, and who had the infinite capacity to allow in more friends, even though she already had plenty. By then, Anna was going into the third grade. She had felt lonely for long enough, had lived a life excluding hope for long enough. And although she hated to concede any point to her mother, she decided to ride this one wave to completion. Maybe the woman had been right this time. She could give the town a chance.

Chapter 16

EVERY YEAR, in June, Hamilton's Community House hosted a Block Party at Patton Park, with food trucks and bounce houses and street performers and face painting. In a town where nothing much ever happened, it was an event, a place to see and be seen, a summer kickoff where you could reliably run into the people you hadn't run into for the rest of the year. Denny always looked forward to it, just as Anna hated it. What she saw as obligation he saw as getting to know the neighbors.

Last year, though, there was a drought. This year was drowned by rain. The month of June had been a washout, and everyone had hoped for better weather in July, but that had been a washout, too. The Community House had begged off the event, pushing it back into August, but it had rained for thirteen consecutive weekends of summer, so by the time the second weekend of the month rolled around, the grass was muddy and thick.

Plus, Denny didn't want to go. Running into the people of Hamilton at the Block Party, once appealing, now was anything but. Who wanted to stand in the rain, eating a burger from A&B's,

chatting with people who looked at him with sympathy while he was impotent, unable to do a thing about the death of his own wife? He would have stayed home if it weren't for Louisa, who, bounding down the stairs and looking out at the mist settling on the front lawn, sank a few inches lower, like a deflated balloon.

"Rain again!" she said.

"Bad summer weather," he agreed.

"Does this mean no Block Party?"

"I wasn't completely sold on it to begin with, to be honest with you," he told her. And then he watched her turn into a puddle, right there in front of him, his daughter with the corn-silk hair who, in the right light, looked a little like Anna. Louisa lay down like a snow angel, arms extended on the floor beside the stairs, wailing like her life was ending.

"There will be other events, I promise you," he said.

"That's what Mom said about *the Ziti Dance*!" she said. And that just about settled it. They were going to the Block Party, even if they had to put on waders and sailor caps.

But it wasn't exactly *raining* in the afternoon, more like *misting*, the way it had been since late May, ruining everything from the cherries to the tomatoes. There were no decent crops, not many decent beach days, and not enough time to dry out. Louisa went upstairs to change into pants and a yellow slicker that Anna had bought her a few years earlier. It was two sizes too small; her wrists came out well beyond the sleeves, tiny little flashes of white that reminded Denny of a porcelain doll.

In the months since Anna had been gone, he had neglected many things, and a big one was the way in which his children had grown. Here was Louisa, right before him, now taller than she had been, outgrowing her clothing. Soon he would have to pack away the last of the things that Anna had bought. He would be forced to walk the aisles of some department store with his daughter, without his wife, making choices on his own, and he hated to think about all the mistakes he would inevitably make, about how he would buy clothing that would be uncool, about how he would mess up, again and again, about how he was unsuited to do this, and about how this was his reality now.

It all felt incredibly unfair, that he was doing this without his wife, that you could lose the person you were meant to share the most fundamental of experiences with, and that you were meant, still, to soldier on after that. How was he supposed to go on living? No one had told him about that, and as the months wore on, the reality had grown only worse. In the first months after Anna's death, Denny had preoccupied himself with the bare essentials of existence, but now he had started to feel again. It was as if his whole body was defrosting, and the parts of him that had been beneath ice were just learning about temperature and pressure and pain once more. Oh, how it hurt. Oh, the terrible ache of seeing all the things that Anna would never see: the first experiences of his children, the pulsing house that would still hold their memories, except now without her. He hadn't known that he would need to make space for his own grief in all of this, but grief had made space for itself.

Patton Park was a strange political and military artifact in Hamilton. It had a nice little playground for kids, of course, with a boat-shaped climbing apparatus that Ben loved to commandeer with friends. But it was also home to a World War II–era tank, which had once been open to the public (after a vandalism event dating back to the 1960s, the tank was sealed, but it remained on display for anyone to see, a reminder of the state's military history). No one ever called the park by its full name, General Patton Park, but because the park possessed a layer of political formality — of Republicanism, even — Anna had always avoided it.

"It's an army park," she always said, even though it was really just a park — okay, yes, a park with a large green tank as a curio, but a park nonetheless.

"It's just a place for kids to play," he always pushed back, but she usually won in the end.

Today, though, Denny felt sufficiently unnerved by the tank. Something about the misting rain, the gray skies, bleak August coming to an end. The tank looked particularly green, like it had recently been repainted (it had not). The park, at just past four in the afternoon, was surprisingly full, given the weather. Vendors had set up on the perimeter, and the Hamilton-Wenham High School Band, all in uniform, were milling around, holding instruments and preparing to play something to the wandering crowd.

"Where to first?" Denny asked, grabbing each kid by a hand, but Louisa shook him off.

"Daddy! My friends!" she said. He had never considered that there would be a time when she would be too embarrassed to be seen with him, but here they were, at a Hamilton event, and here she was, the reluctant next generation, slipping ever so quickly into a phase of life that would exclude him.

"I'm so sorry to offend!" he said. He watched as she waved, demurely, at a few girls she knew from school. "Did you want to go see them?" he asked.

She nodded so fiercely he worried her head might pop off. "I know where to go," she said. "Mom always said if I got lost to come back where I was at the beginning."

"So that's right here, right?" he said. "The car. We meet at the car if we get lost. Understand?"

Louisa nodded. Ben nodded. Denny nodded. A pact. A Block Party in the rain.

Ben wanted to do the moon bounce and the axe throw and he wanted to get his face painted. Circling the park, they ran into Louisa twice, who had looped in with a group of second graders who were as delicate and lovely as she was: soft, tiny girls with pink and yellow and blue rain boots, dancing around and telling secrets and no doubt accepting that this day was the very best day of their young lives. The man operating the moon bounce made each child leave after three minutes, but Ben didn't want to go.

"Time's up, buddy," Denny told him, and he crumpled to the ground like he had never known such disappointment. He wanted to go again, he said, and so they walked to the back of what was now a very long line, a line lacing all the way into the middle of other lines, where the Hamilton moms and dads were making conversation.

By now, most of the town had given up on the idea that Denny killed his wife. If he had, well, he probably would have been caught. That was what the rumor mill had been spilling out, at least. Still, Denny preferred not to see their faces — a little pinched up, a little too tight — when he walked past. He stared at his feet, mostly, when he had to be around too many of them. It was easier than having to talk about the cloud that had settled over them since January, the grief and the chipping away at whatever or whoever had disrupted their lives.

"Why do we have to *wait*?" Ben wailed. He was on the verge of throwing a tantrum, and Denny could see, looking at the line, that another turn on the moon bounce was still quite a long way off.

He was about to console his son — to come up with some lie about how waiting builds character — when a woman holding a child's hand turned around and looked at him with a smile.

"It's hard, isn't it?" she said. "Waiting? We don't like it, either, right, Kate?" The woman lifted the little girl's hand and her head swung along with it. She had dark curly hair and pink cheeks and a navy shirt with a picture of the Hamilton-Wenham Generals on it and for a second his heart stopped, a panic reaction to grief, he realized. A mother and her daughter, standing in line for the moon bounce, the way Anna would have been if she were here. The woman looked nothing like his wife, the little girl looked nothing like Louisa, and yet the scene brought Denny back to a place that never existed, but could have in a parallel universe, if only The Terrible Thing had never happened.

She was Ellen Wilson, he quickly realized, snapping back from grief into reality, a woman Anna had known from the PTO. They had been friends, or friendly, or maybe not-quite-friendly at the end. He couldn't remember. Something had happened, but he could not identify what.

"Ellen, right?" Denny said. "I think you may have known my wife."

"Oh, yes," Ellen said. "Anna. We were all so sorry to hear about that."

Denny could feel that same feeling, rising up like bile, that he experienced when he saw Karen at Market Basket all those months earlier. "Funny," he said. "I don't remember getting a card."

Ellen looked taken aback. "I'm sure... I'm sure I sent one!"

"I'm sure you did. Practically the whole damn town, right? Everyone sent a card. But not a soul can figure out what happened," he said. He was really on a roll now, but then a figure he recognized came bounding up beside Ellen, slapping the meaty palm of his hand on her back and then reaching down to tousle the hair of the little girl.

"Ah, here you are," the familiar man said. "I was looking near the face painting."

It was Sticks, and Denny realized he had never seen the officer out of uniform. He wore a pair of blue jeans and a long-sleeve red and black checked flannel shirt, even though it was August. His hunter green raincoat was open. No gun. No badge. Not today. Sticks was off-duty, but he still held a telltale cup of that Dunkin' Donuts vanilla coffee he seemed to prefer. Denny could smell it.

"Officer Malkin," Denny said, using his most professional voice. He wanted to catch Sticks off guard, since Sticks was always trying the same with him.

Sticks turned around, surprise registering on his face. "I didn't see you there, Mr. Plummer. Welcome to the Block Party. First time?"

"Not nearly."

"Wish we had better weather. Couldn't be more different than last year's."

"Might as well be the theme of the year."

"Got that right," Sticks said. He looked out toward the moon bounce, drinking his coffee. Without looking back toward Denny, he said, "You know my sister Ellen, here? And this is my niece. Kate."

Ellen turned back around again, this time with a look of distinct discomfort. She put her hand on Sticks's shoulder. "We were actually just catching up before you got here. I was saying how sorry I was," she said. Then, in a stage whisper. "About *Anna*."

"Oh, I didn't... I didn't know," Denny said, looking between the two.

"From Rowley to Hamilton, yep. Big change in the Malkin family. I mean, more for Ellen than for me, right?" Sticks winked at his sister. "She married up, is what I mean."

Ellen looked to the ground. "As if there was anywhere to go but up when you come from Rowley," she said, eyes unchanged. Denny was remembering now. Anna had found her untrustworthy. She had trusted her — had liked her, even — and then, suddenly, she had regarded her the way one would a snake in the grass. Venomous. Dangerous.

"Were you friends? With Anna?" Denny asked. Sticks leaned back a little on his heels. Ellen was still holding Kate's hand, swinging an arm absently.

"We were friends. We were friendly. You know. You know Hamilton." Was it Denny's imagination or had she looked over at Sticks first? Was her look asking for his help?

The line had been moving, snaking gradually forward. Their turn in the moon house was coming up.

"Daddy, look," Ben said, pulling on his arm. The kids were taking off their shoes in preparation, and the trance was broken.

"Finally, our turn," Ellen said. She looked appreciative of the interruption. "Nice seeing you, Denny. You take care." She guided Kate inside the house and stepped off to the side, where a gaggle of moms he didn't know had formed to wait out their kids' exhaustion.

He felt Louisa's arms around his waist before he saw her. "Daddy, did you do the moon bounce?" she sang. He hadn't seen her in line.

"We did. Twice. Where are all your friends?"

"Most of them had to go home with their parents." She had taken her raincoat off and was swinging it around her, a fantastic yellow cape, even though it had started to rain again.

"Put your coat on," Denny urged. "It's cold and wet."

"I hate this thing," she said. "It's too small and it's hot."

"We'll have to get you a new one, but I can't do that right this second, and right this second it's raining."

She seemed momentarily poised for battle, the way her mother always had been, ready to fight about anything and everything, but then she saw that there was no point in this particular fight. He watched her slump her shoulders down in concession and put the jacket on. "I. Hate. This. Jacket," she said indignantly, and he watched from the corner of his eye, his other eye on Ben, who was looping in big circles on the lawn, getting his kindergarten energy out. If only his wife could see this now, this perfect family photo, all of them together, her image a tear in the fabric of space. Denny didn't know how long it took before a person started to feel better. All he knew was that each day he felt worse, like life was becoming further and further away from the version of the family that he had created, that he had built. It was as if he were consciously deconstructing a perfect piece of furniture that he had made. Something he loved. Something he now had to destroy.

It was getting dark now. The Block Party was an afternoon and evening event, and although the crowd was thinning, some had decided to stay until dark. "Let's go home and have dinner," he said to the kids. He looked up, one last time, surveyed the party, with its Hamilton denizens, friends and neighbors and almost-acquaintances, and there was Ellen, maybe a hundred feet away, holding a burger, her face blurred from the smoke of a food truck. Kate was by her side, the little girl hopping from foot to foot. She looked tired, and maybe a little cold. But what Denny noticed, as he watched the woman — the one who had maybe once been a long-ago friend of his wife's — was that she stood in a group, talking to another woman he knew. A woman he recognized. One Mimi Mar.

Chapter 17

THE THINGS THAT drew Anna to Hamilton were some of the things that she loathed about it. She loved, for instance, the ambling green hills, property of the wealthy equestrian families, who lived gated lives, not behind privet like in the Hamptons, but just as reclusive, just as out of reach. The houses were beautiful in every season: dappled with red-leafed sugar maples at the peak of October, iced like gingerbread houses in winter, and brought back to life in April and May with a yellow breath of forsythia, followed by plumes of lilac and pruned rhododendron. Now, Anna drove by to see the staggering of allium globes and catmint and white hydrangea, a heady aroma hanging in the air, wealth personified: horse shit and flowers.

That was beautiful, of course, horse shit notwithstanding, even if you could never take a walk on the allée because every allée belonged to someone else. She had chosen Hamilton because of its green spaces, anyway, and there was so much green, especially now. But sometimes she missed growing up in a town, even a small one, where you could congregate and walk into stores and run into people you knew at any old time of day. Hamilton had the coffee shop and a small main street — called Railroad Ave — with a dance school and a consignment shop and a pharmacy. A few intersecting streets offered other small-town necessities: orthodontics, yoga, Pilates, a tavern, a nail salon, and the library, of course. Still, sometimes she wanted more.

She wasn't unconvinced that she could find more here, in Hamilton, though. Anna had let her Life Time membership lapse, but she had opted instead, in early July, for a membership at the Veterans Memorial Pool, a public pool for community members in Hamilton and the neighboring town of Wenham. It was a modest alternative to Life Time, just over two hundred dollars for a family for the entire summer. When she broached the topic of switching allegiances to Di, her oldest friend laughed.

"I love you, babe, but not enough to sit in a pool full of pee for the rest of my summer," she said.

"It's for the greater good," Anna pleaded.

"I believe that you believe that. I really and truly do," Di said.

And so, Anna joined alone.

She knew there was no danger of running into Mimi or Ellen or Karen at the Veterans Pool, which opened later, and which closed at even the slightest threat of rain or lightning. It was a pool for the regular people of Hamilton, the *moms*, not the *mommies*, if such a distinction could be made. The truth was, Anna sat somewhere in between these two categories. She still got manicures at the same place where everyone else got their gels and dips done. She wore a nice pair of VS2 2.5-carat diamond studs daily, only changing them when she was going out to dinner. She had a Cartier love ring from the first Christmas that Denny's business had done well. She wasn't struggling, and no one would have reasonably accused her of having to scrounge around for her next dime, either. Upper middle class, but in Hamilton, that made you poor, practically, and even if you had a million-dollar house (check), it paled in comparison with the three-million-dollar equestrian estates.

Anna's separation from the women at the top of Hamilton's food chain was more academic. The purity test of the town — that the acceptance of its children was predicated on the performative nature of wealth — was what rubbed her the wrong way. Joining the Veterans Pool felt like solidarity, like a way to meet the exact kinds of people who had been cooled by Mimi's shadow for far too long. If Di didn't want to come along for the ride, so be it. There was, after all, more than one way to run a race. Anna had always preferred the repetitive routes. The trick of running was knowing what the course had in store for you. What made this race any different than the scores that she had tackled on the actual road?

Ben and Louisa did not seem to notice the difference between Life Time and Veterans. Slipping green goggles over his freckled face, Ben kissed Anna on the cheek and went careening toward the pool, instantly recognizing friends from kindergarten.

"Andy!" he cried with glee, stomping into the water. Another childhood goal unlocked: a pool full of local kids, doing what they did best, communing via water.

Louisa, too, found a niche. A group of second graders had staked their claim on a series of dilapidated lounges near the shallow end. They had created their own private coven, a circle of whispering girls, happy to be out in the sun, far enough from their meddling parents to dive into the juiciest matters of summer. Anna shaded her eyes and watched them compare their Taylor Swift friendship bracelets, the color of their goggles — Louisa's, a last-minute buy from Amazon, had a glittery band that commanded extra attention, a steal for eleven dollars — and their toenails, all painted in various shades of the rainbow. Within, Anna could feel the tension release. For once, she was in the company of people who would not set her on edge.

She chose a chair close enough to the kids where she could keep watch and they could feel her and far enough away where they could still enjoy a sense of privacy. Louisa was always asking for space these days, and Anna could respect that, the need to be alone, that pulsing desire to have something that belonged only to you. Next to her sat a woman wearing a white and brown flowered one-piece suit with a scoop neck. She was tanned, brown hair grayed at the temples, which Anna could see even from beneath her baseball cap (Red Sox, of course, but navy, not pink). Her nails were not painted, and Anna thought about how few women she knew who walked around without manicures. She could think of no one, in fact.

The woman had a book folded on one leg, *Counterfeit* by Kirstin Chen, one of those heist books for women that everyone seemed to be talking about.

"Is it good?" Anna asked. The book was oily around the edges, steeped in sunscreen.

The woman looked up. Maybe she had been napping. She had thick-lidded, sleepy brown eyes. "Not too complicated," she said. "But who wants to read something hard in good weather, right?" She pulled off her hat and shook her hair and Anna could see now that the woman was actually a little on the younger side, maybe early thirties. The gray had arrived early, that's all. Her skin was soft and peachy. Her hat had left a crease in her forehead, but she was pretty, sweeping her hair up like that, the kind of pretty person who doesn't stop to take stock of her looks.

"I'll take an easy summer book on an easy summer day any day of the week," Anna agreed.

"With this drought, there's plenty of them," the woman agreed. Massachusetts hadn't seen a good rain since early May. The equestrian lawns in Hamilton were still mysteriously green, despite enforced water restrictions, but Anna's own lawn had turned a dry and brittle brown, poky little spikes of dead grass replacing what was once a supple field.

"I'm Anna," she said, introducing herself. She was wearing a cover-up that Denny had bought her once he had started making money, a long caftan, white with brown stripes and tassels on the bottom. It was faded now, with subtle tears along the seams. She had worn it relentlessly, watched it turn from stylish to tattered. Here at Veterans, it didn't matter. She wasn't on display. No one was wearing couture, she realized. It felt a lot freer to be in the company of no one in particular. "Hamilton," she added, because that was a thing you said: "Hamilton" or "Wenham," to specify which side of the line you landed on.

"Mary," the woman said, turning to look at Anna, not appraisingly. Neutral. "Mary Langley. Also Hamilton. My kids are over there. I have a six-year-old son and an 11-year-old daughter. Michael and Charlotte."

"We're new here," Anna said. "Not to Hamilton. To the pool, I mean."

"It's an acceptable place to pass the time when it's hot," Mary said. She flipped the book up, dog-eared the page, and fanned her face. "And it's hot."

"Actually, we were Life Time members," Anna said. "Defectors, I should say."

"It's a bit spendy over there," Mary said, sourly, though not unkindly.

Well, she wasn't wrong, at any rate. Money. Always off the table in these towns, no matter which way you came at it, so Anna changed the subject. "Your son," Anna said. "He's at Winthrop or Cutler?"

"Cutler," the woman said, looking out over at the pool, scanning for her kids. It was the lesser of the two schools, but still governed by the same PTO. South Hamilton, the less affluent side of town, fed into Cutler, the school with diminished resources. Mary didn't seem to have any feelings about it. Not like the way that the Hamilton mommies at Winthrop talked about Cutler, anyway, like the name was a disease.

"We're over at Winthrop. I guess our kids don't know each other. Well, not yet anyway," Anna said. "Mine are Ben and Louisa. Five and seven. Green goggles, all the way over there, and the pink sparkly ones, immersed in the coven."

"Ha. That's what I call them, too. Probably a North Shore thing."

"This is going to sound odd, since we only just met," Anna said. "I'm actually trying something new." Mary was a complete stranger, Anna realized: this pretty young mom from South Hamilton. But this was campaigning. This was how you got to know people, to win them over. She was going to have to get used to broaching the topic, over and over again, if she was going to make any headway between now and the start of the year.

"I'm planning to run for president of the PTO, and I'm doing some initial outreach to see how the community reception is."

Now Mary seemed interested. She dropped her ersatz fan back into her lap. "President? Isn't that Mimi Mar's, like, permanent gig or something?" she asked. She was careful. She didn't seem like she had a horse in the race. She just seemed to understand the long game.

"Well, that's sort of the point." Anna looked out at the water. Kids were everywhere, clearly violating the rules of etiquette when it came to the pool, jumping over lane lines, playing chicken, dunking one another. The lifeguards didn't seem to care. This would never pass muster at Life Time. Also, she didn't really care. There was a spirit of conviviality here at Veterans that was absent at the tonier pool: Di with her rosé, the Hamilton witches in their black robes, prancing around, half dressed for the crowd to watch and admire.

"It's not a permanent gig at all. It's up for whoever gets it. I'm not trying to *take it away* from anyone. I just have some ideas, and I want to discuss them and see if other people are interested in what I have to say," Anna said.

"Well, I'm always interested in new blood," Mary said. "Or, barring that, a good old fight. Who in Hamilton doesn't like to see a little blood drawn now and then?" She laughed, a loud, broad laugh that made Anna think they could be friends, despite the fact that the woman was obviously younger, despite the fact that they didn't know each other, despite the fact that they probably didn't hang in the same circles at all.

"Cheers to that," Anna said. She had nothing to toast except an insulated water bottle, which she retrieved from her beach bag.

Mary matched her with a peeling S'well bottle of her own. "To summer," she declared. "To winning over the snooty snoots of Hamilton, if that's what it takes!" Then she stopped and covered her mouth. "I'm so sorry, I shouldn't have said that. For all I know, you're a snooty snoot! I shouldn't have said that, either." She laughed again, another broad, likable laugh, and Anna knew that she had found a friend in a storm, a comrade in arms, at least one other member in her very small army, ready to fight for the presidency.

"Anna Plummer for president!" she said.

"Why not?" Mary said. "Started from the bottom, now we here." Unexpectedly, she untwisted the cap of her bottle and poured its contents over her head and, shaking like a little wet lap dog, smiled in the hot sun, laughing as she did it. She would make a fine new companion, Anna knew. They were a good team already.

Chapter 18

THE AGAWAM HAD put him in a bad place, set his mind in motion. Unanswered questions. Antagonistic people. But now Denny was faced with further questions. Who was Sticks, really? And where did his loyalties lie?

When Anna was sad or confused or out of sorts, she had disappeared — he knew this, though she thought he didn't — to the museums. The Isabella Stewart Gardner Museum did not have any Gerhard Richter, her favorite. But he knew she liked to drive into the city to see the Sargents, or to walk through the Gothic Room, or to spend time in the courtyard, especially in December and January, when the indoor garden was transformed into a holiday forest, populated by flowering jade, green aloe, and amaryllis. She was, he felt, communing with old friends.

This time, he would be the one doing the communing, though in summer, not winter. Corina offered to take the kids to see a movie in the big reclining seats at the AMC Theatre at the mall, and Denny inched through traffic on Storrow Drive, a slog even though it was neither a weekday nor rush hour. Soon, he realized there was an issue with his brakes. When he depressed the pedal the car continued to slide forward. This had happened once before in a 1979 International Scout he had owned in the Hamptons. But that car had been a stick shift, and he had been able to downshift into first to get the car to disengage. Brake lights appeared on the cars in front of him, and Denny tried again, pressing the pedal all the way down. The car was moving slowly — maybe five miles an hour — but it wasn't slowing down. Rolling ever so slowly, with the brake all the way to the floor, his Volkswagen — Anna's Volkswagen, actually — made slow-motion contact with the Nissan Rogue in front of him.

The car made a crunch. The Nissan began to honk furiously. More brake lights, this time from all of the surrounding cars, too. An angry driver popped out of the car.

"This car is brand new!" the driver shouted at him. He looked like he was in his mid-thirties and wore a button-down linen shirt that was open to mid-chest. "You have *got* to be kidding!"

"Let me take a look," Denny said, getting out and surveying the damage. He had experience with cars. Both vehicles would be fine; the traffic had saved them. The truest definition of a fender-bender.

"I'm not letting you look!" the man said, suddenly shouting. "Let me see your phone! Who were you texting?"

"Calm down, man, let's just . . ."

"Oh no, no way. I'm calling the police. We can wait here and file a police report. I'm not going anywhere."

"Okay," Denny said. Despite a slightly cracked front bumper on his end, which insurance would no doubt cover, both cars appeared operational. Well, there was, he now realized, the issue of the brakes, a true problem.

It was terrible luck. A year earlier, Anna had been in a hit-and-run and the car had been out of commission for nearly a month while it was under an insurance repair contract in Beverly. When Denny had gone to retrieve it, the Volkswagen had been fine — fully repaired, the mechanic assured him — but it had made a strange ticking noise that Denny had attributed to one of the rotors. Now Denny wondered if the brakes or the rotors were to blame, scarring from an old accident, another ghost from his wife's past come back to haunt him.

By the time the police arrived, traffic was backed up for at least a half mile. A tow truck came and towed Denny's car to a repair shop in Malden, which was closer and cheaper than taking it all the way to Hamilton. He'd take an Uber home and deal with the rest of it tomorrow. The Nissan driver left in a hurry once the details were exchanged, but not without offering Denny one last piece of his mind. "Expect to hear from me," he said.

"Some people don't know how to drive," Denny said, under his breath, but he never did hear from the driver again after that.

It wasn't until Denny arrived back at home — not until he had stopped to pick up a pizza, and not until he had spent forty-five minutes listening to Ben and Louisa debate a fight one of them had witnessed in school regarding Magna-Tiles — that he stopped to think more fully about the car. It couldn't have been the rotors, Denny realized, and it couldn't have been the brakes, either. Just a few weeks earlier he had taken the Volkswagen over to Burnett's Garage, in Wenham, for its annual inspection. There were no emissions issues. The car had four great tires. And, to hear the guys tell it, there were no issues with the brakes. The mechanic in a one-piece denim blue jumpsuit and a red baseball cap had slapped the car on the side like it was a thoroughbred. In fact, that pesky ticking had even gone away of late. He hadn't noticed it in months.

"She's ready to go," the mechanic told Denny. So Denny paid the thirty-five dollars for the inspection, got the new Massachusetts sticker, with the little hole punched in the corner that said *August,* another end-of-summer task accomplished. One more thing he wouldn't have to worry about until next August. He had driven back — he remembered this clearly — in the gray, pulsing rain, a day so hot and thick that nature had released itself in the only way it knew how.

Had the inspection missed some crucial detail? Denny knew a thing or two about cars, and brake pads squeaked when they needed to be replaced. He had heard no such noise when he pushed all the way to the floorboards. Just an excruciating silence. No brakes. No resistance.

What, then? Could someone have, what, tampered with the brakes? Or, more likely, caused the brake fluid to leak slowly so that he was more prone to find himself in a situation where the brakes suddenly stopped working? Unlikely. But possible. Kids? Neighbors? Denny was no longer so confident.

Once the kids were settled, Denny busied himself with a martini. Then he headed to the garage, into the bay where the Volkswagen usually lived. The flickering overhead light could not mask the pool of yellow-tinted fluid on the ground.

Brake fluid.

Was it a leak? That was possible, Denny thought. It was possible that the two-year-old Volkswagen Atlas was leaking brake fluid, and that it had lost so much of it that the brakes had simply given out on Storrow Drive, causing him to collide with the car in front of him.

Or maybe — and this was something darker — someone had *caused* the brake fluid to leak.

It was, if he was honest, a possibility he didn't want to entertain, the possibility of his own mortality, and the suspicion that the brakes were another instance of the threatening forces surrounding him, and, of course, Anna. To entertain that possibility was to confront the reality that he was fighting a war that might never be won. That he was battling an enemy. And that he was losing.

Do you have a sec? he texted Di. He had come to rely upon her too heavily, he knew, but she could — and would — tell him if he was being unreasonable. Anyway, he was starting to wonder whom he could and could not trust. His phone rang almost immediately.

"Everything okay?" Her voice sounded a little unsteady, borne, he knew, from concern.

Denny looked at the spot on the floor of the garage again.

"Paranoia getting the best of me, I think," he said. "Had a little fender-bender today on Storrow. My brakes went out. And I'm starting to wonder if maybe someone did something to my car. I know it sounds nuts," Denny said. He considered Sticks's warning at the Agawam and the encounter at the Block Party. Right now what he needed was the comfort of a friend.

"That sounds very scary," Di said.

"Yeah," Denny said. "I guess it was."

"I don't mean for this to come out the wrong way," she said. "But do you think maybe there's another explanation?"

"Under ordinary circumstances? It sure does sound insane," Denny admitted. "But I've gotten used to insane. Also, the car was just inspected."

"I guess I just feel . . ." She coughed lightly, interrupting herself. "I just feel that maybe it's best not to jump to conclusions."

"You mean that maybe assuming that someone breaking into my house and draining the brake fluid from my car is a wild and unlikely thing to happen, and that there is probably a much more logical explanation for what happened today," Denny said.

"Bingo," Di said.

"Thanks," Denny said. "I really did need to be brought back down to earth."

Louisa called from upstairs, even though she was supposed to be asleep. He took one last look at the stain. If you looked at it for long enough, he told himself, you could be convinced that it was just old oil, or water, or something that had been there a long time, the kind of stain that had been on that floor long before a Volkswagen Atlas had ever parked in its spot.

"I'll be right there," he called in response. "I'll be up in a minute." Then, to Di: "I gotta go. Louisa's calling for me. Thanks for talking me off the cliff."

Turning the lights off, he closed the door.

There was no use in trying to solve a mystery like that, he told himself.

Chapter 19

"I CAN HOST it at my house," Mary was saying over the phone. In the few short weeks of their friendship, Anna had become a *telephone* person again, making actual phone calls, chatting, actually listening to another person's voice on the other end, the way she once had in the '80s and '90s. This was a surprising quality of her new friend, the desire to talk on the phone. Most people her age didn't even like the phone anymore, and she almost never met people younger than she was who called rather than texted, but Mary wasn't like most people. She was — and Mary would say this about herself — an old soul trapped in a young body.

"That's why we're so evenly matched," Mary said, right from the start.

Which was true. They did feel evenly matched. Anna felt bad that she preferred Mary sometimes even to Di, but Di was busy anyway, with Life Time and the Hamilton gossip, and so she and Mary made plans to meet at Veterans or to take their kids for an early al fresco dinner of wood-fired pizza at Appleton Farms or to take them to Crane's early in the day before it got too hot and then to Russell Orchards after for cider pops. The party had been Mary's idea.

"You are never going to become president of the PTO without some ridiculous meet-and-greet. You know this, right?" They had driven over to Richardson's, in Middleton, and the kids were stalking the parking lot for yellow jackets, slapping them with flip-flops the way Denny had once taught her to do.

"This is exactly what I do not want to do," Anna said. "An afternoon communing with the women of Hamilton is my precise and sweat-soaked nightmare."

"Well, how else do you intend to get them to vote for you? The people you need to win over — I hate to say this — are the ones on the *inside*. It's all well and good that I like you, and I can tell all of my friends to have your back, but the voting majority are the people *on the PTO*."

Of course Anna knew this, but she had been putting off the abject reality of it, because she knew that the hardest part of becoming part of the PTO would be getting the existing PTO to like her enough to make her one of them. It was also the existentially challenging part, the part that required stepping into a different pair of shoes. Anna Plummer was, after all, the kind of person who wasn't good at pretending, and she was particularly bad at disguising her own sense of distaste, and she had a sour spot — that kind of turned-up-mouth feeling — for the women who disregarded the parts of Hamilton that needed work. The parts of her that needed work, if she really thought about it.

"This part is the impossible part," she confessed to her new friend.

"We literally had entire human beings come out of our bodies. I wish people would stop saying that anything was impossible," Mary said. She lifted a chocolate ice cream cone to her face and sank into it, covering her entire nose. It looked ridiculous. And fun.

"I hate that what you say makes so much sense to me," Anna said. She drew the line at sticking her face in ice cream.

Mary had plenty of other ideas, of course. It should be, she felt, an afternoon party. Garden-themed. Upscale, but not too upscale. Anna had to distinguish herself as a woman of the people who still had impeccable taste. She needed to come with ideas, but those ideas should be tempered. *She* should be tempered.

"Let them get to know you first, *then* hit them with your platitudes about how the world is unjust," Mary said. "Or at least let them get a little drunk before you start talking about that god-awful Ziti Dance."

It made sense. Anna needed this kind of consultation, a second set of eyes to help her see the nuance that she couldn't. Much as she loved Denny, he was too kind for any of this, too forgiving. He would have told her to show up, act the part of Hamilton doyenne, and never mention a word about any of the underpinnings of the PTO. But it went against everything she believed in, to just let the core rot under her eye. There was a way to get at it, and she hadn't seen it before, and now she did, and to reclaim the town was to find a way in and to change the atmosphere and the culture, to force out its terribleness by forcing in goodness. And although she remained unconvinced by her friend's ebullience — that anything could be solved as sunnily and easily as just sticking one's face into a scoop of round, smooth ice cream — she had come to believe, in just a few short weeks, that maybe her hard-and-fast outlook on the world was a little too rigid.

Mary's house, they both agreed, was more neutral. Mary, after all, had grown up in South Hamilton, knew more people, and could draw a bigger crowd, even though her house was smaller and much farther away from, say, Nancy's Corner.

"We aren't multimillionaires, okay?" Mary said. Her house was lovely enough, with a well-tended garden that reminded Anna of her mother's. A charming sunroom, laden with antiques, was the kind of room that Anna could imagine spending a family Christmas in as the snow fell in the backyard. She coveted the blue Murano glass paperweight, the rolltop desk with its inkwell and stained-tip pens, and even the old wingback chair, the leather of which had split in the center.

In the backyard, a lattice archway was thick with tea rose vines, now crossing into their third bloom of the season, tiny white flowers, honeybees buzzing around them. The last week of August, they agreed, would be perfect, right before the school year started, in the late afternoon, after the heat of the day had died down. They could serve cucumber sandwiches and iced tea and lemonade, put the girls in pretty floral dresses and set out tiny crystal bud vases with roses and pansies and other cuttings from the garden and string Edison bulbs along the white picket fence for when the sun sank a little low in the sky and maybe the Hamilton mommies would find themselves temporarily enchanted by a garden full of gnomes and flowers and pixie elementary schoolers, with their pigtails and wide-eyed dreams, and maybe they could all agree that all kids should have that same ability: to dream about a world where they could do anything anywhere, boundless, up to the sky, out to the fuzzy edges of the earth, limited by no person, by no president of the PTO, appointed either by God or by man.

Even though Anna wanted a low-key event, once she got wind of the party, Di insisted on calling her *very favorite* planner over at Special Events of New England for help with high-tops, linens, and glassware. Anna drew the line at a tent, which was not to say that Di hadn't tried.

"They do have these beautiful sail tents, rescued from old ships that are no longer in use," Di pleaded.

"There's not room, and this isn't a wedding," she told Di.

"Everyone wants a tent when it's hot," Di told her. "Half the

PTO's going to be marching around fanning their precious, sweaty faces. Just watch. And anyway, isn't it pretty to stand under a tent in the afternoon?"

"They can drink lemonade, just like everyone else."

And they left it at that.

Anna had to admit, though, that her two friends did make a fiery and commendable team. Mary's house was modest, but in August its garden was bountiful, pulsing with black-eyed Susan, purple ironweed, panicled hydrangea, bee balm, Russian sage, and phlox. It had been weeded and tended to, but it lacked the particular manicured look of the estates along the winding roads of Hamilton. You could get lost in these flowers, and that was exactly the mood that Anna wanted to set.

With Di's help, too, high-top tables had arrived, cloaked in a tidy gingham print, a pale light blue to match the coneflowers and globe thistles.

"Alice's Tea Party, but for adults," Anna said, standing back to admire the work, her friends by her side. It was the hottest part of the day, but she could feel the sun fading. Soon the women would arrive, and Denny would be there to drop off Louisa, for whom she had selected an eyelet sundress and leather sandals.

"Calling some of these women adults may be taking things a little far," Di quipped. She hooked her arm into Anna's and, on the other side, Mary did the same, and the unlikely trio stood looking at the tables, now topped with their little bud vases and mason jars filled with rental silverware. Looking around the garden, Anna felt a surge of optimism, that she could do this, that this party was going to create the kind of forward momentum that she needed.

"Okay," she said, inhaling the August air, the flowers, the heat, the slow smoke coming from some neighbor's grill. "Into the lion's den we go, though this time I suppose the den is ours."

* * *

The women of Hamilton always arrived fashionably late. Mary's friends came first, their joyous kids crashing into the lawn with glee.

"Away from the tables!" Mary shouted, as little girls rolled and bounced underfoot, threatening to tip over the very bud vases they had spent so many hours artfully arranging. Eventually, a group of girls found their way to a small hollow in the back of the yard, where a tree that bent down toward the earth created a natural nook, perfect for shade and for secrets.

Anna stood near the front gate holding a glass of tea and wearing a long, sweeping skirt, hoping to make small talk with the new arrivals. Mary had been generous in introducing her friends, but she had gone off to tend to the rest of the party, so Anna now stood on her own, watching women she didn't really know show up, some of them spectacularly coiffed: beaded sundresses, gladiator sandals that wove halfway up the calf, layers of chunky jewelry that made it look like they had casually run out of the house in a dash (Anna knew the truth). The women who knew one another leaned in for reciprocal air-kisses and offered quick updates on their summer lives. Anna, from her post of relative invisibility, could hear it all, the trips to Amalfi, the swim lessons from the handsome new guard at Life Time, the restaurant that had just opened in Rockport (*divine,* one woman declared).

One by one, they filtered toward her, tilting sunglasses down, offering their hands for a shake, nodding as she explained who she was, considering the air, taking her temperature, surveying the garden, clicking a little — was that actual approval Anna sensed? — and then thanking her and saying they'd be back.

A few lingered to ask questions. Why was she running? some wanted to know. What did she plan to do differently? She and Mary had rehearsed this beforehand, an answer that was both canned and produced to sound as if it were spontaneous. *It's not that there's anything wrong with the current path or leadership! I just think it's always nice to change things up and give someone else a chance at improving our community. I believe that we can and should include more of Hamilton's best and brightest in all of our events, and that's what I'm here to do in my bid for president.*

It was vague, it was optimistic, and it left Mimi Mar out of the conversation, three things that no one could reasonably argue with. Each time she repeated it, Anna felt emboldened, and she could see, on the faces of the women on the receiving end of her mini polemic, that it was working. The idea — that a little bit of fresh blood could improve the community — wasn't necessarily a revolutionary one. Here and there, Anna added in fragments of political commentary. One woman, wearing a long linen sundress, wanted to hear more about events hosted by the PTO, which gave Anna the perfect segue.

"What I *don't* want is for this to be an uneven playing field, the way it is now, with parents having to fight over who gets to take their kid to a pasta dance. I don't want you to have to pay more to have the same access to these services. Everyone should get the same things out of these schools," she said.

The woman in linen considered. Was it all that bad right now, her face seemed to say. "Will it just... make it more difficult for some of us, though?"

"I don't want it to be difficult for *anyone,*" Anna emphasized. "There's space for everyone in this town, isn't there?"

Linen Lady seemed satisfied with the answer, or with the lemonade, at least. She lifted her glass. "Well, cheers to that," she said, chirping like a bird.

The conversation gave Anna ballast, just an added scoop of confidence. When the next woman came around — black slip dress, awfully dressy for the occasion — Anna felt sufficiently armed. She launched into her messaging, talked about how much she wanted equality for the kids, about how unfair it had been, about how maybe *some people* didn't really want things to be all that different in the end. Even if Mimi wasn't standing behind her—and she wasn't—Anna could just about feel her, eyes like lasers, a confounding vision for the PTO that did not comport with her own ideas about what was and what was not equitable or decent.

"It has been the same for a while," Black Slip Dress said, in a way that made Anna think that *the same* was a synonym for *just fine*.

"I don't know any other PTO that keeps the same president around for over a decade, the way Hamilton did with Laura Cox," Anna said.

The woman stepped back, a little surprised. "It's true, she did have an unusually long run," she said.

"Every president here has had an unusually long run," Anna said.

Mary came over just then, carrying drinks. "How is everyone enjoying the party?" she asked, the consummate host. "Has Anna talked to you about her ideas for extending the PTO's scholarship program next year?"

"I was actually just talking about tenure," Anna said, leaning back on her heels. The sun was still full and ripe. Her clothing stuck to her, but she felt strong. Magical, even. The party felt rich with possibility.

"The past is the past," Mary said. "We're here to talk about the future. Isn't that right, ladies?" Was it Anna's imagination, or had there been a flash of something as she said it? Anger? Indignation? But that wasn't right. Anna's imagination was running away again, and she relaxed a bit when Mary raised a glass and smiled into the late-afternoon sun. "To Anna," she said.

"To Anna," Black Slip Dress said.

Di had set up little stations with information cards, printed by VistaPrint, Anna's face smiling back along with a handful of bullet points and some handy sloganeering about why she would be a good fit for the post. Anna watched as a few of the women picked the cards up, looked them over, and, astonishingly, even tucked them into handbags. She thought of her face, sitting on a kitchen countertop, looking up at some Hamilton family a few days from now. She couldn't be sure, but she could feel something at work that was larger than her.

Across the street, a dog barked. A car door slammed. "Did my invitation get lost in the mail?" a voice said, a bit more loudly than other voices at this garden party. And then two faces were before her, Mimi and Karen, their children not with them — probably for the best, Anna thought to herself — both dressed in long, sleeveless sundresses, purple organza for Mimi and a cream-colored linen for Karen.

"It's nice to see you both," Anna said. "It was an open-invitation event. I'm so glad you could make it."

"I wouldn't miss it for the world," Mimi said. The corner of her mouth turned up on the left a little, like she could taste something she didn't like. Her hair was piled atop her head in a mismanaged way, almost as if she had left the house in a hurry. Anna had never seen her quite so uncomposed.

"There's a table with drinks and tea sandwiches in the back," Anna said. "I'm also happy to share with you my campaign information, if you'd like to see that." She smiled big and bright at her adversary, allowing the full measure of the late-afternoon sunlight to hit her eyes. Now would be the ideal time to march right back into that rehearsed speech about improving the *community*.

"A sandwich does sound good right now because I'm famished. How about you, Karen?" Mimi tugged on Karen's elbow, directing the woman to the table in the back. "You ought to save the campaigning energy for the women here. It's not me you have to win over, after all." She looked back, appraised Anna up and down and, seemingly satisfied, headed off toward the food.

Mary slid over on Mimi's heels. "I would have loved to have seen that," she said.

"You didn't miss much, but I think she may have found out a little late," Anna said.

"Did you expect her to come?"

Anna thought about it. Nothing about Mimi ever surprised her, and, if she thought about it, this was no exception. Of course Mimi was going to show up to assert her authority. That was a traditionally Mimi move: to try to bully her way into the situation, to manipulate Anna's party to suit her own needs.

"I guess, if I'm honest, deep down, yes," Anna confessed.

"Well then, the good news is that the worst part is over," Mary said. Mimi had moved on from the sandwich table to the high-tops, a hummingbird trilling from table to table, visiting with other members of the PTO, no doubt spreading whatever information she had about Anna and the event. Anna turned and watched this other version of the campaign, a muckraking born of self-preservation.

"I'm not so sure it is. Over, I mean."

On a clipboard at the front, they had collected the names and email addresses of everyone who had shown up. Sixty-two women in total, not including children or the errant woman who had forgotten to sign. A good turnout by any standards, but particularly on a muggy August afternoon in South Hamilton. A few women stood lingering in the dusk, swatting mosquitoes and fanning themselves with Anna's marketing materials. Their ice-cold drinks had sweat down into the gingham tablecloths, leaving tiny wet tattoos on each small table.

Finally, they filtered out, the women in the gladiator sandals with their knotted little buns and their chunky jewelry and their rattan handbags. Last to swing past the gate was Mimi. She waited as a few of the others said goodbye and thanked Anna and then stood in the low light next to the host.

"I hope you had a nice time," Anna said, not insincerely.

"The cucumber sandwiches were very good," Mimi said. Karen was across the street already, unlocking the car. Anna watched as she fumbled with a key fob.

"Perhaps next time we should stage a debate," Anna said. She raised her own lemonade, first of the day, to the sky, in a mock toast.

Mimi whipped around and grabbed Anna by the wrist. Her grip was strong, fierce, and immediate.

"I am not fucking around, Anna," she said. "I don't want a debate. I don't want a campaign. I don't want any stupid garden parties in South Fucking Hamilton. Don't waste my time and I will not waste yours. Am I making myself clear here?"

"Are you saying you do not want me to run for this position, Mimi?" Anna asked. She was laughing now. What was it about this lemonade — about this night — that made this so riotously funny, anyway?

"I am saying that you do not want to go down this road with me. But if you do, I can promise that it will not end in a way that you will expect." With a quick chop, she brought her hand down on Anna's wrist. The pain was sharp. Anna dropped the lemonade; it splashed up her leg and onto her skirt, and she cradled her wrist in her hand. *She is completely out of control,* Anna thought to herself, and not for the first time. *This is not normal. None of this is normal.* By the time she noticed the climbing stain — a thick, coarse rope of a stain, tightening as it dried — Mimi had already charged off into the growing darkness.

Part III
Winter

Chapter 20

SOMETIMES, ANNA FELT like she and Denny were two big orbs overlapping in the same world. She loved her husband. She could not imagine a world without her husband. But then: She knew the women who would peel themselves back like an onion, tell their spouses every single thing. Denny went off to his work shed in the morning, hat on, insulated mug full of coffee. After she got the kids on the bus, she, too, retreated. Hague Blue office. Fall had come and gone so quickly she had barely had a minute to think about the rustling maple leaves; pretty soon they were dead and scattered beyond the wood. It wasn't so much that she hadn't told Denny about the PTO as much as she assumed he didn't want to know. How could he have walked past her office without hearing the commotion? Without seeing the little placards with her name on them?

ANNA PLUMMER FOR PRESIDENT. He'd have to be half blind.

So she didn't say anything, just told him she was going out with Di, meeting friends at Honeycomb, trying to make friends, whatever she needed to say to make him happier in their cloud of suspended belief.

She wasn't living a secret life, exactly. Or: She preferred not to think of it that way. It was true: Denny had never met Mary or some of the other women from South Hamilton. He didn't know about some of the meetings, the ones where she wore long dresses and knotted her hair up into a banana clip, twisted a rope of pearls close into the nape of her neck and looked convincingly like the Stepford wives version of the Hamilton Mommies that she had always made fun of. Would Denny have cared? Probably not. He might have taken the opportunity to rib her slightly, and he would have been justified, given all the times she had sworn up and down that she would never turn into the women she hated. And she would have bitten right back, anyway. Wasn't the best way to get to the heart and soul of an institution through infiltration, anyway?

In order to actually win the presidency, Anna had to get the votes of the majority of the Hamilton PTO by a secret ballot, and although there was no definitive way to determine who was or was not siding with her, in a small town there were always signs. Since the August garden party, she, Mary, and Di had made it a point to stop by Honeycomb once a week, on Wednesdays, taking the table right by the window — prime seating, everyone knew that — and staying from 10 a.m. well into lunchtime. They waved at the moms who came in, started small talk, complained about the weather, asked about which teachers were assigning too much homework. Was the soccer schedule unusually erratic this year? Oh, definitely. (Anna had signed Ben up, for good measure.) Had anyone noticed that the Hamilton-Wenham Trunk or Treat at Pumpkin Fest had a particularly poor showing when it came to nut-free candy? (On our list to address for next year, of course, Anna wanted everyone to know; she herself suffered from a nut allergy.) The risers in the gym needed replacing; they seemed like an accident waiting to happen. Could the PTO start a fundraiser in 2023? And then there was the annual PTO Spring Silent Auction. If you asked about the hot gossip in the wet, cold months before the daffodils and forsythia pushed, you were sure to get whispered talk of the auction. Which rich families were putting their Nantucket houses up for bidding this year? Who was outbidding whom for the coveted *named* parking spots at Winthrop? Anna had heard these rumors, of course, about the auction and the legacy families who bid, about how you could spend up to $100,000 for — and this was true — a parking space with a little placard that said your family's name on it. But no one had ever confirmed it, not to her. Now the women were coming to her in droves, whispering their equal discontent.

It was surprisingly easy to catalogue the grievances of the local women, who arrived breezily each Wednesday for the unscheduled-scheduled chats. Hamilton was unequal, they realized, and they, too, disapproved of it, but before now they had no one with whom to conspire. Mimi had never lent much of an empathetic ear, had only ever governed by force, but Anna was there to hear the gripes, however mundane. Finally, in Anna, they saw an ally.

By the first week of January, Anna had built up a substantial amount of goodwill with the Hamilton moms. There was a routine by now; in the mornings, she waited in her long parka by the bus, kissed the kids goodbye, and came back in and watched the morning pass in front of her desk while she sent emails and attempted to draft copy for clients while her mind wandered. A few minutes before ten, she drove over to Honeycomb, where Di was always waiting, always in head-to-toe Prada, her preferred brand, the kind of thing that women with means loved to say (every once in a while, you could catch Mary in a hand-me-down, and Anna herself only knew this from Di's *last season* whisperings). Di had never been late for a thing in her life. Matcha latte for Di, hot chocolate for Mary, *pain au chocolat* and a regular coffee for Anna. A notebook out, going over anything they had learned from the meeting the week before. And then, gradually, it was office hours.

"Good to see you, Anna," said a woman wearing a pom-pom-topped hat and a puffy down parka. Her hair was short and nearly scarlet, just a crescent of it peeking out from under the hat. Anna couldn't quite remember her name – maybe Casey or Carly – but she remembered that her son was a year older than Ben, who was now in first grade.

"And you!" Anna said.

"I wanted to run an idea by you. For the PTO," she said. One thing that had amazed Anna was how many people were treating her as if she was already president of the PTO, even though the elections had not yet taken place. It was as if they had merely wanted permission to put another person in office, but they had been too afraid to ask for what they needed.

"I'm all ears," Anna said. Di handed over the notebook.

"I was thinking that maybe we need to organize a book drive," Carly or Casey said. "I'd love to help get readership up in the community."

She added *book drive* to the increasingly long list of actionable items that had been requested from the moms of Hamilton.

The ideas were not bad. Many of them were thoughtful. Some parents were concerned about students who could not afford extracurricular activities. They wanted to host a fundraiser to help fund a PTO "scholarship," which could be awarded to students who might not have the same advantages. Anna liked the idea, but she wondered how she would be able to make something like that work without embarrassing students and their parents. No one wanted a handout, particularly in Hamilton, where the common denominators were money and status.

Anna's own vision for the PTO was complex. She envisioned a space where everyone had a stake in the future of the town and the public school system. She wanted to put the kids' needs first – and she really wanted to dismantle the privilege that seemed to govern the current way of doing things. Mimi Mar's PTO focused on high-octane events. Parents were often asked to donate their summer homes for "charity biddings," and the donated monies were then held by the PTO for future events, to entertain wealthy community members. And so on and so forth. It had always seemed to Anna like a giant circle jerk: the wealthy families of Hamilton putting up their assets as golden trophies, just so that other wealthy families could step in to put money in the coffer. But none of the money was going anywhere. It wasn't making it to the kids, at any rate.

Anna wanted to change that. In a wealthy community, there was no reason that the people at the top couldn't give more to the people at the bottom — and there were plenty of those, Anna knew. They could buy new risers for the gym, sure, and, yes, even support a yearly Ziti Dance, but why not also start a fund to support school supplies, sports, and after-school programming for students who needed extra assistance? Why not establish a confidential scholarship program in which students and their parents could ask for assistance for items not covered by the district — without having to disclose their level of need? Anna could see, quite plainly, the level of disparity between the people with wealth and the people without in Hamilton, and she felt that the PTO could act as an intermediary instead of an antagonist. The question she kept asking herself was: *Why can't we help fix this?*

Her friends, of course, were more focused on the immediate outcome, which was winning the race. "I think we're having what you might call a breakthrough," Mary said. She wasn't wrong. The Wednesday meetings had become unofficial town halls, PTO compilation sessions, opportunities for everyone to stake their claim, should there be a regime change. "It's like everyone has been waiting around with all of these ideas for years and now they're just rushing out."

"I think that means they feel like they haven't been heard, to be honest," Anna said. They had already filled two notebooks in three months of meeting here at Honeycomb. Two notebooks with ideas both large and small, suggested by all different kinds of parents, some of them friends with Mimi and others not. It would be impossible, of course, to include every single idea in any kind of new version of the PTO. Reframing would take time. What were the most important changes she wanted to make? What were the things that needed to happen to make the PTO better, to make Hamilton better?

"You'd want to start with the dance, anyway, right?" Di said. Allow everyone in, was what she meant, but, no, that wouldn't be Anna's first change, not that. She would get rid of the preferred membership, eliminate the ability for any parent to spend more to cut the line, prioritize the actual kids, which had been the point in the crusade to begin with.

"It's the memberships that irk me," she said. "That people can just skip ahead if they pay more. How many people have complained about the memberships?"

"A lot, actually," Mary said. "I don't have the information here, but I have a spreadsheet at home. I can share it with you. I've been going back through the notes and keeping them organized and tracking which issues are most popular."

"Which I guess leads me to another question," Anna said. "Do we think we have any idea what the vote looks like? We're just over three weeks away, and I think we've done good outreach. We have more to do still. But it's not like a normal election. We're not polling people."

Di and Mary exchanged looks. Mary started to laugh.

"I guess I'm missing something fundamental here," Anna said.

"Maybe we've been asking around," Di said. "On your behalf."

"That feels extremely against the rules, but fine. What have you come up with?"

Mary took out a separate notebook, a small black leather one. Anna had never seen it before. She flipped past the first few pages. "To be honest, we've been keeping a tally," she said.

"Like, you've been asking people who they support?" Anna said.

"Pretty much exactly that. Don't act so surprised." Di grabbed the book from Mary and flipped through, pretending to look shocked at some of the information. "You wouldn't believe it," she said. "Simply scandalous."

"What do I actually need? To accomplish this?" Anna asked.

"We think a better question is: How do you get every single person in Hamilton to come to your side?" Di closed the book before she tallied the numbers. "Look, we have every reason to believe that you are in a position to be elected the next president of the PTO."

Anna tugged an earlobe. "I didn't hear you right. It sounded like you just said there are enough votes for me to be elected," she said.

"That's what the lady said," Mary repeated. "A round of beers!"

"Wrong place, wrong time of day," Anna said. "But seriously. How did this happen? And also, how did this happen without Mimi?"

Glances again. It was as if her two friends had developed a secret language behind her back. Mimi's name hung in the air. Anna thought about her meeting with Mimi, at Honeycomb, how different everything had been back then. Sitting at this same table, sunlight in their eyes, Mimi had been the main attraction. If they had stayed for half the morning instead of half an hour, the town would have come in to greet her the way they were now greeting Anna.

"You did this, so don't undersell yourself," said Mary.

"I do want to say something, though. About all this," Anna said.

"Take a bow," Di said.

"No, it's not a valedictory," Anna said. "It's about the . . . other stuff. The bad stuff. It's been weighing on me, I guess."

Mary and Di exchanged glances. They gave Anna the floor.

"It's just that — it's not that I take any of this stuff seriously, exactly. The texts, or the stupid notes, or even the people who have been icing me out. But I do wonder if this is just going to make all of it worse."

Mary nodded. "I see what you're saying. I think it's probably safe to assume that it's going to get worse if you win," she said.

"Right," Anna said. "Am I prepared for that?"

"Only you can answer that question," Di said.

"This shouldn't be this difficult," Anna said.

"Being a star never is," Di said.

In truth, Anna hadn't spent much time entertaining the thought of it — that she could really be the president of the PTO. But now she was close. She could win. She could make a difference in a town where iniquity was practically baked into the *pain au chocolat*. And Anna Plummer realized, suddenly, that she very much wanted this. She wanted to win, wanted to be wanted. For all the things that she had given up because she was sure that she was not quite good enough (Richter be damned), she was following through to the bitter end because she knew that she would be an excellent president — kind, respectful, thoughtful, willing to listen, open to new ideas. If she had given up on things before because she thought she was not quite good enough, this was an inflection point. She was not only good enough; she was great. Hamilton could be great with her help. She believed that, too.

And here she was, one January later, same place, different crowd. Mimi Mar, dethroned, except not really. That was just a vision. Anna had never quite recovered from that look, that one dark look Mimi had given her at this very table. She would not forget that look.

* * *

The forecasters were warning of snow, but for now it was just cold and icy. Anna ducked back into the house before the kids returned from school. Denny never asked where she was going or where she had been.

Denny came in from the shed as the sun was slipping into the trees. "Should we just go out?" he said, rubbing his hands together from the cold. He did have an uncanny way of knowing when she was unprepared for dinner. And she was unprepared. Her mind had been elsewhere, with the little black book and the notes of what to fix in Hamilton and with all the things she would have to do if she actually did win.

"That's fine. We can just head over to the Tavern."

"Whatever you want. Can I jump in the shower?" She nodded. And she wondered what Denny would think of all of this – that Anna Plummer was about to be the Queen Bee. She'd have to tell him eventually, but maybe it could just wait until after the election. Maybe he would laugh and laugh, the way he had when they were just a couple of kids on the Montauk docks.

"Take your time," she said, and she meant it. The kids peeled their backpacks off like snakes slithering out of old skin and darted into the playroom, ignoring her completely. In the family room, she looked at that damned green velvet couch, which had been a mistake. Jewel-toned in the pictures, but they didn't tell you what could happen if you had a dog.

"Alexa, play Joni Mitchell," she said into the silence, and at once the room swelled with music, the kind of melancholy music that Di was always getting on her case about. *Don't listen to that bullshit around me. It just makes me depressed.* Joni wishing for her river that she could skate away on, teaching her feet to fly. A river so long. That song always came on the radio at Christmas, but it wasn't really a Christmas song. It was a song about loss, a song about realizing that what you had was no longer there for the taking. Mimi would wake up one cold morning, Anna realized, and discover that it was all gone: the PTO, the presidency, the reign. What then? What would she fight for? Who would she be in Hamilton when she was just another mom?

The songs cycled through. No one ever listened to albums anymore; no one ever listened to the songs in the right order. Joni Mitchell's career highlights zoomed on the speakers: *Mingus, Blue, Clouds, Ladies of the Canyon*. Anna's eyes were just beginning to flutter shut when she heard Denny's voice from the kitchen, like a ghost, like a lifeline, tugging her back to earth, tugging her back to remind her of all the work that remained undone.

"Are you ready?" he asked. "Are you ready to go?"

Chapter 21

ALL THROUGH THE wrenching fall, Denny struggled to make sense of the pieces. Anna would have said that there were no true coincidences. Sticks and Ellen. Ellen and Mimi. The knotting together of these Hamilton friends and family members. If at first Denny had suspected that this was merely the convergence of people who happened to find themselves in the same place at the same time, he had shifted his perspective. Something about that push at the pool and about Mimi's web of connections had forced his mind into an uncomfortable space. He couldn't explain it, but he knew she was responsible somehow. Was it possible that she had looped in a cadre of like-minded conspirators? The crazier and more outlandish the story sounded, the more Denny began to believe that it was possible.

He had opened a fake Instagram account. Finsta, Anna used to call it, even though he never even would have understood how to operate the social media part of his life if it hadn't been for her. Through the account, he could see Mimi's stories, charting the end of summer and the start of fall. Mimi was at Crane Beach, in August, head tilted back into the sun, arms up as if in prayer. When fall breezed through, her photos displayed a storybook New England landscape: crimson maple leaves, her rosy-faced daughter in a pumpkin patch, a reel of a nighttime walk through Long Hill, in Beverly, where pathways had been converted into glowing coils of jack-o'-lanterns, and a photo of her cheering on the Pats (fair-weather fan as Denny imagined she was) in a box at Gillette, with a caption designed to make people jealous. Thanks to our friend @sama for the epic seats! She had tagged Sam Altman. Speaking of making people jealous, there was Easter, too, a pastel-perfect Mimi Mar standing alongside her family in front of the White House at the iconic Easter Egg Hunt.

Her outward-facing life was perfect.

Ellen Wilson did not have an Instagram account. Denny had wasted plenty of hours on the computer looking for information about her, but he'd come up short. She had married right out of college and moved from Rowley to Hamilton, according to a local announcement in the paper — and, of course, according to Sticks. That was about all Denny knew. What she did for a living, who she was friends with, how deep her allegiance to Mimi lay: all this remained a mystery, and he wasn't sure how to begin to solve it.

There was another mystery that lay right in front of him — his wife's office. Nearly a year had passed now since her death, and Anna's belongings were still where they'd been, as if they were awaiting her return. Denny had slowly started to throw away some of the things that he could bear to part with: shampoos, toothbrush, and other items in the medicine cabinet. But he had yet to deal with Anna's office; it still haunted him. Walking past it at night, he could almost see her shadow in the dark, hunched over a chair, working, thinking, leaning into the present as if it were not the past.

The kids asked for waffles for breakfast. Afterward, Denny dressed them up for the cold, reminded them not to lose their mittens, packed their lunches, and stood at the end of the driveway waiting for the bus to chug by, always at least five minutes off schedule. Normally, he would head back in through the side door, refill his coffee, and duck back out to the shed, but today he walked back in through the kitchen and around to Anna's office. The gray January light made the room look particularly flat and empty, despite the fact that it was full of Anna's stuff. Bookshelves of thumbed-through texts, tiny crystal vases, Wedgwood China in various sizes and shapes — all robin's-egg blue — that she had collected, and papers heaped on a green antique chair.

He could take everything from the shelves — no harm in that, really — and decide what to keep and what to donate. The books that had been Anna's favorites could get passed on to the kids. He'd make space in this room for something else. Maybe an office of his own. Let the air circulate in this brain of his. Let the air circulate in this room, where nothing but old and dusty memories lived.

But he decided to tackle all the papers first. Now that he was in the office, this moody room where his wife had spent so many afternoons, he could see that there was actually paper everywhere. On the chair, of course, but also on her desk, and atop the filing cabinet, to say nothing of the inside of the cabinet itself, a whole world of documents that Denny had never even bothered to think about. This was her domain, not his. When he was making things and losing himself in the art of production, she was here, surrounded by a different brand of work.

In the bottom drawers of her desk he found more unfiled papers and, beneath those, a few notebooks, all of them full. Removing them, Denny came across a stack of card stock placards with his wife's face on them. ANNA PLUMMER FOR PRESIDENT, they read. She was smiling, hair brushed back behind one ear, diamond earrings sparkling in perfect, soft sunlight. The photo was one he had never seen before. All of this was entirely new to him: His wife was a stranger to him. Anna for President? Living in the house with her, he had not known. Had they known one another at all?

The notebooks were full of different people's handwriting, but he found one that belonged to Anna. He recognized her small, tight cursive, the way it looped along, like she didn't even have time to get the words onto paper fast enough. Inside, it read almost like a diary. May 2022. Anna described seeing Mimi at Life Time. The pool. Louisa. That was old territory. Denny knew the story so well by now he felt as if he had been there himself.

But there were other stories, too. A garden party in South Hamilton in August. Mimi with a threat—a karate chop to the wrist. The writing was a journal entry, a simple accounting of what had happened, none of it particularly threatened or scared.

She thinks I am winning. September 2022. *Mary and Di say that there's an actual chance that I could be elected.*

Around fall, the writing turned to other people. Anna had written a few entries on Ellen Wilson, notes that expanded Denny's understanding.

> *I found out from Di that Ellen was an outstanding field hockey player in high school. They competed against each other: Triton and Newburyport. I don't remember her at all. Di says she tore her ACL senior year and had to quit and all of the players knew about it. I guess she had always assumed she was going to be a college athlete of one sort or another. Her brother was an athlete. Makes sense that she would gravitate toward someone like Mimi after that. How else do you rise to the top after high school?*

The brother, of course, was Sticks, another athlete who didn't make it to the pros. Living in small towns with high expectations had set these kids up for failure, Denny could see. Sticks and his hockey career, turned to dust. Ellen, once a field hockey star, now just the third wheel of the Queen Bee of the PTO. And Mimi, of course, joined at the hip with her best friend Karen, stewing in discontent from the age of fifteen.

But then, a more potent discovery. It came only a week before her death. The entry was specifically dated, unlike some of them: December 28, 2022. It had not been written out in full paragraph form but was instead a series of notes. *PTO. Cover operation. Secret society. College admission.* And then, in all caps: *PAY TO PLAY!!!* Whatever it was that the PTO was secretly up to — was secretly covering for — his wife had started to uncover it. Her proximity to it would have put her in danger from the start, Denny now realized, and her success in nearly unseating Mimi Mar would have made her a target.

It broke him apart, to think that Anna had gone through this alone, excavating some hidden world of secret societies and Hamilton demons. But Denny also remembered the feelings he had experienced when he unearthed his wife's private email cache a few months earlier. Perhaps it wasn't fair, but he felt it again, that white-hot rage, anger at having been left behind, with this mess, so much of it foreign, so much of it a mystery. He had shared a life with a stranger, he was coming to realize, a woman who had her own world entirely separate from him. True, as far as he knew, she had never been unfaithful, but wasn't this equally duplicitous, this life of hers, secreted away, unshared? And now, what made him the most angry, if he was honest, was that he couldn't even ask her why — why she had felt the need to keep these things from him, when he would have supported her through all of it; why she had embraced values she had told him she loathed; and why she had gone to such lengths to conceal parts of herself that were soft and tender and in pain. He could have helped. He *would* have helped. Here, in the dusty mess of her office, he could do nothing.

Because sitting in this office around his dead wife's things made him feel particularly useless and impotent, he texted Di. He needed reassurance that he was useful to someone, and maybe help spotting some of the outliers in his wife's group of friends. Hey, did I ever ask you about Ellen Wilson? he asked Di. It was an entrée, he figured, a way into a larger question about the PTO, about who they really were and how they operated, about what secrets they held. Di had been a little quiet these past months. A little less inclined to take his calls. He understood. They were grieving in their own ways, and Di and Anna had been practically conjoined, two faces of the same coin. For all the things he didn't know about his wife, Di held them for keeps, her confidante, the lockbox.

I'm not sure. Anna did. Last year, she texted back.

Thinking back on it, he hadn't seen Di in, what, three months? Not since before the holidays, he was sure, and maybe not even since Louisa's birthday, in September.

I feel like Anna was about to come to some conclusion about her, he wrote.

White bubbles appeared in the text field, and then disappeared. Di writing. Erasing. Trying again. As was her style. He put down the phone and picked up the notebook again, leafing through months of his wife's life, a catalogue of what people wore and what things they said, her observations of the members of the town. Maybe she had been using the book as a tool to remember faces. She must have seen a lot of them. From her notes: appointments each Wednesday with Di and a woman named Mary, an open invitation for anyone from Hamilton to come and chat about the state of the schools and the PTO. He had known about none of this, either, of course.

Denny's phone vibrated. She wasn't anyone specific. She was just a field hockey star who had a very unlucky break and got married to a rich guy to make up for it.

That story, though, seemed a lot like Di's story, too. Di, who had played varsity field hockey through high school, who had gone on to play Division 1 at UMass Amherst until she, too, suffered a game-ending injury, moved back to the area, and, yes, married rich.

It happens to the best of us, he said, knowing she would understand what he meant.

And also the rest of us.

Denny wondered if there really was a distinction.

The Triton field hockey records were largely available through a basic Internet search. How absurd. All this time, he could have been looking at photos of Ellen Wilson from his own computer. She was the same age as Anna, and, in the '90s, beautiful, too, with long legs and hair that slid all the way down to the center of her back. In old photos, Denny saw her leaning down to chip away at a ball, long hair flying loose in the wind, topped only with a light blue ribbon.

That didn't answer any questions about Anna's last entry. *Pay to play* and *cover operation* stuck in his brain as he thought of Ellen Wilson, field hockey stick in hand, her face mutating from adolescence into adulthood. Who had she been? Who had she become?

Ellen had gone to UMass, too. Di hadn't mentioned that, but a *Daily News* piece on the archive mentioned a scholarship—a scholarship Ellen lost because of the injury. But an interview said she was going anyway. He was halfway down into a rabbit hole on his bedroom computer when he heard a knock at the front door. It startled the dog.

"I'm coming, I'm coming," he yelled.

He opened the door and there was a familiar face, Di, staring back at him.

"Oh," he said. "I didn't expect you."

"Can I come in?" She wore a cropped puffer coat, a fleece headband around her hairline, and a large pair of black sunglasses. She rubbed her hands together. They were red from the cold. "I forgot my gloves," she said. "A New Englander who will never get used to winter."

"Warm up, then," Denny said. It was as if she had read his mind. He had just been thinking about how absent she had been, but now here she was, instantly conjured.

"I just thought maybe you needed some help," she said. "It sounded like you were trying to piece something together."

"Yes. No. Well, maybe," he admitted. "Actually, I was just cleaning out Anna's office and I was going through some of her things."

"Show me what you've got," she said. She took her glasses off and put them in a bowl in the hall, the same bowl where Anna had kept her own glasses. Those Denny had moved to a closet upstairs, but he paused for a moment, to take stock. The glasses didn't take up nearly enough space.

Di hooked her arm into Denny's and he walked her into the office, now a bona fide disaster. Halfway through, he had abandoned the task and had gone upstairs to search on his computer, and now the room was just an explosion: papers, books, pieces of art he had taken down from the walls.

"I was thinking maybe I'd paint it another color," he said. "I always hated this."

"The name was something horrific, wasn't it?"

"Hague Blue. Like the Hague." He laughed. "I was thinking maybe just a bright white office. Start over again."

"Of course you were," she said.

They sat down on the floor amid the paper and the books. The room had folded in on itself, far smaller now than it had been before. Di spread her hands out and made a seat for herself among a sea of stuff.

"I didn't realize...about the PTO...the president stuff," Denny said. "Why didn't you ever tell me?"

Di looked up at him. Her eyes were soft. She pressed the center of his forehead with her thumb. "That was your business with

Anna," she said. "I felt like there was a reason she didn't tell you, and I really did not want to get in the middle of it, life and death notwithstanding." When she finished talking she left her thumb there for just a second longer, and he could feel it, the warmth of her hand. She drew it down across the bridge of his nose and held her whole hand to his cheek for a second and looked him squarely in the eye before breaking away.

"I guess I get it," he said, distracting himself, distracting her. "There was a lot we didn't understand about each other, but that doesn't mean we weren't the right fit. I just wish I hadn't found out about it this way." He picked up one of the cards featuring his wife's smiling face. "Mostly, I just wish she had known that I would have supported all of this. I wish I had been better at expressing that to her. It's my fault. I missed too much."

"It's not. You couldn't have prevented it."

"What if I could have?"

"They call it the conditional tense for a reason," Di said. "There are conditions attached. You can't go back in time, so why try?"

"Fair, but it doesn't mean I don't want to," he said.

"I know," Di said, leaning in again. Now the hand was on his arm, just a light touch, feather-light. Soft. Friendly, he thought, although, on second thought, maybe it wasn't. It was hard to read these gestures in a room like this, in a house like this. "I should have told you." Some of the notebooks were stacked before Denny. Di grabbed one and began palming through it. "I haven't seen this before," she said.

"Those are just some notes, I think. That Anna had been taking."

Di stopped to read more closely. "More like weird personality profiles if you ask me. I love Anna to death, but she could really overdo it with the psycho pop."

"Loved," he corrected.

"Right." She sighed. "You understand what I meant." Di squeezed his shoulder in commiseration.

"To me, it read like she was just making notes about everyone for the PTO. And that some people maybe caught her attention more than others," Denny said.

"I wouldn't mind taking a peek?" Di said, with a look that asked his permission.

"Sure, but just leave it here. And keep it between us."

"Between us," she said. She flattened her palm and placed it on his knee. "Just between us."

Denny couldn't understand exactly what happened next. Di, with her cropped hair and long eyelashes and hand on his knee. Di, leaning in, breath on his cheek. For a second, his instinct was to push away, but he also wanted something else, to be embraced, to have someone look at him or hold him or make the spaces in the house that had felt wide and barren since Anna disappeared go away. He had not realized how much he had missed in being alone, every morning, a space in the bed, every night, a hollow. Every moment, carved out by grief.

And Di, too, hadn't she been carved out, made skeletal with this loss?

Later, lying in bed, her head notched into his arm the same way Anna's once was, he would think about it. Was it betrayal or healing? Di was married, of course. That was her own cross to bear.

"Penny for your thoughts," Di said, but Denny missed the silence, the way Anna always curled up after, like morning glory at night.

"I'm not thinking of much, really," he said. He was thinking of the ocean, of the way Anna used to look at it, and of the stranger in his bed and of how it had felt nice until it hadn't, of how easy it was to make a mistake, something you could not take back. He was thinking about how trust was the kind of thing you could misread and about how he had misread something important, something right in front of him: He could feel it in the room, a haziness descending.

"I know it's strange, me being here," Di said. "But I think she would have wanted us to find comfort in one another."

The truth existed somewhere in between, though. Denny wasn't sure he knew what Anna wanted anymore, and he was even less sure that Di really knew. A confidante. A best friend. A stranger. A foe. A new and darker realization began to swirl around. The afternoon light filtered in through the bedroom. Anna had always wanted blinds to block the lights from the neighboring house. He hadn't even been able to dignify that simple request, and he could see now that he had failed her, Anna. Dust swirled in the air.

"It's very hard to know what she would have wanted," he said, but that was a lie, too. What Anna would have wanted was the entire universe, he sometimes thought, but it was simpler than that. She wanted decency, fairness, and other things he could never deliver to her. Or not in life.

"If you want, I can go," Di said. She was sitting up now, shielding herself with the top sheet. Her features were sharper. She had a crease along the top of her brow that he hadn't noticed before. "I'm sorry." She reached for his hand. Instinctively, he retracted. "I'll go."

She turned her back to him and rooted around on the floor for clothing. He looked over at her one more time, studied the foreign shape in his bed, watched as she collected herself, and saw her pick up his wife's notebook that included those last words. He was surprised to learn, upon touching his own face, that it was wet, that the sadness had leaked out. It had been all wrong, allowing Di here, into his house, into his bed, into the space that had belonged only to Anna. But what could he say now? It was done. It was all done.

Chapter 22

MARY HAD ASKED to meet up for dinner, just the two of them. Usually, it was a trio — Mary, Anna, and Di — but Mary had texted early in the week to see about a one-on-one dinner. Anna didn't mind. In fact, she did better one-on-one, she always thought. It was an opportunity to really sink into whatever the other person was saying.

We should go to Newburyport. You always say you're going to show me around and you never do.

That was true. Mary had asked again and again for an insider's tour, and they had simply never made the time.

There's a place I love called Vera, Anna wrote back. The restaurant was loud, so she and Denny almost never took the kids, because they had to yell across the table to hear anything. And they hardly ever had date nights anymore. But Vera served good pastas and chewy-crusted pizzas and it was a warm little place right off Market Square that people knew about but that always miraculously seemed to have enough space for a party of two.

Sounds perfect. Pick me up at 6, Mary said. Now Anna just had to clear it with Denny.

Which turned out to be no issue at all, because there was some miniseries on that he had been dying to watch, so he didn't even blink when she told him she was heading out for dinner with friends, and would he please remember to give the kids vegetables and fruit with their macaroni and cheese this time? (Yes, yes, fine, he promised, though she knew better than to expect it.)

Mary wore a pair of pale blue slacks that cut right to the ankle, along with heeled black boots and a camel-colored wool coat, all clothing that Anna had never seen before.

"Look at you," she said, as her friend got into the car.

"Well, you know, any opportunity not to wear sweatpants in public."

In Newburyport, the giant Christmas tree still hadn't been removed from Market Square. This year, the city had used LED lights instead of traditional bulbs, and the glow cast from them tinged everything blue. When Anna moved to the area in the late 1980s, the city had just started to recover from a period of economic regression. In the 1970s, a city-wide restoration, focused on the area's brick-paved downtown, had been initiated to help drive business owners and tourists. But most of the people she knew were middle-class kids, with parents who worked in the public sector or who deep-sea fished on the weekends. The town had been a bit down on its luck until a commuter rail nosed in somewhere in the late '90s, connecting the area with Boston and bringing better jobs with it.

Now you wouldn't even recognize the place. If Newburyport had once been a place for cheap beers and wayward fishermen, it was now a tony bedroom community, a mirror to Hamilton: UPPAbaby strollers, upscale boutiques, small restaurants that operated with a reservations-only model. Anna still knew plenty of people around town, but she found that the faces looked less and less familiar now, a place stretching beyond its own measure of comfort.

Vera still reminded her of the way Newburyport had been when she was a kid, even though it had been the home of an old ice cream parlor, Bergson's. Inside, she and Mary were shown to a table in a corner.

When a server came over – one she recognized – Anna held up two fingers. Sangiovese, two glasses. The server nodded and disappeared toward the bar.

"Everything is good here, but I can also list my favorites, if that's helpful," Anna said. She didn't need a menu. Even though she never came with Denny, she had been to Vera plenty with Di, and even a few times alone, enough to know the menu, enough to know the wine.

"Order for me," Mary said. "I honestly don't care. I'm so happy to be out of Hamilton, I'll eat anything."

"Even pizza?"

"I'm from South Hamilton. I'll eat pizza."

Anna laughed. She thought of Mimi with a slice. Never in a million years.

She ordered enough food for twice as many people. Prosciutto with burrata. Two Neapolitan-style pizzas. Linguine with clams. A salad that went untouched. They had to send back the share plates; there was no room for anything else.

"I obviously overdid it," she said.

"I'm okay with it, honestly," Mary said.

Mary, Anna noticed, had been drinking quickly. She was already moving toward the third wine by the time they made it to the pizza. Her face had flushed, and she seemed hesitant to make eye contact.

"I have a feeling we're not here to talk about the pizza, though," Anna said.

Mary looked up and put down her fork. Sitting back, she laced her hands in her lap. She went to say something, but nothing came out.

Anna waited.

"I'm sorry, I'm trying to think of the right way to have this conversation," Mary said. She was quiet again. This time, she began to chew on the inside of her cheek, meditatively, in the same way that Denny sometimes did, former tobacco chewer that he was.

"Denny does that."

"Does what?"

"Chews his cheek when he can't think of what to say."

"You know, I've still never met him," Mary said, and then proceeded: "Here's the thing. I wanted to meet here because I wanted to talk to you about Di."

Her newest friend coming here, to her hometown, to talk about her oldest one. A competition for her affection, maybe. Anna couldn't yet tell. She studied the face looking back at her: earnest, kind. Still that gentle spray of gray hair at the temples. Large chandelier earrings, down nearly as far as her shoulders. So out of style they were nearly in style. She should have known that Mary and Di could never really be friends. Foolish of her to imagine a world where all three of them belonged together.

"What about her? I do know she can be difficult and demanding, but, you know, she's basically my family," Anna said.

"That's the thing," Mary said. She reached a hand, searching. For Anna's hand. Anna pulled back. "Is she? Your family?"

"I guess I don't really know what you're getting at." Anna could hear her own voice turn cool. She didn't care for the implication. To feel jealousy was one thing, but Anna had no patience for women who initiated grievances among women.

"I think — and this is hard to say to you — but I think that she may be friendly with Mimi," Mary said.

"Oh, that's what you're worried about?" Anna leaned back and sipped from the wine. She had never spent much time thinking about the wine, but it wasn't very good. Slippery, a little rust on the palate, a hiccup of acid and then gone. A short burst on earth, grapes that turned to dust. Wasn't it all like that, really? Just a moment and then life extinguished. All those winemakers, making a fuss, battling the sun and the rain and the snow and the hail, out in the field picking their grapes by hand, and for what? An average bottle of wine. A bad bottle of wine. A good bottle of wine. Whichever one you ended up with, it was gone at the end of the night. Finished. Forgotten.

"Di, well, she's friends with everyone. It's her thing. I wouldn't put it past her to work extra hard to get Mimi on her side just so that she doesn't lose her social status at Life Time," Anna said.

"I ran into her," Mary said. "She was having dinner. Not just her. She was with Mimi and Ellen. Two weeks ago."

"She didn't tell me about that," Anna said.

"It was in Beverly. Some new place. I'm sure she was counting on the fact that practically no one we know eats out in Beverly."

"Or maybe she was counting on the fact that she was just going out to dinner with a few women from Hamilton and that it was no big deal," Anna countered.

"Also possible." Mary drained another glass of wine and turned to get the attention of the server. Anna put her hand on her friend's arm.

"Don't," she said. "I think you've had enough."

"I'm just trying to make myself a little nicer," Mary said. "The mediocre wine helps."

The Beverly restaurant, Mary told her, was formal. Dark. The women were at a table in the back, and when Mary excused herself to use the bathroom — she was at a dinner for work — she walked past, and they averted their eyes. They did not want to be seen.

Anna listened. Di hadn't mentioned anything about the dinner, it was true. But then, it was just as possible that her friend hadn't wanted to upset her. Di had a tendency to keep close to the vest information that she felt might be prone to rocking the boat. As much as she was invested in Anna's success when it came to the PTO, she was also a society woman in town, and Anna had no doubt that Di was still working the rounds, ensuring her own value in Hamilton.

"Look, when it comes to Di, she may just be trying to smooth things over so that things are easier for her and the kids," Anna said. "I don't exactly blame her, given the kind of shit I've put up with." Hadn't it been Di, after all, who had dragged her over to the police station to file the report in the first place? Di who had backed her decision to run for PTO president, no questions asked? All these years, Di had calmed her down and walked her off the precarious cliffs and also had been there when Anna needed her most. She couldn't quite entertain what it was that Mary was implying – that Di was somehow on the other side of all of this, the side that was perpetuating text messages and emails, the side that had pushed her own daughter into the pool. That wasn't Di.

"I am only telling you what I saw. That's all," Mary said.

"I appreciate that, I do. Maybe we should just leave it at that," Anna said.

Mary didn't seem offended, just quiet. She picked up a piece of pizza and devoted her full attention to it. Anna watched her friend, the way she folded the little triangle before biting, the way her nose nearly touched the end of her food and how she didn't even care. The truth was that they hadn't known each other for very long, and if you had to put one friendship up against the other, she was always going to take the lasting, resounding one, the friend who had been there for every twist and rumble of her life. Those childhood days when she was stuck in her attic bedroom, grounded for one reason or another, sneaking onto the extension landline, coiling a telephone cord around her index finger, talking in whispers into the night so that her mother wouldn't catch her.

When she met Denny, Di was the one she had called first. "I don't know if it will last," she said. "It's probably just a summer thing." But Di told her to trust the sweet summer breeze and to drive out to Gin Beach in Montauk and to believe that love could last for longer than just the summer. She believed Di when she told her that you could build a life and a love and a marriage from the scaffolding of those pink and hazy summer days. Just kids, she had been thinking. But it's only ever just kids, Di told her. And Anna believed that because Anna wanted to have something to believe in.

"Do you think that maybe you're just jealous of Di?" Anna said. She could feel bile rising in her throat. It was the wrong thing to say, or it was the right thing to say, or it was just a *thing* to say.

"If you have a question for me, just come out and ask it," Mary said.

"I thought I just did."

"I'm not jealous of you and Di." Mary sighed and put her hands in her lap. "You know, if anything, I'm... as worried for myself as I am for you."

"What's that supposed to mean?" Anna asked.

"It means that I have kids, too. You're not afraid of these women, but maybe you should be."

"Then you can be afraid for both of us," Anna said. It sounded ridiculous, being afraid of Mimi Mar. Being afraid of Di! If anything, Di had been irritated with Anna, but hardly in a dangerous way. And anyway, that was a long time ago. Field hockey: a bust. Anna was in New York with an exciting life while Di was back at home, and if she had ever been jealous of the big life that Anna was living, well, she hadn't exactly said so. She didn't want New York, she didn't want the Hamptons, she didn't want to be exceptional; that's what she always said. She only ever wanted to be comfortable. Anna never really spent much time thinking about what it was her friend did want; she took her at her word — but sitting in Vera, she did think about it, for just a minute.

"We can get the check," she said. "I'm ready to go." She would pay. During their short friendship, she had already grown accustomed to the discomfort in Mary's face when the bill came at more expensive restaurants, despite her husband's job at Baupost in the city. She watched Mary fumble for a wallet for just a second too long before relieving the tension.

"I've got it," Anna said. "Let me get it."

On the way home, it began to snow, an unexpected spray of flurries along Route 1. By the time they reached Ipswich, the houses were already covered with a tidy first layer of snow, like frosting. The crumb layer, the bakers called it. Anna was always surprised by how moved she was by an evening snow flurry, by how stark the beauty was. You could see it a million times, that first cover of snow in darkness, and never tire of it.

"Do you want to talk about it?" Mary asked. The silence had all but consumed them, ever since dinner.

"Not really," Anna said.

"I'm sorry," Mary said. "I really didn't mean …"

"It's fine."

The roads were all roads that she had driven down with Di a million times, smoking joints way back before weed was legal in Massachusetts, driving down back roads in a beat-up Volkswagen Golf in the late '90s, speeding in the snow in winter, stopping just as the headlights hit a flicker of light in a deer's eye, just in time to see a whole herd cross the road in the puddle-black of a winter's night. They had driven off the road one of those nights, lost their grip in the snow, looping too fast around a turn right around here, on a night not unlike this one. With the car settled in a ditch, they called a friend on a flip phone and he hooked a tow hitch from his Jeep Wrangler onto the back of the car and flipped their car out like it was a little toy.

Back then, they had been having the time of their lives. Wild. Untethered. Unattached. No consequences. They worked as cocktail waitresses in the summer after college and tucked wads of cash into the black cloth aprons they wore around their waists and went out to the Thirsty Whale after work and played Golden Tee with the local boys and drank ice-cold Bud Lights and smoked Parliament Lights inside, because you could still do that then. They drove home with one eye open, tracking the lines of the roads with the headlights, not sober, barely surviving, living off French fries and egg sandwiches and iced coffee from Dunkin' Donuts, keeping spare bathing suits and towels — it all smelled like mildew — in the car, even well into the fall, for drives out to Plum Island in summer. It all jumbled together: fall, spring, summer, winter. Anna had come back for one year after college, tumbled around before she got her life together again. Going nowhere. Swearing she would get it together again.

And all that time, she knew Di as well as she knew herself, could see in her friend her own reflection, knew the disappointments and the thrills. Or she thought she did. Looking at this same stretch of road all these years later, Anna was starting to wonder how much she really knew, how much she could trust about herself and about her memory, what was real and what was imagined. For all these years, she had constructed a life around the people she knew and trusted, and now she was beginning to have her doubts.

They crossed into Hamilton. The snow was beginning to accumulate. Anna slowed down, watched the trees sway in the night wind.

"It's pretty," she said, mostly to herself.

Mary nodded in the dark. "I've always loved the snow at night."

"They'll cancel school tomorrow, I think."

That much was probably true. A snow day. Magical, maybe. A respite, like when she was young, a day unspooling without plans. Pulling up to Mary's house, Anna felt clear-headed again, reborn in a winter storm, a person full of possibility. In the morning, all of this – a white world – would be sullied with footsteps and car tracks. But now, it was still, perfect, clean. Mary opened the door, leaned in as if she was going to say something, thought better, raised her hand in a little wave. She walked back toward her house and, when Anna looked up again, she was gone in a swirl of white.

Chapter 23

You're a witch.

But who was the real witch now?

When Di left, the house felt like a deflated balloon, a space that couldn't quite retain its normal shape. Denny pulled on pants and a sweatshirt and wandered around the rooms upstairs, inspecting things he had never finished. Anna had wanted to replace a rug in Ben's room. It was frayed at the edges. The dog had peed on it. It was old. Now Denny lifted his son's bed at the edge, pulled the rug out and started to roll it toward him. He should have done this a year ago. He had waited. He had ignored it. The rug, like so much else, had just become background noise. Beneath it, the oak flooring was a slightly darker color. Hard to see the damage while it was happening.

Denny slung the rug over a shoulder and brought it downstairs, depositing it near the front door. He had left Anna's office a mess, piles of paper everywhere. Di had been a distraction, and a purposeful one. One minute they had been sifting through the detritus of his wife's life, the next she had been smoothing the side of his face with a hand, then leading him upstairs, and he had not protested, had needed some kind of reassurance that he was still human, still a person with a true and beating heart.

Back in the mess that he had left behind, the moody blue room gave him new clarity. They had been talking about the notebook and then they weren't. They had been looking through notes and then they were looking at each other. Di had known about the office and had come over unannounced, but had she come over to comfort him, or had she come over to distract him? Now Denny wasn't sure. The notebook with Anna's handwriting in it was gone, now in Di's possession, but there were other books piled around the office.

Before Di showed up, Denny had been leafing through another notebook, the small black one, in someone else's handwriting. He returned to it now. In it was a list of names, some of them familiar, others not. On the first page was Di's name and then a name that he had heard a few times. Mary.

The book was full of to-do lists, divided by Mary, Di, and Anna. Unconquerable tasks. Questions, it seemed, asked by local community members. Notes written in red, black, blue, and purple. Maybe a code for them to follow, or maybe just a way to keep things interesting: switch pens, switch colors, make it lively. Mary's handwriting, Denny learned, was looping and large, a happy cursive that filled the small notebook's pages. She had designated tasks to Di and to Anna, had bullet-pointed things to remember and to address, where they were meeting, what they needed to take care of, what was next on the agenda.

All three of their names were printed on the first page. Diane Maguire. Anna Plummer. Mary Langley. A trio, in ink, and the first proof of the friendship that Denny had ever seen.

* * *

Six months after they started dating, Denny and Anna planned a trip to Vietnam. Anna had gone to the consulate in New York to get them visas, which were necessary to enter the country. She met him for dinner that night with a pink laminated piece of paper with his face on it.

"The adventure of a lifetime is set to begin," she said. She wore a cowl-neck gray cashmere sweater and a smoky gray cocktail ring and tall black designer boots that were in desperate need of a polish, and her big eyes popped when she talked about all of her plans: the egg coffees in Hanoi and the Phong Nha caves near a farm stay she had booked and the War Museum in Saigon that a friend told her they needed to visit. They would take sleeper trains and eat Bún chả and buy tailored clothing made from silk in Hội An.

Over dinner, they planned the whole thing out, leafing through copies of Lonely Planet and Frommer's, highlighting restaurants and destinations of note. They had a whole month, all of his vacation time stacked together, the kind of adventure you can still take while young with no kids.

A week before they were scheduled to go, Denny got cold feet. He couldn't explain it, exactly. It was something about the hold Anna had always had over him, something about the way her eyes shone in the dim light of restaurants, the way her witchcraft had always worked on him. He couldn't just pick up and go to Vietnam, visa or no visa. He had work to do. He had obligations. He wanted the best of it all — the ability to stay with her without the commitment.

"I have bad news," he told her. They were at dinner again, this time at Little Park at the Smyth Hotel. One of those restaurants that they used to go to all the time back when it was just the two of them, one of those restaurants that they would find insufferable once they had kids: Everything was small and expensive and kind of forgettable, beetroot everything, dry-aged duck when it would have been just fine without the aging.

She seemed to know before he told her. She was a witch; he wasn't kidding. He could see her face fall before the words even came out, and she stopped him.

"You aren't coming," she said.

"It's just work," he lied. "I just can't do the trip for that long."

"I see," she said. Beetroot tartare, that was what it was. He watched her push it around her plate, fumble for a bite, turn it up toward her mouth. No satisfaction in the bite, no payoff. What could you expect from a vegetable masquerading as something else, anyway?

"I expect you to keep me in the loop," he said, reaching for her hand across the table. She recoiled, as if stung. One thing he would come to learn about Anna, right from the beginning: You could only violate her trust once, and this was the only time he would push his luck. On the street that night, he hailed her a cab, pushed the hair out of her damp face, and kissed her underneath a streetlamp and told her that he didn't want this to ruin things, knowing that it would still leave a delicate scar. Every day that she was in Vietnam, riding a train up the country's spine with a friend who took his place at the last minute, he thought of how stupid he had been, and vowed never to make the same mistake again.

The longer she was away, the softer her tone became over text. She sent photos of the things she saw at the markets: cobras and starfish tucked into glass bottles of so-called snake wine that she threatened to bring back with her, green-rinded oranges, parasols made from silk. The karst cliffs in Phong Nha looked incredible, he had to admit.

We waded through mud today, a text read, in the middle of the night. At the farm stay, they served pizza. It's a village of mostly locals.

She was supposed to come home to her own apartment in Astoria, but he drove all the way out to JFK to pick her up when the month was over; she came back in late January, just as Tet was about to begin. Her absence had opened up a space in him, something large and unhealed, and he realized that he needed her, that she was a part of him, her fierceness, her assuredness. She had known they were right from the beginning, and it had been him. He was the one who had lacked the trust and foresight. Always him making the wrong choices, failing to see what was right in front of him, in its sweetness, its simplicity, its perfection. He had been so stupid. He opened his phone, searched for a photo of the caves. There it was: a photo of Anna from a trip he had never taken, covered in mud, smiling like she had never experienced life so fully. He was twisted by it now, doubled over with grief, racked by pain so acute that he thought for a moment that one of his organs was set to explode. But no, he reminded himself. This is just what it feels like to lose a part of yourself. This is what it feels like to die without dying.

Mary, Denny learned, lived in South Hamilton. She was so easy to find, right beneath his nose the entire time. He drove to her house in the afternoon, past the rolling equestrian farms, where the hedges were now winter-anemic; you could see right through to their sprawling estates. Mary's house was small and pretty. Denny could imagine Anna at the picket fence gates, taking stock of a summer garden, memorizing the things she would do to their own house: the lattice arch with the vines crawling up, the sunroom on the side that almost looked as if it was leaning into a snowbank, the brass whale above the portico on the front door. He took a breath and walked up the path, which no one had cleared of the inch or two of snow that had recently fallen. Blue snow, like the night that Sticks had come to his own house, crisp, crunchy, fresh, and also filled with omens. Ophelia in a frozen river. Denny had never asked if her eyes were open or closed, but he had imagined her with a halo of flowers around her head, even though he knew that dead people never really looked, in real life, the way they did in the movies.

Denny took the skinny, aged bronze knocker in his hand. How many times, he wondered, had Anna stood at this exact same door without his knowledge? A thin woman with auburn hair, slightly gray at the temples, came to the door. She looked confused, as if she knew him, as if she had always known him.

"You're Denny?" she said, opening the door wide. It was a question, or it wasn't a question. "Come in, of course, come in." She swung the door wide, but he didn't really know why he had come, or who she was. The house was disorienting. He could smell reed diffusers, like the ones that Anna put out from Farm + Sea. "I'm sorry I didn't introduce myself at the funeral," she was saying. "Everything was just so…"

He remembered almost nothing from those days. Wearing a black suit, he had stumbled into the funeral home and made decisions as a woman with pursed lips and a tight-clipped bun asked him questions about his wife's preferences. Did she prefer roses to calla lilies? (Yes, he said, this he knew; she hated the smell of lilies.) Did he know how many people would be in attendance? Would he be driving in the processional, or would someone else be assisting? Who would be speaking on his wife's behalf? During those soft and blurry first days, when he felt like the air had been sucked out of every room he walked into, the funeral home was another dark corner where his mind would wander, another place where ghosts followed him. Even if Mary had come up to him at the receiving line, he probably wouldn't have remembered her. He was, himself, a corpse, leaning against the fabric wallpaper just to survive. Di brought him ceramic mugs filled with lukewarm water, which he sipped until he could feel his cheeks come back to life. He was crepuscular, an animal alive only at the edges of dawn and dusk. All other times, he was in a trance, skirting the mortal world and looking for the spaces where the dead and the living danced. He couldn't find it. No one ever could, not even in those first days when death and life were at their nearest.

"I wouldn't have been in a position to talk then anyway," he told Mary. It was a miracle that he had survived, that he had been able to get through the year. "Sometimes, I'm not sure I can talk now. I go up to people sometimes and say crazy things, you know."

"That's an interesting quality," she said.

"Is it?"

"I think so. I like people who say crazy things."

"So did Anna," he said. "She always enjoyed it when I broke loose, even though it didn't happen very often."

Mary's house was a jumble of things: an old credenza overflowing with books, vases of flowers that had dried and were long overdue for the trash, various antiques in different stages of disrepair.

"This way," she called, already a step or two ahead. Before he knew it, he was following her into the bright sunroom, where she had somehow grabbed two teacups and an electric kettle. How had she gotten them so fast? She pointed at the cup, asking a question without saying anything at all.

"Why not?" he said. Without asking, he took a seat on a Barcelona chair. It sank disproportionately low to the ground, forcing his knees up toward his chin.

He could hear noise from the other room. "One of my kids is home today," Mary said, by way of explanation. "I thought it was strep, but the test was negative." Something from the kitchen crashed.

"Fuck! Excuse me just a sec?" Mary disappeared back into the hall, leaving Denny in a stranger's sunroom, admiring the snow from the Barcelona chair.

What he wanted was to look around. A secretary in the corner could hide secrets, he figured, but whatever had crashed would likely only take a few minutes to resolve — not enough time to leaf through a stranger's belongings and sink back into the deepest chair on planet earth. Instead, he concentrated on the items on the table before him. The table was actually a trunk: red leather with brass buckles, topped with a few crystal pieces, Murano perhaps. One was curved and blue, an ashtray from the 1960s, he thought. In it was something he thought he recognized — a small brass button, the size of a pinkie nail. Anna had worn a cardigan with buttons like that, he remembered now, black cashmere, five buttons down the center.

Mary was soon back. She held a rag against her hand, where, Denny guessed, she had cut it in the kitchen.

"Kids," she said, and rolled her eyes a little. Denny nodded.

"Well, I don't have to tell you," she said. She lowered herself onto a settee across from him but didn't make eye contact. Instead, she looked out the window at the snowy yard.

"I live in a jungle gym," he said, trying to keep the conversation going. "Anna was the person who kept my life together."

"I assume you came to ask me about her," Mary said absently. "There isn't much I can tell you. Well, maybe a few things that would be helpful. Honestly, I thought you'd come sooner."

"Why is that?"

"I did try," she said. "I have to be very careful about what I say." She leaned over and picked up the button. "Do you ever feel like people are watching you, Denny?"

He thought about Mary's words. Watching. The scrawled word *Killer* that had appeared on his door. Di showing up unannounced. Sticks always being just a step ahead. Denny didn't answer.

"I can tell from that look that you do," Mary said.

"I've never really thought about it quite like that," he said.

"Hamilton," she said. "Always someone sticking their nose in your business, right? Even when I met Anna, that was something that irritated her about this place. She was always talking about how when she was growing up, people knew plenty about each other but still kept to themselves."

"That was something that definitely bothered her, yes," Denny said. "She never told me about you. I don't even know how you met. That's been gnawing at me, actually. That there were things about my wife that I didn't know. That I still don't know."

"Veterans Pool. I'm from here originally. I think she needed an ally."

"She always had Di."

Mary went quiet for a moment, ran a hand through her hair. Denny now noticed that she was younger than he had originally thought, maybe even a decade younger than he and Anna. "Some people put all their cards on the table. Anna was like that. I loved her for it."

"And you?" He wanted to know how she viewed herself, this mysterious friend of Anna's whom he had never met, the woman holding her button.

"I'm like her. See something, say something. I'd say that's why we got on so well. Until we didn't."

"Something happened with the two of you?" Denny asked.

"Right at the end. A few weeks before she died." She leaned over, holding the button between her index finger and thumb. "I had this feeling. Anna was running for the president of the PTO. I assume you know that."

"A recent discovery," he said. "But I'm learning. I think Anna was afraid I wouldn't approve, but the funny thing is that I would have supported anything she did."

"She was going to win."

"There are a lot of people who wouldn't have liked that," Denny said.

Mary thought about that for a second. "Yes. But she knew that. *We* knew that. And we knew that Mimi knew it. Every week, we met at Honeycomb, and it's not as if Mimi didn't know about the whole strategy."

Denny sat silent a minute. He had no reason to trust this woman – this friend of his wife's whom he had just met – but he was out of reasonable choices. "I found a notebook of hers," he said. "There was something else."

Mary said nothing, just looked straight ahead, hands folded neatly in her lap.

He cleared his throat. "She wrote that the PTO was a cover operation. There were a few notes. Cover operation. Secret society. Things like that," Denny said.

Those words were met with more silence. Mary did not move, but there was a nearly imperceptible twitch. Denny saw it. Something had caught her off guard. "Well, I don't know anything about that," she said.

"Why would she have written it? It seems like a strange thing to write. And only days before . . ."

"I really don't know," Mary said abruptly. "Who knows why people do the things they do?"

Now Denny was interested. He tried to prop himself up on the sinking chair. Mary was still holding the button up in the air like a magical charm. "When you met with my wife," he said, "what was it you had the feeling about? You didn't say."

"It was Di," Mary said. "All along. It was always Di."

Chapter 24

THE PTO ELECTION was two weeks away. Anna had put out of her mind the dinner with Mary. In fact, she hadn't spoken with her since. Instead, she had relied on Di for information about the ebbs and flows of the polling. On Wednesday, the day designated for their regularly scheduled tête-à-tête at Honeycomb, Mary sent a group chat saying she was sick. It was for the best, Anna thought. She didn't want to sit in uncomfortable silence, nor did she want to explain to Di what their third-wheel friend had said. At some point, they would have to face the uncomfortable reality of it: a jealous friend who would never fit the same way that Di and Anna had. That's what she was telling herself, at least — that all of this was because of jealousy, that Mary had felt the twinge of a thirty-year friendship brushing against her nascent one. The other feelings that had risen up Anna pushed to the back of her mind.

On Saturday, Anna told Denny to sleep in and she and the kids drove to meet Di and her kids all the way out to Salisbury Beach, even though it was winter.

"Mom said I could do as much Skee-Ball as I want this time,"

Louisa told Ben in the car. That wasn't true, of course. There was a limit. Forty dollars. But that could buy a lot of Skee-Ball, even accounting for inflation.

"Mom, did you say that?" Ben asked. He always wanted to play the sucker games, the grabber that got the tickets that no one ever won, and anyway, even if you got the ring of nine hundred tickets, it bought you one stupid little lollipop, twenty bucks for something that cost a dime at CVS.

"Not exactly," Anna said. "But I'll let you do way more Skee-Ball than those grabber machines that you seem to love so much."

"Totally unfair," he whimpered.

"You're right," she said. "Totally unfair."

Di had bought her boys cotton candy, which was the first mistake. She let her sticky kids loose in the arcade with a card stocked with money. "I really do not care what they do," she said. "It's Saturday. Let them exist." Henry and Ben were over at the grabber, a toy that always succeeded in grabbing money, if never a toy. Di had gotten herself a Slush Puppie, for no apparent reason, blue raspberry, in the middle of January, and her tongue and teeth were stained blue.

"You are so weird sometimes," Anna said.

"Oh, good, you're finally here. I apologize for not getting you one, too," Di said.

"Believe me, I'm not offended. It's nice to see Ben and Henry playing together. They haven't seen each other in a while," Anna said.

"I know. Henry got moved around a little." Henry had, in fact, undergone a complete transformation. His move from T-ball prospect to soccer whiz was first. Next, he had been promoted from First Grade A to First Grade B, and the scuttlebutt among the Hamilton Mommies was that First Grade B was the class with the *advanced* students. Ben was in First Grade A, so the boys saw less and less of each other these days.

"Well, anyway. I'm glad to see them together again."

Di smiled and held up her index finger. "Hold on, just one second," she said, pulling out her phone. "I have to let the man of the house know what time I'll be back. What time do you think we'll be home?"

Anna looked at her watch. It was just past noon. She'd give the kids two hours to get their energy out. "Say two? A little after if we get pizza?"

"Thanks," Di said, dashing off a text. "All set now."

All four kids had disappeared into the grim dark of the arcade, which looked exactly the same as it had thirty-five years earlier: peeling linoleum floors, a pop of neon lighting here and there, grizzled employees waiting for the shift to end. Joe's Playland had no doubt stayed the same since it opened in the 1950s, always a year-round respite for the local kids who had nothing to do on the weekends.

"Amazing how this place never changes," Di said, reading Anna's mind.

"One of the few things that always stays the same."

The stasis was something, though, that Anna couldn't entirely wrap her head around. Here in Salisbury, where the linoleum crumbled under her feet and the best thing to eat was a piece of pizza with crust the consistency of cardboard and sauce that was 90 percent sugar, staying the same was just fine. She and Di could comfortably slip into old versions of themselves: sweatpants and hoodies, Slush Puppies that turned their mouths blue. Joe's compressed time turned them back into the teenagers they had been a long time ago, and so it was easy to forget that they were also mothers and wives and citizens, that Di was also the kind of person who wore overpriced yoga pants and thick-soled vanity sneakers to the grocery store, just in case she ran into anyone from the neighborhood.

"I always feel like a kid when I'm here," Di said. "Come. Let's take a photo." She pulled Anna by the hand and brought her into the photo booth, which looked as old as they were. It was probably the same booth where they had taken photos the day of their eighth-grade graduation, when Di's mother had paid for them to come down to the beach and the arcade in a limousine, a motley crew of teenagers. Di inserted a five-dollar bill and made ridiculous faces as the lights flashed, and Anna looked right into the mirror that showed her reflection, fine lines creeping up around her eyes now. When the long strip of black-and-white pictures printed out at the end, she handed it over to Di.

"You keep it," she said. "Something to remember us by."

"As if I ever need anything to remember you by. I can't seem to get rid of you," Di said. She folded the strip in half and tucked it into the pocket of her jeans. That was true, Anna thought. Di had never quite been able to get rid of Anna, her perpetual sidekick, always around, always there.

"Maybe you've never really tried," Anna said. It must have been her imagination, the way her friend looked at her, just a moment too long, before sticking her blue tongue out.

"Beat you at a game of Skee-Ball," Di said. And off they went, to tackle the demons of Joe's Playland.

When she got back home, something about the kitchen was different. Anna could not quite put her finger on it. The bowl in the center of the kitchen island looked almost as if it had been disrupted. She had left in the morning and there had been a handful of avocadoes ripening. Now she noticed that all of the fruit lay over to one side, as if someone had rearranged them on purpose.

"Denny?" she called out. "Are you home?" She hadn't noticed, pulling in, whether or not the Jeep was in the driveway. The house was midday-January dark. She walked around the kitchen, turning on the lights as the kids went upstairs to change into sweatpants.

"Daddy isn't here," Louisa called from her room. "The Jeep isn't here!"

Good to know, Anna said to herself. Something else about the kitchen felt wrong. On the edge of the island, Denny — well, she assumed it was Denny, at least — had brought in the mail and stacked it in a tidy pile. On the top was a Hallmark card, in a pink envelope, addressed to Anna in sloping ballpoint letters, perfect cursive, no stamp.

She slipped her finger beneath the seam of the card, and in the process gave herself a paper cut. *Fuck,* she said to no one. As she said it, a flurry of pink and white glitter — hearts, actually — fell out onto the floor. Annoying. A glitter bomb, the kids called it.

Anna pulled the card out. A brown dog, sitting in the sun. *I'm sorry for your loss,* the card read. A pet sympathy card. She opened the card. Unsigned.

She wondered if it was some kind of message from Mimi, a joke that was supposed to be funny, about the upcoming election. To drive over from Nancy's Corner to leave it in her mailbox, though, well, that took some nerve.

When did this come, she texted Denny, sending a photo of the envelope.

No idea, haven't seen it.

You didn't bring this in?

No. Be home soon. Just stopped by Home Depot.

Someone had been inside the house, her house, stacking the avocadoes to one side, lining up the mail so that she would the card when she came in. From outside, Anna suddenly became aware of a faint barking. The sound was from beyond the property line. Hank. Someone had let Hank out. I'm sorry for your loss.

She was at the slider in a flash, then out in her own icy yard yelling for the dog. "Hank! Hank! Come here, boy!" Anna could hear the faint bark again, but the more she yelled the stronger the bark became. Soon, it sounded like the bark was approaching, and then she could see an outline of a dog cresting the hill between her neighbor's property and her own, his brindle fur covered in mud.

"Good boy," she yelled. "Oh, good, good boy!" He was missing his collar and one of his hind legs looked like it had been scraped up pretty good, but he was okay. Just cold and a little nervous. He rubbed up against her legs and licked her cheek when she bent down to pet him on the head.

She had been out. And someone had known that she was out. Anna could not allow herself to believe what any reasonable person would have told her. *I have to let the man of the house know what time I'll be back*, Di had said. What if it had been a lie? Anna had been away for two hours; Denny had been at Home Depot—that much would have been obvious to anyone driving by the house. The Jeep was always parked in the driveway and never in the garage. Di would have known that.

But no. This was ridiculous. Just another tailspin. The only thing more absurd than believing that Mimi Mar was harassing her was believing that her best friend was. Was this paranoia? Who could reasonably say at this point? Nothing had happened to the dog. Another childish prank. She debated whether to text Di and tell her what had happened, but she thought better of it.

What if, what if, what if, her brain said, and so she didn't. *This is probably nothing. This is just some teenager fucking with me, trying to scare me. I am being brought to the brink of insanity.*

Anna brought Hank inside and wiped him down with a towel she kept on a hook by the door—what Denny called the Dirty Dog Towel. Louisa and Ben had come downstairs and were sitting in the kitchen, arguing over which Minecraft character was better: Steve or Alex. It was a game that Anna did not understand or enjoy, something having to do with robotics that had also made its way into the Lego universe (another domain that belonged to her kids and to Denny and squarely not to her).

"When is Daddy coming home?" Louisa asked, seeing Anna walk back in with the towel.

"He should be home soon," Anna said. In her head, she

was already having a conversation of her own, rehearsing what she would say when Denny showed up and asked about Hank, who was more his dog than he was hers. The dog had gotten out, she would say. The collar had slipped off in the woods. It was nothing to worry about; he had come when called. Yes, they had a good time at Joe's. No, they didn't have anything planned for dinner. Sure, Chinese sounded good.

To give the rest of it a name was to make it real. Someone had been in the house. Someone had planned to be there in her absence, and had left a card there for her to see it, and had removed Hank's collar and let him out into the woods, where there were fisher cats and God knows what else, where the boundary between yard and woods was blurred, where anything could have happened on a bleak January afternoon.

Anna had promised to read the latest installment of Captain Underpants to the kids — their recent obsession — but she felt winded, so she corralled them into the family room and turned on *Bluey* and allowed them the gentle purring of anthropomorphized Australian dogs instead, while she went into her office to sit at her desk and stare out the window for a minute. Her computer, she noticed, was still on. She moved the mouse and the screen saver blinked back.

A Word document flashed to life. Black Times New Roman font. Size 36. (*Aggressive*, thought Anna.) **Go big, go home**, the words on the screen said. A message, and not at all a subtle one. When Anna went to close the file, she found that it had been saved to her hard drive. Document name: PlummerForPresident.doc.

Dragging the document to the trash, she listened for the satisfying crunch, the telltale virtual shredding of garbage. Over and done with. Gone. Whatever all this was, Anna Plummer refused to fall for it. When she looked down at her phone, she noticed that Mary was calling. Without thinking, she sent the call to voicemail.

The conspiracy theories could die in the mailbox, as far as Anna was concerned.

Denny didn't ask about Hank, even though he must have noticed the missing collar. That was one of his superpowers, and, if she was honest, one of the things that Anna appreciated most about her husband. When she needed him to ignore something, he did. When she needed him to pretend that an issue was less than the sum of its parts, he was willing — and able — to will it away, to bury it under a hill of other, more pressing concerns. Anna hid the card that had been stuffed full of glitter at the bottom of the trash bin; she would not speak of it, and if Denny stumbled upon it on trash day, he didn't mention it, either.

For dinner, they drove out to Kowloon on Route 1 in Saugus. The parking lot was full, probably with tourists who had learned that the restaurant, open since the '50s, was up for sale. The previous summer, when Covid had everyone scared to sit in a restaurant full of germs and other people, the owners set up a movie theater in the lot so that people could still feel like they were going out in the world. But Anna and Denny were still living in New York back then, out on Long Island, where a million people had decamped during the pandemic, crowding the beaches and the restaurants and the tiny little stores that lined every hamlet, making it feel like its own small hospital ward.

Now that they were settled into their Hamilton life, they were Kowloon regulars. Bob Wong, working the front, showed them to one of their favorite tables in the room with the fountain in the center. Anna let the kids order Shirley Temples with extra maraschino cherries. For herself: a piña colada with a rum floater, served in an ersatz pineapple.

"I've always wanted to do this," she said to Denny.

He looked at her like she was crazy. "They're sixteen dollars," he said under his breath.

"Sometimes it's worth the price for something you love."

He frowned, looked down at the menu, which was more like a leatherbound book, and shook his head. "Is everything okay with you?" he asked.

"You mean because I ordered a piña colada in a pineapple?"

"That, and you just seem a little...preoccupied," he said.

"I am enjoying the company of my family on a Saturday night at the Kowloon," she said. She had put on a long purple dress, with black leather boots and a three-inch heel. A coral necklace, looped twice around her neck. Hair up in a tortoiseshell clip. Maybe she was feeling a little fancy. Maybe she was trying to shake off the threat of the afternoon, trying to piece together how all of that could have happened in one day: Skee-Ball and blue raspberry Slush Puppies and glitter bombs and the dog getting out and the note on her computer and Denny none the wiser. He loved to call her a witch, but she had no magical powers. That was what she was always trying to explain to him. She was painfully mortal, painfully human, just stumbling through this life like everyone else.

"Whatever floats your boat," he said. He ordered a Miller High Life — also unlike him, Anna noted — and a pu pu platter for the table. The kids loved to watch the fire leap at the center, even if they were ambivalent about the actual food. "What did I miss today?" he said.

"I won Skee-Ball," Ben said.

"You can't *win,*" said Louisa. "I mean, he beat me. That's what he's saying."

"Everyone gets their time in the sun," Denny said.

"A good way of looking at it," Anna said. Even if it wasn't true. Even if the scales were tipped. Even if certain people made sure the scales remained skewed and uneven. Even if the world was unfair, as her own kids had put it earlier in the day. Even if there was no righting any wrongs, no matter how hard you worked at it, no matter how hard you tried. Someone was always going to be waiting at the door with a glitter bomb, with a warning, with some kind of retribution.

Denny lifted his Champagne of Beers sky-high, and there, in the dining room that was designed to look like some kind of far-flung boat in a Southeast Asian sea, they made a toast.

"To Saturdays," he said.

"To cherries!" said Louisa.

"To Skee-Ball," said Ben.

"To drinking piña coladas," said Anna. "To enjoying every last minute of it."

Chapter 25

DI IN HIS BED. Di with his children. Di, his wife's best friend. The button held in the air was a talisman, Denny realized, a thing with magical powers that he was supposed to understand but did not.

"That button," he said.

Mary nodded. "It was Anna's. I found it in my mailbox. I assume it was sent as some kind of warning."

Warnings had been everywhere, swirling around him, Denny knew, even if he had been ignoring them. The message on the door, of course — that had been the obvious one, but there had been more subtle ones, too. Di's appearance at his home, he now knew, was not an accident. She had come to get him off the scent. All this time, he had put his trust in the wrong person, pursuing a lead and telling her everything he knew, while she no doubt went back to the very people he was chasing.

"How far does this go?" he asked.

"I don't know very much," Mary said. "I have suspicions, and that's about as far as it goes. As you can see, I've stayed out of it. For good reason. Safety in distance." A noise came from the other room and a little boy peeked his head in. "Here's my good reason now," she said.

The little boy waved. He was small, about Ben's age, though a little taller, with a spray of freckles across the bridge of his nose. Mary excused herself a moment, and Denny could hear the television from another room in the house. In a minute, she was back, smoothing the settee with her hand before sitting down.

"How much did Anna know?" Denny asked.

"I honestly have no idea. I met her for dinner. I told her I had some thoughts about Di. She didn't take it well. She pretty much stopped speaking to me. A few weeks later, after everything happened with Anna, the button appeared, and I took myself out of it. I know exactly who those women are, and I can't . . ."

"I understand."

"But do you?"

"I think I'm starting to."

"I wish I could help you more," she said. She stood up from the settee, brushed off invisible lint from her pant legs. "I hope you understand why I can't be involved in any of this. It's dangerous. They're dangerous. It's not just Di. Or Mimi. There are connections here. In this town."

"Like Ellen, for instance," Denny said.

Mary didn't answer. She tipped her head back a little. Denny could see a necklace with a charm in the shape of a star — something he hadn't noticed before — sitting squarely in the nape of her neck. "Ellen Wilson obviously comes with a side of the Hamilton Police Department, and that's a road I don't want to go down. I'll leave it at that."

"Until recently, I was under the impression that Ellen and my wife were friends," he said. "Well, maybe I shouldn't say friends. I knew that Anna didn't trust her completely. But they had a *friendship*. That's what Anna had always led me to believe. It's what Ellen certainly led me to believe when I saw her not long ago."

"Ellen wanted you to have that impression," Mary said.

Denny chewed on his cheek. Ellen wanted him to have that impression. Ellen wanted Anna to have that impression. Sticks wanted Denny to back away from the case entirely. It had all been connected, right from the start, from the moment his wife meddled in the milquetoast dealings of the Hamilton PTO. A dance for little kids. A bid for equality. She had exposed some raw, pink underbelly in a town where no one wanted anything exposed. Still, he felt unsettled. The scribbled penmanship. His wife's notebook. Denny had extended grace to too many people, had spread himself thin listening to the stories of Hamilton, and where had it gotten him? He had been running in circles, listening to different versions of the town, but maybe they were all a little untrue. Mary could just as easily be protecting her own version of a story. He wanted to believe her. He wanted to believe that someone had been looking out for his wife. But something about the way she had bristled at those words, *secret society.* He couldn't be sure.

"How deep do you think this goes? The police?"

"That I can't say," Mary said.

The idea that Sticks was involved in his wife's murder was, of course, equally unfathomable. Blue snow, blue lights, the man at the door informing him of a man's worst nightmare. Could he have known all along? Hamilton was, though, the kind of shiny town where everything lived beneath the surface. The houses were beautiful, those huge equestrian properties, but anyone who had ever lived inside a home that was built in the 1700s or 1800s could tell you plenty about rot, about termite damage and knob-and-tube wiring and beautiful pine flooring that was so soft that it took on the shape of a high heel if you walked on it. A house that was old and beautiful on the outside was actually just full of quiet decay, and maybe that's what Hamilton was, too, a place where faces were painted on, where everyone was quietly spoiling on the inside. You couldn't see it. You couldn't know it.

"I should probably get going," Denny said. He pushed himself up from the sunken chair. Mary was tall, much taller than his wife, and he found himself looking squarely into her eyes. She had a sadness about her, which he only now noticed. At some point she must have put the button back into the Murano crystal ashtray, but she picked it back up and handed it to him.

"You should keep this. It really belongs to you, not me," she said. "I'm sorry I couldn't help you more."

Denny reached out. He wanted to give her a hug, but they weren't friends. He realized he might never see her again, this stranger, this friend of his wife's who had spent so much time with the person he had once shared a life with. He reached out, patted Mary on the shoulder, the way you would a friend, even though she was not a friend. She was just somebody that somebody used to know. "I'll show myself out," he said, heading out of the sunroom, past the clutter of antiques and old, aging things, toward the door, and out through the snowy walk, into the cold, clear January day.

When Denny got home, a squad car was parked in his driveway. Same scene, different year. Denny had not seen or heard from the Hamilton Police Department in months. He had left messages inquiring about Anna's laptop; those messages had gone unanswered. Once, Sticks had texted, saying that the laptop was "still being forensically analyzed." That was last summer, six months ago. Denny had come to believe that the laptop, like the engagement ring, was another casualty, an item lost to the chaos of death.

Denny parked right next to the squad car and got out. He tapped his knuckle on the window and smiled, expecting to see Sticks looking back at him, but it wasn't Sticks. Instead, an officer Denny had never seen before rolled down the window. A kid, Denny thought, no more than twenty-five.

"Mr. Plummer, Officer Malkin sent me over here. I'm sorry to bother you," the officer said. He was nervous, Denny could tell. He didn't make eye contact when he was speaking. Instead, he looked straight ahead through the windshield, facing the empty woods.

"What's it you need?" Denny asked. "Here to follow up on a year-old crime that no one's done anything about?"

The young officer cleared his throat. "I'm here to take a look inside, if that's okay?"

"What did you say your name was?"

"I didn't," the officer said. "It's Smith, though. Aaron Smith."

"Sticks didn't want to come over himself, I take it?"

"He got caught up on another case he's been working on, you see. That's why he asked me if I could just stop by." The kid cleared his throat again. He really was a kid. Denny could see scars on his face from where there had once been acne, probably only recently cleared. Sticks had been invisible for the better part of a year, except the time Denny ran into him and Ellen at the Block Party in August. No follow-through. No interest in the case. So why was he sniffing around here now, sending his minions over to investigate, when the meat of the murder was so clearly elsewhere?

"I see," said Denny. "And what was it he wanted you to take a look at, exactly?"

"He was just wondering." The boy stopped and opened a bottle of water from the cup holder in the center console. Denny could see the boy's hand — it looked like it was shaking. "He mentioned that Mrs. Plummer had an office?"

Well, wasn't that a fucking coincidence, Denny thought. Nothing in this town was a secret.

"I'm afraid it's all packed up, you see. I broke it all down just this morning."

"Maybe you could pass along all the stuff that was in it to Officer Malkin? He'd be interested in seeing whatever it was you packed up. Sir." The boy was trying. Denny had to give him that. He had obviously been given stern instructions from Sticks to come back with the contents of his wife's office or not to come back at all.

"I'm afraid I can't do that."

"You can't?"

"On account of you not having a warrant, and all."

"Oh. Yes. Well, I guess I can understand that."

"You can tell Sticks that if he needs to talk to me about any of the things in my house, he can reach out to me directly," Denny said.

"I'll let him know," Officer Smith said.

"One other thing," Denny said, leaning into the frame of the squad car. He could feel his size compared to the boy's. He felt sorry for the kid, who had been caught in between a bad boss and an angry widower, but what choice was there now? They were all in too deep. "Let Officer Malkin know that I'd like my wife's laptop back. He's had plenty of time to analyze its contents, or whatever he's been doing with it over there. He can bring it over here or I can come get it. Private property and all that. I sure wouldn't want to have to file a police report against the police." Denny laughed a little, but the young officer didn't seem to find the joke funny.

"I'll relay the message."

"Much obliged."

Denny gave the car a loud pat with his flat, open palm and then turned to walk in to the house. Whatever was in the office was of interest to Sticks, and to whoever was in Sticks's circle. Denny imagined a dinner party: Ellen, Di, Mimi, and Karen, with Sticks at the head. Spouses in attendance, candles burning down to pretty little beeswax nubs. Glasses of red wine; tiny filets mignon, rare; pommes purée; and the skinny little asparagus that used to make his wife insane. *Who buys these stupid little things, anyway? They are insulting to actual asparagus.* A demi-glace and, for dessert, *tarte tatin,* one perfect white tablecloth, maybe everyone at Di's midcentury oval table, the one with the Kardiel Milla dining chairs, which he had always coveted, even though he made things out of wood, not leather.

He could picture this imaginary (or was it real?) dining scene, a bottle of Opus One opening up in Di's Riedel swan decanter, everyone a little drunk, a conversation unfurling about Anna, nuisance that she was, and about how to fix a problem without creating a different one. Husbands off to the family room to watch football and nap, the unspooling of an idea, of a plan, a joke at first and then more serious. They could do it, couldn't they?

At first, it was just an idea, and then it was an idea that became the seed that was planted, something growing, developing roots. Stopping a cancer like Anna had purpose. Hamilton was a place worth preserving. She was messy and they were tidy, clean people who believed in their tidy, clean town. Believing in the same things kept them together. Believing in the same things kept them whole.

A dinnertime conversation. A joke, even. The kind of story told among friends that gradually took on a distinct shape. When had their eyes become little pinpricks, when had the wine turned their tongues the color of blood, when had the color drained from the room, when had everything turned cold, when had someone stood up to draw the thick velvet curtains in the dining room, when had the loud voices in the room turned hushed, when had they realized that they had started to develop a plan?

Mimi. The kind of woman who would push a little girl into a pool. Oh, come on, they all knew it. Ruthless to a fault. She would do anything to maintain her social status, and no one doubted how far she would really go. It was true. She had come from nothing—few knew it, but she had grown up dirt-poor in some Podunk town in Maryland—and look at her now, look at everything she had become, clawing for freedom, clawing, clawing, clawing, unwilling to give up everything she had fought so hard to achieve.

Ellen. Just a second-rate field hockey star who had only made it as far as UMass. Not as pretty as the other girls, and sure, she had gotten out of Rowley, but who even looked twice at Ellen Wilson? Well, Mimi Mar did. Mimi put trust in Ellen, took her under her wing, fluffed her up and made her feel important, and that was enough. It was enough to be part of something, to be part of the PTO, and it was enough to want to defend that something if it was under attack.

Karen. A blank canvas. Denny could barely even remember what Karen looked like when he wasn't standing directly in front of her. Mimi's careful stooge. She would do anything for the Queen Bee, Denny knew that and so did everyone else: Mimi and Ellen and probably even Anna.

Sticks. A has-been high school athlete willing to protect his sister at all costs. Denny hadn't seen it before, but he saw it now, that desperation, that common bond, these two locals who had never really made it out of Rowley after all.

And that left Di. Smart-as-a-whip Di, who always existed in Anna's shadow. She could have gone to Haverford, like her father, but she settled for Division 1 UMass instead, and for what? For a sport that failed her. She came back to town just like everybody else, while Anna was off living a life, all that exciting shit she had done in her twenties and thirties.

More than once, Anna had stumbled into bed—in the city, in Montauk that first summer, and in Hamilton, long after they moved—loose-lipped about Di. Di had always wanted to write books, she had always wanted to see the world, she had once hoped to travel after college. Di had these *aspirations,* but she had gotten stuck, and the bottles of rosé seemed to pile up on the countertop. It wasn't really all that shiny and happy being the tallest and most alive and most centered person at the party after all. Denny had shaken all this off the way he had shaken every bit of Hamilton gossip off. Upper-middle-class ennui. The chatter of the town. The sound of his wife's voice was so far off now, like the sound of crackling radio when you were losing a station, back when that was a thing. If he had only been listening, he thought now. If he had been paying attention. Then what? Could he have stopped the force of nature that was Anna Plummer, pulled her back from an inevitable edge?

Could he have stopped Anna's fate, if he had been listening to the sounds of the radio, if he had turned the dial to make it clearer?

Sticks would be back. Denny was sure that he had not seen the last of the officer, that whatever treasures his wife's Hague Blue office held were now of interest to a crowd. The bus would be back soon, returning his children to him. He was a different man than he was in the morning, when he had bundled them in hats and gloves and warm winter coats and shuttled them on, kissing them goodbye, telling them to have a good day, wondering how much of this they would remember when they were older. He knew so much more now. Every single moment that followed that first moment — a frozen Ophelia in a river — had led him here, to the driveway outside his house, where he finally knew. He knew. He knew it all now, memories come back to haunt him like a curse.

Chapter 26

DIANE FOLEY WAS the tallest girl at the party. That was the first thing that Anna Denton noticed. It was the last weekend of summer, that weekend just before Labor Day when parents and kids have all just about given up. Anna herself had just about given up. Most weekends, she either holed up in the attic with a book, despite the interminable and oppressive heat, or sprawled out in the spiky grass of the backyard and imagined herself running through a sprinkler, which her parents refused to invest in. "Waste of water," they said. It was a rare moment of agreement between them.

Still, somehow, her ever-arguing parents had met friends — friends! — through one of the Welcome Wagon women who came by with coupons to the local businesses and a jar of beach plum jam for them to sample (too tart, Anna herself had decided, though her mother oohed and aahed at the *localness* of the whole thing). Which was how they had been invited to a barbecue at the Connors's house, over on Broad Street, in a tidy little gray house with a small backyard and a wide, spacious living room with brand-new skylights that allowed all the summer sun indoors. Truth be told,

Anna had never seen anything that modern before; she had only ever lived in houses that were older than sin, as her mother put it, afflicted with termites and rot and all kinds of other problems that her parents were always talking about on the phone with contractors.

The house was within walking distance of their own. Anna had chosen a flowered sundress from Laura Ashley, purple and pink and white, with tiers that made her look a little like a wedding cake.

"It's a little dressy," her mother observed, but Anna didn't care. All summer, she had been in shorts and T-shirts, bored to tears and wishing she had some occasion to change into anything else — even a bathing suit. Finally, here was a chance to pretend that summer hadn't been one giant and complete disaster.

Kaitlin Connors was hanging around the backyard when they arrived, wearing jean cutoffs and a faded Guns N' Roses T-shirt. Anna's mom wouldn't let her buy *Appetite for Destruction,* a tape she coveted. She had flipped through so many tape decks at Sam Goody, and studied the macabre metal art (it was a giant cross, with each of the five band members' faces — turned into skulls — superimposed on the cross), wishing she could just take the tape home with her and memorize all the words to "Welcome to the Jungle" and "Paradise City." That summer, of course, was the summer of *Lies,* the summer of "Patience," and Anna had none for her mother, who would turn the radio off any time she heard Axl Rose crooning. *Just a little patience. Oooh.*

Dear lord, could she use that patience now. "What are you *wearing*?" Kaitlin asked. She was old townie blood. Her father worked for the water department. He had been born in Newburyport. His parents had been born in Newburyport. If anyone could lay claim to the legacy of the North Shore of Massachusetts, it was the Connors family. Joe Connors was a volunteer fireman who bought thirty-racks of Bud Light for all the guys in the neighborhood when he wasn't busy getting bruised on the weekends down at the North End Boat Club. Marie Connors was from Newburyport, too, South End; she taught math at the high school and was one of those ordinary teachers who believed that you could do just fine by heading off to a state school, moving home, marrying a football star and planting roots where you grew up. No need to see the world if you lived in the prettiest little place on earth.

"I was hot," Anna said by way of explanation. She pulled the dress out a little from her body and fanned her face. Kaitlin just laughed. She had long blond hair, like every other girl with a cute '80s name. Jennifer. Amanda. Ashley. Melissa. Tiffany. It was pulled back into a ponytail with a hot pink scrunchie.

"*That* is why I have shorts and a T-shirt on," Kaitlin said. "Well, come on. Everyone is over here. We have grape tonic and Doritos. My mom doesn't care what we eat at these things."

One hurdle crossed, Anna thought. Kaitlin ushered her over to a long white plastic table, which had clearly been set up with younger guests in mind. On it were bottles of generic sodas from Market Basket — tonic, as Kaitlin and half of Massachusetts called it. Grape soda, yes, and orange, too, plus root beer and cream soda, not that Anna could ever tell the difference. A bag of Doritos, already decimated, lay open on the table. Anna eyed it suspiciously.

"You have to get those early," Kaitlin said, shrugging.

The Smartfood, though, was still relatively untouched. Anna stuck her hand into the bag. "My mom won't buy this," she told Kaitlin.

"In our house, that's health food," Kaitlin said. "Popcorn and cheese."

From the corner of her eye, Anna saw a girl she vaguely recognized from school. Green eyes. Tall. Tomboyish. Cropped hair cut just below the ears. Anna had a strange sensation, almost like she knew that this person — a person she knew nothing about, really — was going to be involved in her life somehow. She was just a kid. How she could have understood that Diane Foley was about to become her friend was some kind of kismet, she would later believe. But it was true. Anna could feel it even then, right there in Kaitlin Connors's backyard, that their lives were set to align.

"Hey, Di, over here," Kaitlin called. Di had been talking to a much shorter boy who was also in their grade, but Anna could tell from the glazed-over look in her eyes that her interest was limited. "Yoo hoo!" Di loped over in what Anna would come to recognize as her signature gait: long, graceful strides that almost seemed to sidestep anyone that got in the way.

"Nice dress," Di said. It was hard to say whether or not she meant it. Like Kaitlin, she wore jean cutoffs, which rode higher on her tall, slim legs. White T-shirt, V-neck, stretched out a little. Green eyes. A headband right in the center of that short hair. "Your mom got Smartfood!" She reached over Anna for the bag.

"It's my favorite, too," Anna said.

"You to go Kelley," Di said, mouth full of popcorn. "But not my class."

"No," Anna said. "But aren't we both in Kid Stop?" That was the after-school program held in the South End, where her mom insisted on sending her so that she could meet other kids.

"Hey," Kaitlin said. "You guys wanna go inside? Play video games?"

"My mom will kill me," Di said. She put her hands around her own neck, simulating strangulation. "She's really against it." Anna smiled. Her own mother was exactly the same way.

"Mine, too," she said. Di smiled back. Even in her stupid dress, on a stupid hot evening, with the smoke from hot dogs and hamburgers billowing up from the grill, it had never been so easy — it would never again be so easy — to make new friends. They poured themselves big plastic cups of grape soda. Tonic! They found a cool patch of crabgrass over by Marie Connors's raised beds of tomatoes and cucumbers. Kaitlin went inside for a notebook and colored pencils, and, in the waning August light, they wrote their futures out, playing a childhood game called MASH, figuring out who they would love and where they would live, and what they would grow up to be, as if three girls could ever truly predict the future with just these simple charms.

Had she missed something on that stifling August day, all those years ago? There was the smell of charred hot dogs, the purple ring that the grape soda left on the plastic table, the heavy, thick air that came around that time of year. No relief from the heat. Di's eyes were so green, they looked the way the water looked in midsummer, emerald and glass, shiny and practically transparent.

One night, during Anna's freshman year of college, she came home for a long weekend, and she and Di drove up to UNH, where Kaitlin was living the high life, as they liked to say. Up in Durham, she was sharing some beat-down house with a bunch of kids from school, and it felt romantic and grown-up; it was where Kaitlin would fall in love, first with a kid named Scott, and, later, with heroin, snorted off dashboards in cars and then shot up in dark New Hampshire alleyways. *We knew her when,* they'd say later. *Way back in the day.*

It was cold for October, with a threat of snow, the way it used to feel back before the climate made everyone feel on edge all the time, and Anna and Di got high before driving up. They felt good, or they felt great, or they felt invincible, the way best friends always feel when they're young and in the middle of conquering the world, and then right before they pulled into the driveway — it was littered with cheap cars that were all on the verge of ending up at some New England chop shop — Di looked at her. Anna would never forget it. Emerald gone from those green eyes for just a second.

"You know, you're not so great," she said.

"What?"

"You're not so great. You're ordinary." Di was staring straight ahead, looking at the windshield. Through the windshield. Into the veiled and velvet black of the night.

"Believe me, I don't think I'm that great," Anna said. She moved to get out of the car. Di was high, she was high, this place in the woods was giving her the creeps, and all she wanted was to be inside, even if Kaitlin's house was as terrible inside as it was outside.

But Di grabbed her by the wrist and looked at her dead-on.

"We all end up in the same place in the end," she said. Then she let go and tipped her head back in an uproarious laugh, clocking herself hard on the headrest. She shouldn't have been driving, Anna realized. Anyway, what did it matter what people said when they were fucked up? Just a bunch of words with no meaning. No one ever remembered it in the morning.

Anna had, of course, remembered it in the morning, but the hard edges of that night had been softened with the length and roundness of their friendship. She went back to New York, Di went back to western Mass, and it was just another dumb thing that one had said to another, part of a catalogue of sins. All long relationships have them. If there had been festering resentment, Anna hadn't thought of it much, or at all — not the fact that Di hadn't done the things she wanted, because Di had ended up in a fortunate position. She was beautiful, with those emerald eyes, and well-liked by everyone. She had carved out a position for herself in Hamilton. When Anna talked about moving back to Massachusetts, it had been Di who suggested Hamilton in the first place. "It's not as stuffy as you think," she said.

"Even with all those horse-loving rich people?" Anna asked. She had been scrolling through countless houses on Zillow, and the ones that came up first were outrageous: multimillion-dollar homes with acres to keep up, facades that were sure to chip away at any reasonable person's bank account.

"There are plenty of normal people here. Newburyport isn't like it was when we were kids, either, you know." That was true. She didn't know anyone who hung out at the North End Boat Club anymore. After Kaitlin died, the Connorses moved up to New Hampshire, way into the mountains, to get away. All the locals complained about the rising costs in town, the newly expensive restaurants, the skyrocketing real estate. Everything was more desirable now, even their diminutive little hometown, where nothing important had ever really happened.

"Is it hard to make friends?" Anna had asked.

"I've met some people through the schools," Di told her. "The PTO, actually. I know it's probably not your scene." Even back then, Anna had wondered, privately, how she would adapt in a town where the main social interactions revolved around moms and the engines of their drama.

But Anna had taken the bait and convinced Denny, even, that Hamilton was worth sinking their teeth into. They drove up on weekends from New York with the kids, looping around the back roads, trying to figure out where they could envision themselves. Hamilton. Wenham. Ipswich. Merrimac. West Newbury. Even Essex and Gloucester. Di met them at showings, pointed out how lovely Hamilton was in spring, had them over for dinner at her sprawling estate on Bridge Street – the right side of South Hamilton. The good side of the tracks, if you were keeping score.

"You were right. It isn't half bad," Anna told Di. She found the town charming. There was an actual polo club, and a store where you could get your initials monogrammed on a beach bag. She could envision the kids growing up there, an idyllic northern Massachusetts life for them all, close enough to see her mother on the weekends, not too far from the beach, setting down roots in a new enough town where she still had at least one old friend.

"I told you," Di said. "And there are nice people here, I promise." Di had a group of friends, she said, women that she met sometimes on the weekend for wine at the Black Cow. "You just have to get to know them a little."

All of that sounded convincing, and Anna had been convinced. Hamilton seemed like a dream, and it was a dream: Di in her sprawling house, the other women in their equestrian estates, Nancy's Corner or the nicest parts of South Hamilton, even, with riding lessons for the kids and memberships at the nicest clubs and husbands who went foxhunting or played golf at Myopia Hunt Club (members only, of course).

Even when she moved into her perfect little house, though, she could never fit in at Di's parties. Mimi Mar looked disapprovingly at her outfits. They weren't nice enough. Karen Pistoulia brushed something off of the shoulder of her dress. "Just a little…dust," she said, implying that Anna was unkempt, that she couldn't get herself together, not even for one evening among women. Ellen Wilson always smiled and waved at parties or out at Patton Park, but Anna knew better than to call her for dinner plans. She had her own friends.

All of that eventually left Di, who had become a centerpiece, too, the main character in this small town, even if Mimi Mar had been parading around like a peacock pretending to be the most important person in all of Hamilton. Diane Maguire was not president of the PTO, of course, but she was a swirling brand of energy, fiery and interesting and surrounded by Hamilton's most important people. Queen Bee? Maybe not. But a person of influence. A person with friends. A person who knew how to conduct the orchestra.

"They do seem to love you here," Anna said to Di at one of her friend's parties. It was spring. They were sitting on the veranda, taking stock of the newly sprung daffodils.

"Big fish, small pond," Di said, raising a glass of rosé. The sky was the same color, fading salmon.

In that moment, Anna remembered the drive up to UNH. *You're not so great,* she thought, looking around at the giant house with all its trappings. *None of this is so great.* The friends seemed vapid. The party was dull. The parties were all pretty dull. She preferred Di when it was only the two of them at Anna's house, gorging on chips and terrible reality TV. She did not say this, though; instead, she raised her own glass of onionskin-pink wine and toasted to the party, to her friend's good fortune, to the emergence of spring, and to their luck in having survived the winding and long path of friendship.

"To the big fish," Anna said.

"To the small pond," Di said.

And for a minute, they were right back in Kaitlin Connors's backyard, a black bag of Smartfood between them, just a young girl in a Laura Ashley dress and a much taller girl in cutoffs, the one with the emerald eyes, the one no one could take their eyes off, especially Anna Denton.

Chapter 27

THAT NIGHT, AFTER the kids were asleep, Denny collected all of it: the notebooks, the stray papers, the photos that had amassed on the floor of her office. Packaged it into boxes. Took it out to the shed, where he had long ago installed a paper shredder. Would he regret destroying any of this, the information that could prove guilt? Possibly. But the alternative, he reasoned, was that someone else could end up with it, that Sticks might end up with it, and Denny could not bear the thought of more of his wife's belongings falling into the hands of the incompetent — and, for all he knew, criminal — officer.

He didn't have much time, he knew, but Denny snapped quick photos of some of the journal pages, most of which were written in Mary's now-familiar cursive. He also took a photo of one of the pieces of card stock bearing his wife's image: ANNA PLUMMER FOR PRESIDENT. Then, one by one, he turned years of her life into compost — long woven ropes of paper that the shredder spit out in indignation.

"I don't like it, either," he said to the shredder, the third time it jammed, as if it had been a sign to keep the pages intact. He remained unpersuaded. It had to go. All of it.

Sticks would be back soon. Denny knew that for sure. When he was finished with the shredding, he mixed the papers with sawdust from an ongoing project and shoveled it all into a green wheelbarrow that he kept outside the shed. Spring would have been a better time, he realized, to try to hide something as conspicuous as a mountain of papers and sawdust, but what choice did he have? The summer before, he had started to clear a space for a fire pit before the Conservation Commission had stopped by to tell him that he was not allowed to remove any trees — dead or alive — without a proper permit. Still, the space where the dead birches had once lain remained, an area that was now covered with snow, leaf debris, and mud. It was an okay hiding space if he could make quick work of it, a task that would be doubly difficult in the cold and the dark.

Denny was halfway through digging a hole in the back and filling it with the combination of dust and shredded paper when a cruiser pulled up, now for the second time in one day. Denny pulled out his phone to look at the time. He had been working in the dark with a headlamp, trying to attract the least amount of attention possible from the neighbors, who tended to call Conservation at the drop of a hat, though Denny suspected that the cruiser had nothing to do with the neighbors and everything to do with whatever other mess he had stepped in.

The car pulled all the way to the end of the driveway, right near where Denny's shed stood. Headlights on, glaring angrily at the shed itself. A dark figure got out, but the car engine remained on, with steam billowing up; it was that cold out. Denny, standing back in the woods, found himself shivering, from the cold, yes, but also in anticipation of whatever lay ahead. A reckoning, he figured. Two men in the night.

He heard boots crunching through the snow, even though he could not see the face of the shadow that approached. But he already knew it was Sticks. And then a voice called out in recognition. "Plummer, you there?"

Denny stopped. Nothing much he could do now besides admit that he was out in the woods, shoveling dirt into a hole in the middle of the night. Certainly nothing suspicious about that, unless you were a cop investigating exactly the kind of thing that might look suspicious, like a person shoveling dirt into the woods in the middle of the night, in January, in Massachusetts.

"Yep, back here," Denny said. No use lying about it now. Sticks could see the headlamp anyway. It wasn't exactly inconspicuous.

"Whatcha got back there? Evidence?" Sticks came closer and shielded his eyes from the headlamp.

"I wouldn't say so, no," Denny said, putting the shovel back into the wheelbarrow. "Honestly, I just do clearing by night so Conservation won't get on my case. You know how it is."

"Actually," Sticks said, "I do." The Hamilton and Boxford Conservation Commissions were notorious for busting homeowners for clearing their own land without permission. Remove a dead tree from protected land and you were looking at a hefty fine, and it wasn't unusual for homeowners to do yardwork by cover of night to avoid nosy neighbors and the watchful eye of the town.

Denny stepped back, admiring the wheelbarrow as if it were a piece of art. He took some satisfaction in the clear irritation it brought to Sticks, this back-and-forth, even if they did agree on the Conservation Commission. Ordinarily, Denny wouldn't be so smug with a cop, but here the man was, on his property, snooping around in the middle of the night. Eat or be eaten was how he saw it.

"You know, Conservation aside, you've got a wheelbarrow of dirt out here in the woods in the middle of a January night," Sticks said, taking a step closer. "A normal person might find that a little...odd." He made a sniffing noise, as if he was trying to detect something in the air.

"I might ask you what would make an officer take a casual drive over to a civilian's house in the middle of a January night," Denny spat back. He took a step closer. The headlamp, he knew, was making it difficult for Sticks to see, and the more difficult it was for Sticks to see, the less likely he was to stumble onto the mix of sawdust and shredded paper that Denny was not-so-artfully hiding in the wheelbarrow.

"I'm sure you're not accusing me of anything untoward, Mr. Plummer," Sticks said, shielding his eyes again. "After all, you did scare off one of my junior officers today. Or maybe you've already forgotten?"

"You mean the kid you sent over here to browbeat me into giving up my wife's personal belongings, when I still haven't gotten back the last load of stuff I handed over to the Hamilton Police Department?" It could go on like this for hours, Denny was relatively certain. He wanted to be delicate with Sticks, but he also wasn't about to be walked over, not on his own property. This had gone too far, and the surprise visit — two surprise visits, if you counted the earlier one — had just about pushed him to the limit.

Sticks put his arms down by his side. In the dark, Denny couldn't be sure, but it almost looked like the officer was reaching for his firearm.

"I'd be careful, Mr. Plummer, about what you're insinuating." It was now the second time Sticks had used words just like these, the first having been over at the Agawam, many months earlier.

Denny thought about asking about the gun but thought better of it. *Best to let a sleeping firearm lie,* he thought to himself. Instead, he took up a different line of inquiry, one that he knew would also rile the officer. But at least it stayed far away from guns.

"Seems like a lot of people around here need to be careful. Isn't that right, Officer Malkin? My wife needed to be careful. What were those words you used? *Ligature marks,* right? A lot of coincidences, though. Her running for the president of the PTO and all.

If I were a more suspicious person, I might start thinking that there were some people in this town who didn't much like the things that my wife was getting into."

Sticks took a step forward. Maybe Denny had overstepped after all. "I was driving by here, you know, on duty, and I saw a strange light coming from the woods. I stopped to investigate."

"Are you explaining it to me, or to the people who will come investigating later on?" Denny said. His voice was steady, but he was worried now. He was staring into the dark eyes of power, the kind of person who could find a woman dead in a river and hide the truth because the truth betrayed secrets that he didn't want revealed, secrets that he knew too much about. Inside, Louisa and Ben were sleeping. Push too far and Denny might find himself frozen in the haul-out, poor Ophelia's forever soulmate, just another senseless tragedy, a man claimed by nature. It was clear to Denny now: There were no accidents, no coincidences, not in Hamilton. Ellen Wilson's brother, Sticks, this small-town cop, had staged this poor performance from the start. A prime suspect to divert attention from a murder had given plenty of time for the trail to grow cold. Now Denny was a nuisance. An interference. A man who needed to be handled. And Sticks was ready to do the handling.

"Plummer, don't make things difficult," he said. He had dropped the honorific, a sign of his growing irritation. "I'm just telling you how these sorts of things sometimes play out." His voice was gravelly, gruff. He sounded like a television cop, Denny thought, full of bluster, like he had memorized lines from crime shows.

"I'm sorry to have wasted your time, Officer," Denny said. "You'll find nothing amiss here. I'm happy to call dispatch and let them know if you'd like." He stuck out a hand, a temporary peacemaker. If he could hold Sticks off until morning, maybe there was a chance for both of them.

Surprising maybe even Denny, Sticks grabbed the hand with his own meaty paw and pulled down. For a second, it was just a generous gesture between two men, but then the officer pulled Denny in, and even with the headlamp shining in his coal-black eyes, he whispered, "It's cold at the haul-out, Plummer. January is the worst time of year." He released Denny's hand and gave the man a little shove backward, making him stumble into the muddy snow. Denny watched Sticks disappear then, a silhouette fading toward the headlights. Sticks was a problem that needed solving.

It was a fitful sleep, haunted by ghosts. Anna came to him that night, maybe the memory of her or maybe whatever remained of her in the house. Had he disturbed the dead, he wondered, riled her in destroying her papers? Neither he nor Anna ever had much use either for religion or for any sort of belief in God. They had passed this floating agnosticism along to their children, the bombastic, celebratory mood that accompanied all holidays but that omitted any mention of a host. No one being could have created a world as complex as theirs, they reasoned. Couples quarreled over all kinds of things — money and sex and communication — and surely Anna and Denny had their share of battles, but one thing they never fought over was whether or not God was in the details of their lives. When a person was gone, that was it. Evaporated. Dust.

Well, that was what he had believed. But Anna was everywhere now. He could almost see her in his peripheral vision, and sometimes, if the light was dim in the evening, he could swear she was there, sitting at the table, or curled up on the couch. Now, waking up from a terrible night's sleep, Denny was convinced that he had been visited by her, that he had somehow disturbed the dead. What did she want, this spirit, this being who was not at rest? What could he bring her that might provide some semblance of peace?

It was early, the time of day that Anna had always preferred to keep to herself. Hank was curled up in her space on the bed.

"Is it warm where you are?" Denny said to the dark. "Did you feel it when you went?"

"I didn't feel a thing, Denny. You don't have to worry about that." It was just a voice in the dark.

"Did you know? Before? Did you know what was going to happen?"

"I think everyone knows when they are going to die. Maybe not right away. But everyone has an idea that death is coming for them."

He reached out in the dark, but there was nothing, only the cold chill of the room. She liked it to be set to 65 degrees. They never fought about God, but they fought about the thermostat, especially in winter. Even in the year since her death, he had not been able to will himself to set the temperature higher.

"I am doing my best," he said. "I miss you. I don't know why I haven't said it more." But who was there to say it to, really? His kids, who were too young to understand? Inside, every time he breathed, he felt pierced by glass. That was what it was like, having Anna ripped from him in this unpredictable way. She was supposed to be here. They were supposed to have time. Summers. Ski seasons. Long evenings looking out at the blushing dusk. People were always wanting more, filling emptiness, failing to see what was right there, but what he wouldn't give now for a chance to do the whole thing over again. Rewind the tape, start from the beginning, and sink into every stupid last moment, get drunk on the things that hadn't even mattered.

"I know," the voice said.

"Is it enough?" he asked.

"Is anything ever enough?"

Of course nothing was ever enough. That was classic Anna. Nothing was ever enough for her. It was why she had abandoned art. Gerhard Richter. He was a better artist, and so she had abandoned her own lesser skill and instead became a capable copywriter, turning the often-unfinished ideas of others into brilliant phrases and paragraphs. Pouring her artistic skills into projects that bore no true trace of her. Nothing was ever enough for her, the world could not contain her, and that was her problem: It was never, ever enough. Denny loved her for all of that, for her grandness, for being too bold and beautiful and wild and wide-eyed to even be contained. He loved her because of all the ideas that she had swirling around inside her, the things she was too afraid to put on a canvas, the pieces that she felt no one would ever really understand or appreciate. All that raw material was now gone; she was now gone. He felt it: the rawness, the echo of grief, its true reverberation, how it could just go on forever and ever. The things he had never told her, the life together they would never finish — the thought of it swelled inside him. A murder is an elimination, he thought, not just of a person, but also of a marriage, of a family, of an entire way of life.

"You were enough," he said. "You were so much more than enough."

"Don't go getting all sentimental on me now, Denny," the voice said.

He laughed, in spite of himself. A slip of light was starting to appear at the base of the trees. Hank was snoring still. In the last year, the dog had lost his spark.

"I'll untangle it, you know," Denny said.

"There's one more thing," the voice said. "But you're close."

Anna — or whatever figment of Denny's imagination was approximating her in this early-morning hour — was right. Denny had scratched the itch, and he had slowly pieced together what he believed to be a reasonable explanation for how he had gotten here, to this place, alone in a bed, a widower and father of two. His wife had been targeted. Of this he was certain. He now knew the players and their roles, he thought, but he was not yet sure of their motivations, or how they related to one another. And he still wasn't sure how he was going to be able to prove any of this to anyone. Sticks, Denny now knew, was either involved or was protecting the people who were, meaning that the police department was just as dangerous as anyone else in Hamilton. And if Anna had somehow been lured to the haul-out by friends and foes without her own husband knowing, and had remained missing for days, who was to say that the same could not happen to him, too?

Some guiding force pointed him, in the ink-dark, to his computer, where he logged in, once more, to his wife's email account. He had read every email up and down, he thought, but maybe he had missed something. Had he? He could feel his body overtaken by something – grief, or the heavy weight of a spirit inhabiting him, who could tell? – guiding him toward the search bar. Email search: "secret society."

And there it was, an email he had never seen before, dated December 28, 2022, from an account called anonmouse@gmail.com.

> Dear Anna,
>
> Excuse the intrusion, but I'm a concerned *mouse* worried that you have gotten into something that you cannot get yourself out of. I can't say much about this over email (or at all), but the PTO is more than what it looks like. It's a secret society of women working behind-the-scenes to get their kids into elite colleges. They will do anything—anything—to make sure that their kids succeed at the expense of others. These women have political connections. They have connections to law enforcement. THEY ARE RUTHLESS. Do not trust anyone.

It's more than a school dance. It's a social structure. The promises they make do come true. They've never had a non-member as president. If you were to win, the danger of you discovering their secrets would be too great.

Be careful out there.

—Anon Mouse

Only a few days before she disappeared — before she died — Denny now knew, Anna had received this final piece of information. The PTO was more than just an organization of well-to-do parents. It was a society where members conspired to pay a tithe in exchange for the ultimate certainty: entrance into the right schools for their children, a lifestyle that was acceptable in towns like these. With Mimi at the helm, all of this remained private and closed off. She had at her disposal, Denny knew, the Hamilton Police Department, and probably plenty of other high-powered organizations. It was unclear to Denny how far up the food chain her power went.

As was Anna's way, she had written back a few hours later. It was right there in the thread.

Dear Mouse,

Tell me your secrets.

—Anna

The anonymous emailer waited two days to reply.

Dear Anna,

I've been thinking of the best way to respond to you, so I hope you can forgive me for taking my time. I'm putting myself in some danger by telling you all of this. I'm probably putting you in some danger, too. Please take care of yourself. Please take care of your family. I can't tell you who I am or how I know what I know, but I hope that you trust that it's true.

This covert operation has gone on in Hamilton for a long time. The kids who get into Ivy League schools get in with the help of the PTO. The parents who pay to belong to this organization do it with the understanding that they are buying a ticket to the future.

In the early '90s, a woman named Pam Jansen moved to Hamilton from Wenham. Her daughter was rejected from a bunch of schools: Tufts, Harvard, MIT, Penn, Columbia. It was one of those mysteries. The girl was perfect on paper. In every club. Perfect GPA. Sophisticated. Smart. It just didn't make sense. Pam thought that maybe there was a better way for parents of means to make sure that their kids could bypass these archaic rules that enslave us to college administrators. So, when her son was a sophomore, in 1992, she came up with a bribery scheme to help him. The PTO just happened to be a convenient way to conceal her tracks, with their built-in connections to schools, financial incentives, and conduits between parents.

Ever since Pam, the PTO has essentially been a cover operation. The president is elected, and she appoints a vice-president, secretary, and treasurer. The organization has a list of vetted contacts. People within the community who know and support them. People in the state. Senators. Representatives. People who can determine futures. The master list of members and supporters is saved in a file on one laptop that always remains with the president. The four PTO principals have access, but only the president takes the computer home. The documents are never transferred. There's a unique payroll system. It's entirely off-the-books. They're ghosts.

Members pay for the privilege of getting in, and the PTO is very selective about the process. I could spend all day giving you a primer on how the operation works, but the truth is, you don't need to know all of this (and the less you know, the better off you are). What you need to know is that they don't want you to run because you threaten their ability to do what they have been doing, which is control their own futures and the futures of the people who pay into their club.

I hope this is helpful, and I'm sorry that I can't tell you more. These people are dangerous. These people will do anything for power and success.

Don't trust anyone. Look around every corner. And stay away from the PTO. I'm not kidding when I say that they're dangerous.

In good health.

—Your Faithful Mouse

After that, Anna wrote back twice more, but it was into the void; no more emails arrived. Denny had never needed a sounding board so badly, had never wished for a partner so fervently. He had always been solitary in his work, the kind of artist who thrived on time spent alone in a shed, but this kind of problem was bigger than him, bigger than Anna. It was a problem that bubbled beneath the crust of a respectable-looking town. There was a reason that Anna couldn't tackle it herself, even though she was strong-willed and bold. Unstoppable force, immovable object. Which was stronger in the end? It was the force: The force would win. Anna was just another object in the way, and they had numbers, so many of them, pushing her out of the way, making her yield: She had no choice but to yield.

Denny now realized that his wife had stumbled onto genuinely grave danger, the kind of danger that could get a person killed. A secret society might be hard to believe, but there wasn't much about any of this that was easy to believe, and if his revelation about Life Time and the pool incident with Louisa had taught him anything, it was that Mimi Mar was cold and unyielding, like New Hampshire granite. Whatever mess had started with the Ziti with Your Sweetie Dance and had escalated with the PTO elections may have been only that: a mess. But the minute that Anna discovered a wide and flowing river of deceit, that just may well have sealed her fate.

The Gerhard Richter painting that had followed Anna around for so many years, Denny knew, was called *Candle,* or *Kerze* in German. In 2011, it was sold to a private collector for over eleven million pounds. Sometimes when Anna was feeling bad about having abandoned some of her creative pursuits, she looked the painting up on the Internet and stared at it. Denny had caught her doing this before. She would close the browser just as he was walking into the room, but he knew. This was one of the things he knew about his wife: that she had some regrets, and that these regrets lingered. They had a long half-life.

And maybe that candle, with its tormenting glow, kept her thinking of other things. She wasn't painting, but she was planning. Planning to make Hamilton better. Planning on ushering in a better generation of kids. Always planning. Denny could see the candle himself now, the flame slightly blurred.

"When the time is right, I'll be here to help you," the voice said. It was Anna's voice, or it was his voice, or it was just a whisper in the emerging light. But Denny knew that he would put the pieces together. Anna had left a trail for him to find, breadcrumbs leading him to a destination.

"Thank you," he said to the ghosts he didn't believe in. "Thank you."

One year. At the bottom of the stairs, Denny looked at the markings on the wall where he had notched the growth of his children, now a year without their mother. Louisa had grown in leaps and bounds. Anna had never been tall — diminutive in stature but never in substance, she liked to say. But Louisa was proving to be a counterpoint, sprouting faster than her father could account for. Ben was a smaller, softer version of his parents. Was it Denny's imagination, or was his son a little quieter and more reserved now? He was sensitive to the world around him, and he could recite obscure facts and figures about it.

"The lion's mane is the longest jellyfish in the world," Ben said over breakfast. The house felt more empty than usual, like a hole had opened up that morning, just for them.

"No, it's the Portuguese man-of-war," Louisa said.

"It's the lion's mane!" Ben said. He knew about these things. His best friend from school, Liam, was as studious and knowledgeable as he was when it came to sea animals and their accompanying factoids. "It can grow to be almost as big as a person."

"Disgusting," Louisa said.

Denny didn't find it disgusting, though. He was fascinated by what lurked below in nature, by how other species survived. The ocean, so calm and serene on its surface, hid so many secrets beneath. You never knew what you might find if you dipped a toe below. A black-tipped shark, hunting for prey. A school of angel fish, dancing in the afternoon light. Or a lion's mane jellyfish, tentacles searching for something to hold on to. *We are all just full of secrets,* Denny thought. *Every last one of us.* Anna had been full of secrets, and he had his secrets, too, even now, a year later.

He was still reeling from the ghost. Was she real? Was he? Now it was time, Denny knew, to put the last pieces together, to make right what had been made wrong a whole year ago. The center of his world had been set askew, corrupted. It was up to him to correct course.

All those sea creatures were more dangerous than they looked. Anna would have used the word *insidious.* The danger was the kind you couldn't see immediately. Maybe a bear looked ferocious, its fangs glistening, threatening to draw blood. But it was the jellyfish that could get you. Wasn't it the box jelly, after all, that could kill a person with just a single point of contact? Wasn't the box jelly the creature that had defeated the indefatigable Diana Nyad, who had doggedly pursued the swim between Cuba and Florida multiple times before finally achieving her goal?

Box jellyfish crept up in the middle of the night, caught unlucky swimmers by surprise, injected them with venom so poisonous and toxic that they could not go on. The venom was a paralytic, entering the bloodstream swiftly and effectively. Anna had found herself, too, amid a community of box jellies, women so swift and poisonous that extrication was impossible. You could scream, but who was there to listen, after all? It was a sea full of them, box jellies, pulsing in the night.

Sticks, of course, was a lost cause, and he wasn't going to get anywhere with Mimi. But Denny wondered if he might still have some luck with Di. Her husband, Mark, worked long days in Boston as a corporate lawyer. He wouldn't be home until evening. Denny considered a peace offering, something that would feel organic and natural. He never stopped by Di's house, not even when she and Anna were at the peak of their friendship, and it would stretch the limits of credulity to think that he would be doing so now, unless he needed something from her.

Denny was good at making people need him, though. That was the art of being a furniture maker: He produced beautiful things that people didn't know they needed that they suddenly made space for in their lives, that they suddenly had to have. He could make people fall in love with items, like the Windsor chair that he had recently made with no distinct owner in mind. It was just sitting in the work shed, waiting for someone to find a home for it.

As the kids continued to fight over the lion's mane and the Portuguese man-of-war, Denny thought about the Windsor chair left in the shed, and how after the bus came he would load it into the back of the Jeep and drive it over to Di's. He knew, in a deep and hot kind of way, that Di had been involved somehow with Anna's death. She had known. She had been involved. She had been there. She had helped cover it up. Di, who had curled up against his wife in the years when she was still in the process of becoming a person. He knew it as surely as he knew anything, even without proof, even without words.

He needed to see her, the cold and calculating look in her eyes, the loop her mind took when he said *Anna Plummer.* If she asked for an explanation about the chair, he would just look at her the way she had looked at him the day before, with a mixture of want and need. It was a chair that needed a place to live, and he was a person who was in the business of delivering to people the things that they weren't quite sure they wanted.

Denny didn't see Di's car in the driveway when he pulled in, but the lights on the first floor were on and a cotton ball of smoke was rising from the chimney. One of Anna's favorite parts of Di's so-called estate was the floor-to-ceiling stone fireplace in the home's family room. She said she wasn't jealous of the things Di had, but he could tell that the fireplace was the one thing that his wife envied.

"I don't want a house like that, but I want a fireplace like that," she often said, knowing that they could never have either.

He was careful to open the back of the Jeep in such a way that the chair didn't slide. He didn't want to scratch it, nor did he want to risk it slipping out, since the driveway was graded. He was parked slightly uphill, and the chair tipped toward his stomach, and he caught it at an awkward angle, assuming the wood's full weight. A chair like that was heavy, substantial. It could last a lifetime if you treated it well.

Di must have heard him in the driveway, because she opened the door and called to him from the granite steps. "What's going on here?" she called. She wore a matching gray sweatsuit that, though generic, somehow looked intentional on her. A delicate string of pearls lay close to her neckline, and her blond hair was pulled back from her face with a wide cloth headband, also gray. "I wasn't expecting company," she said, gesturing to her outfit by way of apology.

"I didn't mean to come by unannounced," he said, repositioning the chair and hoisting it up from the bottom so that he could carry it and still walk straight ahead while talking. "I wanted to bring you this."

Di took a step back into the entrance of her house. She appraised the chair, looking surprised. "A Windsor?" she said. "Well, it's beautiful. What should I do with it?"

"Anything you want." Denny was stopped at the front step. "May I?" he said. Di had blocked passage any farther and was looking the chair up and down.

"Oh, yes, yes. I'm sorry." She stepped back, letting him in.

The chair was elegantly turned with a deep stain. She could bring it into the first-floor study, but instead she stood staring at it. Denny could smell the fire blazing.

"Did you want me to bring this anywhere for you?" he asked.

"Maybe just leave it for right now," she said. "I was actually . . ." She trailed off. Denny's tactic of offering a gift did not seem to have softened the visit. Di was in a hurry to get him out. The fire. The notebook. He wondered if the two were related.

"I see. Well, I guess I'll be going then."

"Denny," she said. She reached out for his arm. For a moment, he thought she was going to say something tender. He looked at her, at her deep green eyes. Something electric flashed in them. She paused and held his arm for a second and then dug her hand into his arm. "After this, it's over," she said. "You don't come back here." He moved to extract his arm, but she held on tight, her nails digging in. "Walk away from this and everything goes back to the way it used to be. Do you understand me?"

He didn't want to hurt her, so he spun around to release her grip, and noticed, as he did, a small table near the door. On it, there was a crystal bowl. A familiar glint of gold caught his eye — what looked like a button. As soon as he saw it, Di's eyes followed his.

"What is this?" he asked. He reached out and grabbed it. The button was the same as the one Mary had held up in the light of the sunroom. Tiny and gold. The button from a cashmere sweater. There were no coincidences, is what Anna would have said.

Di opened her palm, and Denny handed her the button. How did she know that he would give it back? Like Anna, she, too, was a witch. Her power was intoxicating. "Call it a memento," Di said. "Let's just say that a few of us have them. To remember what binds us to one another." She rolled the button in her fingers and made a fist, as if to say, *All gone.*

"What now?" Denny asked.

"Now you go home," Di said. "Live your life. Move on. This never happened."

"And what if I don't agree to that?"

"Things will probably be better if you do," she said.

"But it did happen. You took something from me," Denny said. "I want to know why."

"You're too trusting," Di said. "You open your heart so easily. I like that about you, actually. Anna did, too."

"If you thought I was onto you, why didn't you try to stop me?" Denny asked.

"Oh, I did," Di said. "We all did. How quickly you've forgotten about your brakes."

Denny nodded. In retrospect, that made perfect sense. Di, who knew him best, could have gotten into the garage herself. How silly of him not to have seen it.

"It wasn't that I didn't love Anna, by the way," Di said, offhandedly. "That was complicated."

"There are just some things that you love more, though, right? Like making sure your kids get into Harvard."

Di looked at him with a cold and clinical glare. She clearly hadn't expected him to know so much about her — or about the PTO. "I don't know what you're talking about," she said.

"It's funny," he said. "You don't have much sentimentality when it comes to protecting what you did. But you'll go to such lengths to protect the PTO." For a moment, he considered mentioning the secret society but thought twice. There was danger everywhere; powerful people surrounded Di. He could get hurt the way Anna had, and he knew exactly how close he was to finding himself at the haul-out.

"Denny, I'm going to give you some advice that's for your own good," Di said. "Forget that we ever had this conversation." She took a step forward. She was not strong enough to hurt him, but he saw something in her just then — something unrecognizable. There were consequences to knowing the truth, she was saying. Whatever answers lay on the other side, he didn't want them, did he?

"Stay away from my family, Di. That's not a request." He turned his back and walked out.

"You have a good day, Denny Plummer. I do hope to see you around."

The heavy door closed behind him with a whisper.

Denny went for a long, restorative drive out toward the Artichoke, where Anna used to run. It was far, so far from Hamilton. He had always marveled at the fact that she had gone all the way to Newburyport just to get out of the car to stretch her legs. But people love what they know, and she knew that, every crest and turn of the road, where the flowers sprang up and where the road dipped down and even where the tar needed replacing. No one could have loved a place more than Anna loved that spit of road, and now it would never again know her sweat or her laughter, the way her own unique gait sounded coming around a bend at magic hour. They had taken that from the world.

He drove the loop twice, caught a shy doe hesitating and then bounding out in front of a snowy beat of bushes, before making the winding loop back. It was late in the day. Denny had gotten nearly nothing done, besides delivering one single Windsor chair, confirming his own worst instincts, and battled with himself about what to do next. Conclusion: He had no idea.

Pulling up to the house, he noticed something strange. There was something wrong with the front door. Normally, Denny went in through the garage, but this time he parked on the side of the house and walked up the path that flanked it. The door had been forced open, allowing in the dusty late-day light. He barely touched it and it swung open, almost as if it had been expecting him, as if the house knew he would be coming.

The house, of course, had been expecting him. Or someone had been. Because there, in the hallway, Denny saw the final warning. Hank lay motionless, eyes shut, a dried pool of blood beneath him. It was too late. It was always too late.

Chapter 28

DI CALLED TO see if she wanted to come over for a bit in the afternoon before heading out for dinner, and she was relieved; she wanted to talk about the emails, and she wanted to talk about them with Di. Besides the conversation with Mary, Anna had kept the information to herself, except for scribbling down a few notes in a moleskin. The women of Hamilton, she now believed, had something precious to protect, and it was the well-guarded futures of their progeny. By getting in the middle of the natural order of wealth and privilege, Anna Plummer had gummed up the machine.

Ben and Louisa were playing a game where neither one of them could talk until one of the adults said some kind of magic word. Blackout or Fake Out or Black Magic – Anna couldn't remember what it was, but both kids had surrounded her in the kitchen, pulling at her as she tried to scramble upstairs to get ready, their lips pulled taut.

"What? What *is it*?" she said to them, but they refused to speak, waving hands in front of their lips.

"Mmmmm," Louisa mumbled.

"Mmmmm," Ben said, by way of response.

Whatever that was — that game — it was Denny's problem now, Anna thought. Upstairs, she pulled out a pair of black jeans that she almost never wore and a black short-sleeve cashmere sweater. She had bought it a few years ago, one of those sweaters that had no true season. The night was cold, but why not, she figured, fingering the gold buttons that ran all the way up to the neckline. It was pretty and she felt bad about having spent so much money on it. She switched out her diamond studs for chandelier-style earrings — a little old-school, but she was into it — and pulled on black boots with a heel and an ermine-colored sweater for over the whole outfit, a sort of slouchy thing that she could at least use to keep her warm until she got where she was going. Hair back in a quick ponytail, she looked at herself in the mirror (acceptable, yes) and bid adieu to her own reflection.

Denny had fallen prey to the kids' game. How they had persuaded him to say the secret word, she would never know, but they were dancing around him in the kitchen now.

"I won, I won," Ben was squealing in delight, meaning that Louisa was appropriately miserable. His gain was always her loss, as was the way with siblings of a certain age.

"He cheated," she said, stomping a foot. "He drew a picture for dad! Do-over! I want a do-over!"

"You didn't say I couldn't," Ben said, sensing the injustice of a long-awaited win against his big sister being stripped away from him. "Dad? No one said! It's not fair!" He erupted into a pool of tears. For a second, Anna had the sensation that she was outside her own body, watching the three of them from beyond the kitchen, her tiny and perfect son, her precocious daughter, her temporarily hapless husband who couldn't figure out how to soothe them both. But she was just as quickly snapped back into the reality of herself.

"It's okay," she said from the hall, and they all turned to look at her. "Louisa, your brother won, fair and square, okay?" Anna's word was gospel, and they all knew it. Louisa would sulk, but she would accept her mother's decree. Ben shook off the bout of emotion. Denny rose to face the kitchen island.

"Where are you headed and what time will you be back?" Denny asked.

There were two boxes of Kraft macaroni and cheese on the counter, Wednesday-night dinner for three.

"Out with friends. I'll be back late. Don't wait up," Anna said. She walked over and kissed each of her children on the head. Louisa smelled like the watermelon shampoo, Ben slightly of sweat. When she leaned into Denny, she smelled sawdust, cold air from the shed.

"Have a great time at Bradford," she said. "See you tomorrow." Then she walked down to the garage, where the recently repaired Volkswagen was waiting.

Di's normally well-lit driveway — she kept lights on even in late afternoon — was dark. This struck Anna as strange. Also, there was a car that she didn't recognize parked in front of the carriage house, a black Mercedes GLS 450, with tinted windows. Only one light was on in the entire house, and it looked like it was in the back, although the porch light had been left on. This was also strange. Still, Anna didn't think too much of it as she parked the car in the pea gravel driveway, which Di had just had redone last summer. Walking to the granite steps, Anna stopped twice to unearth the small stones from the heels of her boots, and in so doing noticed a sound coming from somewhere. Was it the woods behind Di's house? It sounded like a rustling or even a dragging sound. Anna could not quite tell. For a minute, she held her breath, not even in a conscious way, until, suddenly aware of the bruising cold, she moved forward to the steps.

The front of Di's house was hulking, slabs of granite that had failed to impress Anna, three pieces so large it had taken a crane to deliver them. They were graduated in size, organic and beautiful, shaped by a mason but not absurdly so; they were meant, Di always said, to look like they had been plucked from the ground and placed there by accident. The mahogany door had two gaslit sconces on either side and a brass lobster claw knocker on the front, but no one ever used it, preferring the bell instead. Tonight, though, Anna held the cold, unforgiving metal in her hand and allowed it to thunder in a satisfying boom. She could see no light coming from the front entrance, but Di, also dressed smartly in black — turtleneck sweater, black jeans, similar black heeled boots — appeared breathless, as if from nowhere.

"Come in! So sorry, I was in the back," she said, ushering Anna through the door.

Anna stood in the large vestibule, allowing her eyes to adjust to the dim light. "Di, can you turn on the light?" she said.

"I'm afraid I can't do that," her friend said. Her voice was different.

Then, Anna felt the way she imagined a sailboat felt when the sails were being drawn down. No more wind. She was being brought to her knees by some external force, and it took her a minute, in the dim and hazy light, to understand that she had been grabbed from behind, that someone had put pressure on her in a place where she was being drawn into unconsciousness, that the things that were familiar were at once not familiar at all. The ground was where her face was, the ceiling was at a funny angle, and then her eyes closed, only to abruptly open a few minutes later, when she found herself sitting upright in a chair, a belt cinched around her waist, her head aching something awful.

"Where am I?" she asked. At first she thought she was alone. The room was very bright and unfamiliar, but then, no, she realized she knew it. It was the room above Di's garage, the so-called carriage house, which Di had started renovating during the pandemic but had never finished. They had envisioned it together: a plush room for visitors with oak floors and custom built-ins, but the momentum had waned, like so many other pandemic projects. Now the room was just a space where spare items collected. Empty Amazon boxes. Rugs that Di didn't want any longer but that she didn't know what to do with. Things that had no use in the main house but that she wasn't quite ready to part with.

Because the carriage house was not yet finished, it had no real decor yet. The light was harsh, just a wired construction bulb that hung from the ceiling. Anna looked around and saw that she was sitting on an old Windsor chair — probably just another thing that Di had decided she no longer had any use for — in the room's center. Her arms were taped loosely behind her back, and as she tried to swing them to get herself free, she heard footsteps coming up the stairs. Soon she was joined by a suite of people. Di walked in first, her dear old friend. The betrayal ran deep. Anna wanted to say something, but she realized her mouth had gone dry.

Behind Di came more people. Karen Pistoulia, also dressed in black, was next. Karen wore leggings and a tight-fitting sweater, along with a skullcap; she had tucked her hair up into it, like a common criminal. Behind Karen, Anna watched Ellen Wilson emerge from the shadows. She looked sullen and gray, like the idea of this had made her sick. Had she missed the memo about the attire? Her green oversize sweatshirt didn't comport with her fellow kidnappers' outfits. She wore her hair back in a taut braid.

When Mimi Mar walked up next, clad in Lululemon leggings, a zip-up hoodie, and a black Gucci fanny pack, Anna was not surprised. But she was surprised to see the final woman ascending the stairs. Mary Langley, in boots that came up nearly to the thigh. Mary, who had tried to warn her about Di. Here she was, part of whatever this was. In on it, too.

Mimi cleared her throat. She wasn't about to cede leadership to anyone else, Anna figured, or not now. "Maybe you're wondering why you're here?" Mimi asked.

Anna said nothing, just looked straight ahead, at the space where she and Di had planned for the built-ins. Not Hague Blue like her own office, but a mint green that they had selected from the same Farrow & Ball catalogue. It was called Middle Ground.

Mimi walked over to Anna and turned her hand into a small fist. She tucked the fist under Anna's chin. "We did warn you, didn't we? Gave you plenty of chances to back off of this little... experiment? Didn't we, Di?"

Had Di winced at the mention of her name? Di Maguire, her lifelong friend, gone over to the other side. It hadn't taken much, just the temptation of power, just the threat of ruin in one small New England town. Or maybe it was all those years of jealousy, built up over time. *You aren't that great.* It was true, Anna thought. She wasn't that great. She should have reminded Di. Neither one of them was really that great, when it came down to it.

Anna swallowed. She wondered if she could will herself to speak. She opened her mouth, but no sound came out. She swallowed a second time, and this time she was able to eke out a few words. "What are you going to do?"

"What are we going to do?" Mimi asked. She walked around Anna in a circle. "Karen, what are we going to do?"

"We are going to find a solution to a problem," Karen said, in a singsong kind of voice. Karen had always irritated Anna more than the others, maybe because she had no distinct personality. Mimi's stooge. Then, out of nowhere, she started actually singing: "How Do You Solve a Problem Like Maria?" from *The Sound of Music.*

"Karen, please shut the fuck up," Mimi, who was clearly over it, said.

Karen's face turned into a frown. Anna could see she had just been trying to lighten the mood. None of the women seemed to know what to do. Mary stood paralyzed at the top of the stairs. Di stood in the center of the room, but she was also not moving. And Ellen stood looking out the window at the driveway, her back to Anna. Only Mimi had the fortitude to look straight into Anna's eyes.

"Now what?" Anna asked. Her arms ached from their awkward position.

"How much do you know about me?" Mimi asked. She had walked over toward Anna again. This time, she stopped directly in front of her, and squatted, looking right into her eyes.

"I know that this is what you want," Anna said. "To be Queen."

Mimi ignored this. "You don't know as much about me as you think. I grew up in a shithole town in Maryland." She offered up a little laugh. "I don't want to be *Queen.* I just don't want to be… what I was when I was there. I consider myself fully reformed."

"From what? Poverty?" *If I can keep her talking,* Anna thought, *maybe I can figure out an end to this story that isn't tragic.*

"Yes, actually. You hit the nail on the head. I didn't want my financial situation to define me. And now it doesn't," Mimi said, standing up and brushing herself off. She patted Anna's head in an act of faux kindness. "I had nothing. And now I have plenty. Given the two circumstances, I prefer the latter."

Anna's throat was sore and dry, but she knew she had Mimi engaged. Better to keep talking.

"It's sort of extreme, don't you think?" she asked.

"Extreme is food banks. Extreme is searching the couch cushions for gas money. We all have our own definition of extreme," Mimi said.

It was hard to argue with a psychopath who also made a genuinely good point about socioeconomic disparity, Anna thought.

"Can I ask you anything I want?" Anna said.

"At this point, I suppose it doesn't matter."

"What *is* the PTO?" Anna asked.

"I inherited it from someone before me. I won't bother with

names, because I don't think they're important. But the PTO is a group of parents — let's face it, mothers — who pay a premium price for certain... *guarantees.*"

"You inherited it from Laura Cox." Anna said. It was a declaration, not a question. Anna had learned a lot from Mouse's emails, but not everything. Was it worthwhile to show her antagonist how much she knew, or to hold back? Would they let her go either way? Anna considered this. She was sitting in the equivalent of Dexter's death den, minus the plastic sheathing, and she had a feeling she wasn't going anywhere anytime soon, no matter what she said. At the very least, she wanted to hear the parts of the story she hadn't yet heard.

"A regular Sherlock Holmes," Mimi said, smiling.

"And the point of this is to help with, what, college admission?" Anna asked.

"Oh, that's just one of the perks!" Mimi said. "We have connections at colleges. Our members include alumnae at the Ivies, of course. We can't promise acceptance, but we have a pretty good track record. But there are other benefits. Classes with the best teachers at Hamilton-Wenham. Improved grades for students who, shall we say, *are not thriving.* We have the *best* administrators on board, let me tell you, and they can change grades in the blink of an eye. Prime positions on sports teams. Court clerkships. Internships at the country's best magazines. Jobs at hedge funds after college. There are, of course, some other added benefits that don't necessarily have anything to do with our children. Waived speeding tickets. No jury duty. An easier time with the building department. That sort of thing. And don't think for a second that we stop there. We're a regular fucking Federalist Society. Once you're in, you're under our wing for life."

"And this is all for a hundred dollars a year, or whatever that premium membership costs?"

Mimi began to laugh. “That’s the advertised fee, Anna. There’s also an unadvertised fee — one hundred thousand dollars a year, and all your hopes and dreams come with it. But we’re closed for 2023, I’m afraid. So sorry. And anyway, you wouldn’t qualify.”

Anna stared, wide-eyed. Even with Mouse’s lengthy description, Anna had failed to get to the heart of the true cost of the PTO’s secrets — that Hamilton was pulsing with its own underground, a river of money, a river of darkness. Anna had never even thought twice about the architecture of bribery, that you could pay into a system that just bumped you up in the world, that the PTO was just a front for elevating kids — and their parents — into more decades of wealth and privilege. She thought about Harper Mar and the fact that the Top Student award had been given to the same girl, every single year. She thought about Henry, Di’s son, and about how his interests had suddenly mutated. He was into soccer now, Di had said. He was going to be goalie. He was going to be captain. He had been moved from First Grade A to First Grade B, and none of this had ever registered with Anna, except now it did; now it made sense.

“Not that I have a hundred thousand dollars, but I am wondering what otherwise disqualifies me,” Anna said.

“Ah, yes,” Mimi said. “Well, we’re extremely selective about our members. For instance, they have to be part of our *sorority*.”

“So the Chi Omega thing? That was real?”

“Sisters for life,” Mimi said. She made a symbol with her hands, crossing her index fingers and bringing her thumbs toward one another so that they nearly resembled a heart, the universal sign for Chi Omega. Had Di been in the sorority? Anna couldn’t remember. She remembered her friend pledging, but what the group had been, well, that was lost to the dust of time. But now she watched the other women as they each formed the symbol. *Chi Omega.*

“Is this some sick thing where a bunch of sorority sisters pledge in blood to uphold the virtues of their oath or something? Is that how it worked with Antonin Scalia and the Federalist Society? Are you going to tell me they're all members of Chi Omega, too?"

"Good to see you haven't lost your sense of humor, Anna," Di said. It was the first words her friend had spoken. "The fact that we are all Chi Omega is just a way of vetting trustworthy candidates. It's not some kind of blood truce. You watch too much TV."

"How many people are members of this?"

"Fifty-seven," Mimi said. "Everyone signs a non-disclosure agreement. It's legally binding."

Anna had to stop herself from laughing. *Not the place,* she told herself. The absurdity, though, of forcing people to sign an NDA for a crazy scheme that was completely illegal. Were they all idiots? Who would even enforce it? Still, they had all fallen in line, Anna supposed, fifty-seven women, which, quick math told her, came to over five million dollars. You could control a lot of officials with that kind of money, year after year.

"To be honest, this is a lot more complicated than the secret society version I was running with in my mind," Anna said.

"We prefer to be called the Generals," Mimi snapped back.

"The Generals. Whatever."

"You knew all the important parts," Di said. "And every time we tried to convince you to let it go, you just kept pursuing it."

"But you helped me!" Anna said. "You told me to run for president! You helped me plan parties!" Di, in particular, Anna thought, had been at the root of this betrayal. Di and Mary had sat beside her, supporting her, knowing that it was all a sham. Why had they done it?

"You're rigid, Anna. You've always been rigid. I knew you weren't going to give up on an idea. I told you at the very beginning that it was stupid, but you didn't want my advice," Di said. "So I figured I might as well control the narrative, if you weren't going to give it up."

That, Anna felt, was the ultimate sucker punch, the faux friendship. It was her own Chi Omega. Her sorority of sisters. All of it had been a lie.

"You suggested I go to the police! You came with me to file the report," Anna said. She wanted to hear Di say it. She wanted a full recitation of the truth.

"I thought if you felt like there was more danger, maybe you'd back off. And I knew the police wouldn't do anything," Di said.

"The police," Anna said.

Di nodded. The police, Anna now realized, were never going to take a report seriously. Not if they were on the Generals' payroll.

Anna looked over at Mary, who had until now refused to make eye contact. She realized that she had misjudged her friend. Hadn't Anna misjudged everyone, though? Friendship with Mary had been rooted in sympathy. Girl from South Hamilton, so *deserving* of Anna, but all along, it was Mary who had been sending out warning flares, telling her to get out, and Anna who had been too stubborn to listen. The silence was thick, but Anna could almost feel those words floating above, the words of admonition. *I told you to stop. I told you this was dangerous. I told you there were things you didn't want to hear.* Yeah, well, the things she didn't want to hear, to be fair, didn't seem like Skull and Bones crazy. And this shit was definitely Skull and Bones crazy.

Mary had said nothing to Anna since they arrived at the carriage house. She looked at Mary, and Mary looked back.

"I really did think we were friends," she said.

"Actually, I think you pitied me," Mary said. She wasn't entirely wrong. Anna had believed that something was *difficult* in Mary's life, that there were *money troubles* or *gambling troubles* or *addiction troubles,* the kind of troubles you just don't talk about when you're from New England. But the things that Mary had been keeping to herself had nothing to do with shame. Her buried secrets had been for want of a better future, of buying into a dream. She was socking it away, all right.

"In the end, I guess I didn't really know you," Anna said.

"I guess you didn't," Mary said. "Small house, big bank account. My husband works for the Baupost Group. You always seemed to forget that about me. You saw what you wanted to see. And I let you."

That was true, and there wasn't any point in denying it.

All of this, though: It was…ridiculous? That was the only word Anna could come up with. She would have been less surprised if Ashton Kutcher had shown up, announced that *Punk'd* was being revived, and told her it had all been a big joke. Anna wondered if this coven of women knew how insidious, weird, and, yes, crazy this all looked from the outside, or if they had operated within its limits for so long that they had just started to accept a lack of boundaries as normative.

"Does this seem normal to any of you?" she asked.

"Who has the time or patience for normal?" Mimi asked.

Maybe, Anna thought, they were all just delusional. Maybe power had made them drunk. Or maybe they just didn't care.

Anna shivered at the thought. "Just explain this to me, because I genuinely don't understand. Why would a secret society like *the Generals,* with half of Massachusetts on board, be so threatened by one person?" Anna said.

Mimi and Karen exchanged glances. "You're not the *only* irritant to us," Mimi said. "Why don't we talk about those emails. I'm sure you were wondering who sent them." She paused and walked around Anna in a circle, momentarily contemplative, maybe waiting for Anna to say something in recognition. The emails. Of course Mimi had known all along.

"That was Sarah Saunders," Mimi continued. "Our former treasurer. At some point, Sarah grew a conscience. She and her husband

and daughter moved to Winchester and started getting the state police involved. Sarah thought that since she had the entire roster of contacts saved, she could go around the order of operations."

"I can't imagine that sat well with you, Mimi," Anna said, acting as if the revelation did not bother her. Her own response was bait. But Mimi didn't go for it.

"We've worked hard," Mimi said. "This is our masterpiece." The Generals, Mimi seemed to believe, deserved to be protected — and Anna believed that she believed this. A delusion, maybe, but her delusion. *Their* delusion. Anna could empathize with the desire to create something. She had been a stalled artist herself; what would it feel like to have put something in motion in the world, something larger than herself? Probably magnetic. Probably powerful. Probably important. A feeling like that — to know that you were responsible for lifelines and futures, to know that you could make things happen — could have become addictive, and fast.

All told, Mimi said, there were 218 officials on the Generals' payroll, paid in cash, yes, though not in suitcases. It had taken a long time to establish the pipeline — nearly the entire eight years of Pamela Jansen's PTO tenure, though she had been successful in getting her son into Harvard in the end. "Pure persuasion," Mimi said, with a smile. But once the Generals were up and running, there was no stopping them. They developed a system: quarterly visits and payments, check-ins that looked like accidental meetings (Anna had witnessed one between Mimi and Representative Murphy at Honeycomb, after all), requests that never held any kind of paper trail. They recruited new members through the sorority, encouraged the right kind of people to move to town and encouraged their daughters to join Chi Omega, a pipeline operated in a circle. What were the checks for? Requisite fees, so far as their husbands knew. They might as well have been joining a country club. They were permitted to share with their spouses a little about how the organization worked, if it was required to get the money, but otherwise, the organization remained tight-lipped.

All of this made Anna wonder, once more, about Sarah Saunders, a woman she had not known, but who had jumped into her own world to warn her about the Generals. That had been a risk. "What happened with Sarah?" Anna asked.

"She was a lot like you, actually," Mimi said. "Willful. Unable to see others' perspective. She was the first PTO position holder since 1992 to leave."

There were, Anna knew, consequences to going against these women. Certainly there were consequences to going against the Chi Omega code, whatever that was.

"I assume she discovered that moving to Winchester and telling people about the Generals wasn't going to work," Anna said.

"We put an end to that. Plenty of parking tickets. Her husband got called for jury duty every month for a year. We thought she'd learned the lesson, but I guess she saw some potential in you," Mimi said.

"But she's alive?"

"We don't discuss our methods of punishment with nonmembers, Anna," Di said. "Mimi has been more than generous in giving you information about Sarah."

"It's okay, Di, we can tell her," Karen said. "Sarah and her husband have decided to move to the Midwest. At the urging of some very forceful state officials."

"I guess I still don't get why I'm here," Anna confessed. "If Sarah was the problem. I didn't go to the authorities. I fell into all of this. And I can fall right back out. You can let me go and we can all just live our lives. See each other at the Citgo and act like we don't even know each other, just like every other person in Massachusetts who doesn't give a shit about their neighbors." No one said anything, so Anna kept talking. "I could move to the Midwest. I could move to Laurel Canyon. People can start entirely new lives,"

Anna said. She realized she was begging. It was the only time she could ever recall begging for anything.

"Maybe, for some of us, this is personal," Mimi said. It was casual, but Anna could see she meant Di. Di, the girl Anna had met all those years ago, back in the shortening days of summer, back when Kaitlin Connors was still alive, back when you could still get away with jumping off Indian Rock into the Merrimack without someone calling the cops, back when riding a bike around town after dark didn't seem so dangerous. Jealousy, that was part of it — Anna could feel that in her bones — but there was something else, too, a drive to ensure that her children could live a tony Hamilton life in perpetuity. The estate, the carriage house, the rose garden in spring. Success in their futures. Anna looked at her friend, still the tallest in the room. Those emerald eyes had lost their shine. They still had a choice, all of them, to back out, to send her to the Midwest alongside Sarah Saunders, but Anna already knew that whatever was set in motion had been set in motion a long time ago, and had less to do with her being a threat and more to do with her being an irritant, and that they could eliminate her — that it was a flex. It was the ultimate proof of who they were as the Generals, the manifestation of their power. It had ripened, then rotted. Anna was here now, in a room with the fetid reminder of it.

What if, Anna suddenly realized, it wasn't about what people had to do, but about what they wanted to do? What if they were all here because of desire? What if she had misread the discomfort in the room? What if it was only her own? What if Mary had kept her close to keep her off the scent? What if Mimi had hunted her like prey? What if Karen followed the lead? What if Di had always wanted Anna gone? What if savage instincts just needed a place to run wild? What if things that had always seemed illogical and cruel and mad were just a matter of appetite?

Anna was beginning to see appetite in the eyes of her captors.

They had an appetite—not for her so much as for power. To kill: That was the ultimate wielding of power.

"You don't have to do it," Anna said. She was speaking to one of them, to all of them, to their appetites, to their egos.

"It's already done," Di said. And it was.

They say that your life flashes before your eyes when you are dying, but that is not what Anna Plummer experienced. In real time, she had been knocked unconscious. *Ligature marks,* Sticks had said, but it had been tidier than that. A Gucci belt, slipped effortlessly from Mimi Mar's cinched waist. It took two women to exert the force, but it was surprising how quickly something that had been there for so long suddenly wasn't.

The buttons were Ellen's idea. "We need some kind of contract," she said, once they were all in the car. Mimi was in the driver's seat, Karen shotgun, Di and Ellen in the captain's seats in the second row, with Mary riding in the back next to what had once been Anna. Or maybe she was still Anna. No one talked as they slipped from discussion of what they might do into the action of what they were carrying out. But now they needed proof that this had happened, and proof that they were indebted only to one another. "I just think we should... seal this somehow."

"I agree," Di said.

"What is she wearing?" Mimi asked, turning around. They hadn't left the driveway yet. The car was still off. They could all see their breath. Di had sent her children off with the nanny for the evening, banking on her husband having dinner and drinks with colleagues in Boston for the night. But their good fortune wouldn't last forever. They had to get moving. A crime was only as good as its worst perpetrator.

"Black sweater, black jeans," Mary called from the back of

the car. She looked down at Anna, noticing the sweater's details. "There are buttons here," Mary said. "Gold ones."

"That settles that," Mimi said. "Everyone gets a button. No questions asked. We can deal with it when we get there."

A silence consumed the car as Mimi engaged the engine. She drove slowly from Di's house, out through the dark roads of Hamilton and toward Ipswich. Trees rose up like skeletons, bony fingers reaching toward the sky. They passed no cars on the road, saw no other headlights as they inched toward the haul-out. It wasn't yet late, but it was cold, and most houses blew tufts of smoke from their ancient chimneys. People were at home now, safe and snug in their beds, but not the upstanding women of the Hamilton PTO. Not them. They were out and looking for a place to hide the body. They were out and looking for a place to store the evidence.

"Call your brother," Mimi told Ellen as they got closer to the Ipswich line. "Call. No texts." They couldn't risk any mistakes, not now, not after they had been so particular, not after they had come so far.

Ellen nodded in the dark. She punched a few numbers into her phone. It rang twice before someone answered on the other end. It was Sticks, who had clearly been expecting the call.

"Hi," she said a few seconds later. "The car is at Di's house." A pause. "Yes. Yes. Right, where we talked about. Yes. Yes, it's all set. I'll be gone by then." Then she hung up.

"It's all set," Ellen said. "He'll take care of the car." Sticks would come for the Volkswagen, moving it to the haul-out once everything was clear. In a week or two, he'd pin it all on the husband, because it was always the husband, in every episode of *Dateline*. Di could help with that. She had known them the longest. There would be enough to arouse suspicion, at least, even if there was no hard evidence. A little unsolved mystery, gossip floating around town, leave the books open for just long enough and then abandon the whole thing entirely. The last piece of the puzzle, proof they were untouchable.

"Fucking fantastic," Mimi said, concentrating on the road ahead. "One less thing to worry about."

At the haul-out, Mimi parked in the darkest spot, beneath a thicket of trees. She pulled the dark car in as far as she could so that it was nearly invisible from the road. "Karen, I want you to stand here near the road. If you see anyone driving by or anything happening, you let us know." Karen nodded, like she had been waiting her whole life for this unique opportunity.

The others lined up at the trunk to help with the body. They pulled the buttons off the sweater, one by one, and slipped them into their pockets. They came off with surprising ease. That was all they needed. A pact. An agreement among friends. After this, they could go back to being the upstanding members of the Hamilton Fucking PTO. President, vice president, and, of course, *premium members.* Life as it should be, all smoothed over in a small town.

Anna was wearing a slouchy sweater. It looked less suspicious in the middle of January, like she had simply gone out for a walk and lost her way. Weren't they all just losing their way, after all? Wasn't everyone always just losing their way in adulthood? One big clusterfuck. Proof that life wasn't an accident.

The snowpack was low for this time of year. Global warming had come for them, too, even all the way up in Massachusetts. At least there was something, a chill to work with. One side of the haul-out had a shallow embankment of ice and snow, and it was hidden from trails and from the road. It would make a good hiding place for a few days.

The river was moving slow and thick, and they placed her on the side, where she would be found, and hopefully not be swept downstream. Mimi trekked back toward the car, making sure their footsteps were invisible. By now, they all blended together; it was impossible to tell who had stepped where, and by morning, it would be completely indecipherable.

"Let's go," Mimi called. Di followed right behind. She didn't look back at Anna, who was now just another part of the Ipswich landscape, as natural to winter as the falling snow.

Ellen was next, but before she trailed behind, she held Anna's hand for just a second, and slipped a ring from a finger, a diamond that had once been Anna Plummer's mother's engagement ring. Now it was Ellen's own memento of the dead.

Ophelia did not feel the cold. Last memories: a Montauk sunset, the day she married, the piglet pink of her children's toes as they squirmed when they were babies. Had she felt the final moments, or just the fierce betrayal? Death was dark, but it was not cold. It had come for her. She had waited for it. She had opened her arms, and it had embraced her in the carriage house.

I love you, she thought, as the hitched last breath was leaving her body. She was talking to Denny, to Louisa, to her sweet little boy, Ben. The things she had wanted to do, well, those opportunities were now gone. Gerhard Richter. Sonic Youth. There was never enough time, she had not had enough time, and all the battles she had fought, maybe they were the wrong ones. Now she would never know.

I have always loved you. A body. A porcelain doll. A light extinguished.

Epilogue

DENNY DROVE ALL the way down to Hopkinton while the kids were at school, because he wanted to surprise them. The dog was named General. He was black, with a tuft of white fur at the jawline and liquid eyes. “A litter drop from Tennessee,” the program coordinator had told him over the phone. General. But that name, he thought, felt a little too militant. He’d have to ask the kids to weigh in. Maybe something a little softer, like Rover or River.

He slipped a leash onto the dog and walked him down the narrow halls of the shelter. The animal was shy at first, and held back on the lead, but once Denny took him outside into an area that had clearly been designed for potential pet owners — a chain-link fence was obscured by tall plantings — the dog jumped up and down and licked him on the face. Denny found a tennis ball on the ground and tossed it in the air, and he jumped up on his hind legs and retrieved it, as if he had always been waiting for this opportunity to prove his mettle.

“Well, I guess that settles it,” he said. “You’re coming home with me.”

He had long ago donated Hank's old belongings, but he stopped by a PetSmart off the highway on the way home for a new bed and some toys and a bag of food, plus a new food and water bowl set for him.

"Daddy, he's so cute," Louisa cooed, as she stepped off the bus. And he was, this dog, this symbol of renewal, this symbol of the new life the three of them were carving out for themselves. They weren't forgetting, but they were learning to move on.

This life, he thought to himself. *You earn it. You have to learn to keep it.*

Every once in a while, Denny would get an order for a delivery near Nancy's Corner, or he would pass over near Honeycomb and drop in for a coffee and there would be Mimi or Di or Ellen Wilson. They'd look at one another with the faraway gaze of people who used to be acquaintances, who had been involved in their fucked-up lives and had somehow managed to get out of them. Only once had he spotted Mary Langley at the gas station in South Hamilton, and she had pretended not to know who he was. Hamilton had gone back to being the uninterrupted town that it was before Anna Plummer moved there. It had been sanitized, freed of her spirit. Denny knew what lay beneath the surface, but to survive was to ignore it. To survive was to tread lightly upon the crust.

He briefly considered going back to New York, but what was there for him, anyway? He had built a business in Hamilton, and his kids were happy in Hamilton, and it now housed his life, the shell of it. He could soldier on here, a general himself. He could — he would — make Hamilton home, in the way that Anna would have expected and wanted. Stay quiet, stay the course. He was of the belief — foolish or otherwise — that if you left dangerous things alone, they would leave you alone, too. Wash your hands of them. Hornets wouldn't come for you if you weren't interrupting the nest.

Only once had he been jolted awake out of this dreamlike state, when an article appeared below the fold on the front page of the *Boston Globe* announcing that the body of a Winchester woman had been found washed up off the Aberjona River. But these things happen in towns like that sometimes. Bad luck, Denny thought. You do hate to see it.

One afternoon, in the mail, Denny received a package from the Hamilton Police Department. Wrapped in bubble wrap was Anna's laptop. It had been completely scrubbed of anything important, but it was there, just the same, an artifact of his previous life.

> I thought you might want this back. Sorry we couldn't find anything of use on it. We've decided to close your wife's case. In the end, her death has been ruled "inconclusive."
>
> —Officer Malkin

This was over, then. What the Ipswich River had claimed he could never have back, but they would all move on, rebuild, erect a new life precariously on the delicate topsoil here in Hamilton. Rewind. Start over from the beginning. Suck the marrow out of life. All of that Thoreau bullshit. If there was a lesson in all of this — Denny did believe in lessons, at the end of the day, or had come to believe in them, at least — it had less to do with redemption and more to do with a stab at happiness. Oh, maybe the secrets kept people sick, or maybe it was the secrets that were necessary for survival. The secrets — it was the secrets that kept small towns alive.

Even Anna Plummer had known that much.

Acknowledgments

To my agents, Caroline Marsiglia and Rick Richter, for continuing to help me to pursue my dreams.

To my inimitable editor, Vivian Lee, a collaborator and friend. And to my team at Little, Brown. I wrote two books in short order, back-to-back. This team is fluid, and I think of books as connected, so I offer thanks, too, to Morgan Wu, Jessica Chun, Gabrielle Leporati, Sabrina Callahan, Pat Jalbert-Levine, and everyone else who had a hand in bringing both works to life.

To my writing friends, who have been my sounding boards for the past few years, and who have offered strategies and ideas and plenty of memes and snark, just when I needed them most.

To my non-writing friends, so many of whom showed up when I was on tour, bought books, brought cakes, brought flowers, watched my kids, cheered me on, told their friends about my books, and convinced me that writing wasn't just some crazy dream shared by the creative class.

To my family, who finally got to see me on the cover of the *New York Times Book Review* — and boy, were they proud!

To my husband and kids, who have mastered the art of waiting for me to finish "just one more sentence." Thanks for your patience.

To the people of Gaza. I do not give up hope. I will use my platform as a microphone. I still believe that words matter.

About the Author

Hannah Selinger is the author of the critically acclaimed debut memoir *Cellar Rat: My Life in the Restaurant Underbelly*. Her work has appeared in numerous national and international publications, has been nominated for a James Beard Award, and has been anthologized in the *Best American Food Writing* collection. She lives in Boxford, Massachusetts, with her husband, two sons, two dogs, and one Russian tortoise. This is her first novel.

RAISING READERS

Books Build Bright Futures

Thank you for reading this book and for being a reader of books in general. We are so grateful to share being part of a community of readers with you, and we hope you will join us in passing our love of books on to the next generation of readers.

Did you know that reading for enjoyment is the single biggest predictor of a child's future happiness and success?

More than family circumstances, parents' educational background, or income, reading impacts a child's future academic performance, emotional well-being, communication skills, economic security, ambition, and happiness.

Studies show that kids reading for enjoyment in the US is in rapid decline:

- In 2012, 53% of 9-year-olds read almost every day. Just 10 years later, in 2022, the number had fallen to 39%.
- In 2012, 27% of 13-year-olds read for fun daily. By 2023, that number was just 14%.

Together, we can commit to **Raising Readers** and change this trend. How?

- Read to children in your life daily.
- Model reading as a fun activity.
- Reduce screen time.
- Start a family, school, or community book club.
- Visit bookstores and libraries regularly.
- Listen to audiobooks.
- Read the book before you see the movie.
- Encourage your child to read aloud to a pet or stuffed animal.
- Give books as gifts.
- Donate books to families and communities in need.

BOB1217

Books build bright futures, and **Raising Readers** is our shared responsibility.

For more information, visit **JoinRaisingReaders.com**

Sources: National Endowment for the Arts, National Assessment of Educational Progress, WorldBookDay.com, Nielsen BookData's 2023 "Understanding the Children's Book Consumer"